W9-CIG-358

Praise for Susan Kandel and the Cece Caruso Mysteries

"The delightful Cece Caruso is back . . . These saucy, well-crafted mysteries are a lot of fun."
—*Boston Globe*

"Entertaining . . . witty . . . readers should give Cece a warm welcome to the legion of perky female sleuths."
—*Publishers Weekly*

"Susan Kandel is guilty of penning an utterly original, artful and nicely noir novel of murder and intrigue—all dressed up in fabulous vintage Hollywood fashions. Yum!"
—Mary Kay Andrews, author of *Little Bitty Lies*

"As sparkling as a spilled packet of Sweet 'N Low."
—*Washington Post Book World*

"Fizzy fun."
—*Los Angeles Times*

"Cece once again thwarts evil while looking smashing and providing dry commentary. . . . a satisfying whodunit . . . Cece's got charm and moxie to spare."
—*Oregonian* (Portland)

"A well-spun plot and clever writing."
—*Entertainment Weekly*

Washington County

February 2010
WASHINGTON COUNTY LIBRARY
8595 Central Park Place • Woodbury, MN 55125

"Cece Caruso, the protagonist of Susan Kandel's breezy mysteries, has her quirks . . . but while Cece's vintage clothing fetish gives her a certain loony charm, it doesn't get in the way of her genuine talents as a sometime sleuth."
—*New York Times Book Review*

"Kandel offers up a race against time, a nail-biting chase and some unexpected twists and turns."
—*Denver Rocky Mountain News*

"Fun and frothy."
—*Orlando Sentinel*

"Thumbs up to newcomer Kandel's series for its snappy dialogue and carefully worked-out plots."
—*Kirkus Reviews* (starred review)

Dial H for Hitchcock

ALSO BY SUSAN KANDEL

I Dreamed I Married Perry Mason
Not a Girl Detective
Shamus in the Green Room
Christietown

Dial H for Hitchcock

A Cece Caruso Mystery

Susan Kandel

HARPER

NEW YORK • LONDON • TORONTO • SYDNEY

HARPER

This book is a work of fiction. The characters, incidents, and dialogue are drawn from the author's imagination and are not to be construed as real. Any resemblance to actual events or persons, living or dead, is entirely coincidental.

DIAL H FOR HITCHCOCK. Copyright © 2009 by Susan Kandel. All rights reserved. Printed in the United States of America. No part of this book may be used or reproduced in any manner whatsoever without written permission except in the case of brief quotations embodied in critical articles and reviews. For information address HarperCollins Publishers, 10 East 53rd Street, New York, NY 10022.

HarperCollins books may be purchased for educational, business, or sales promotional use. For information please write: Special Markets Department, HarperCollins Publishers, 10 East 53rd Street, New York, NY 10022.

FIRST EDITION

Library of Congress Cataloging-in-Publication Data

Kandel, Susan, 1961–
    Dial H for Hitchcock : a Cece Caruso mystery / Susan Kandel. — 1st ed.
       p. cm.
    ISBN 978-0-06-182667-2
    1. Caruso, Cece (Fictitious character)—Fiction. 2. Women detectives—Fiction. 3. California—Fiction. I. Title.
    PS3611.A53D53 2009
    813'.6 —dc22   2009022016

09 10 11 12 13 OV/RRD 10 9 8 7 6 5 4 3 2

To my nieces and nephew: Zoe, Amanda, and Spencer Brown

Acknowledgments

I'd like to acknowledge my former editor Carolyn Marino, whose sage counsel I will miss; and to thank my editor, Katherine Nintzel, for her enthusiasm and quick eye. As always, I am grateful to my agent, Sandra Dijkstra, who is tireless in her support. Thanks also to Taryn Fagerness, and Elise Capron in her office.

The Hitchcock literature is fascinating and endless. As I worked my way through it, Donald Spoto's *The Dark Side of Genius*, though somewhat dyspeptic, was extremely valuable. I turned to Patrick McGilligan's *Alfred Hitchcock: A Life in Darkness and Light* whenever I needed answers to specific questions, and to Jean-Pierre Dufreigne's *Hitchcock Style* whenever I needed inspiration. Peter Conrad's brilliant *Hitchcock Murders* deserves special mention, as does Francois Truffaut's revealing book-length interview with the ordinarily tight-lipped director.

I'm sure I traumatized my daughters by letting them watch *The Birds* too early in life, but they have always been a big part of my work. I wanted to thank Maud in particular for the metaphor on page 139; and Kyra for catching a contradiction in the final chapter. As for my husband, Peter, he introduced me to the concept of the Macguffin back when we were in grad school and it stuck, proving once again that he brings good things to my life.

Chapter 1

They write books about women like me, who cancel weddings and then go on the honeymoons by themselves.

Yeah, cracked the little voice in my head. *Freudian case studies. Fat ones, with footnotes.*

Thanks a lot, I said to the little voice. *I'm not crazy. Besides, cruising around the Caribbean by yourself isn't so bad. Sea air is famously restorative. You can have room service at four in the morning. And no end of me time.*

Plus we'd prepaid. No refunds.

I vowed to have a terrible time.

In penance for ruining the best relationship of my life for reasons bafflingly vague to everyone but myself, I left my trousseau behind.

No vintage pineapple-motif Cole of California sarong, perfect for showing some leg while foraging in glamorous ports of call for well-priced raffia souvenirs. No pre-hippie-era, cayenne pepper red Pucci bikini with coordinating terrycloth hat. And forget about the 1930s peach silk charmeuse negligee that clings like body lotion.

I wore baggy gray sweatpants seven days running.

I refused all invitations to sit at the Captain's Table.

I swore off men forever.

Then I came home to my Spanish Colonial Revival bungalow in West Hollywood and discovered that the faucet in my turquoise-tiled bathtub had been leaking the whole time I'd been gone and was half an inch away from flooding my entire house.

So I needed a man.

Estuardo Gomez of Handy-Rooter took care of my pipes, but who was going to take care of the rest of me?

Bachelor Number One appeared later that evening at the beautiful old Orpheum Theatre on Broadway. He was tall, dark, and handsome, but it still hurt like hell when he stepped on my toe.

"Sorry," he said. "Is that seat taken?"

"Yes!" The woman sitting next to me threw her beige cardigan across the seat. "My lover is on her way. She's been unavoidably detained." The woman had an anxious look on her face and plastic-wrapped dry cleaning enveloping her feet, like swaddling. "She's a neurologist, if you must know. There was an emergency."

"Maybe you meant this one?" I indicated the empty seat on my other side.

"That's the one," Bachelor Number One said with a smile.

I smiled back. Then I felt the smile crumble. Fighting a sudden desire to weep, I sputtered, "Actually, I don't know. About the seat, I mean. I think it might be taken. That could very well be the case."

The bachelor scratched his head. "Well, are you with someone?"

"That's rich," the woman with the beige cardigan muttered.

I looked at her, completely unsure of myself now.

"Am I with someone?" I repeated, as if translating from the Croatian.

A blonde in a robin's-egg blue dress squeezed past us to a seat at the far end of the row. "Sorry. Close quarters here." She was juggling red licorice and a large bucket of popcorn.

"I told you I wanted butter," said her bald boyfriend, snatching the bucket out of her hands.

"Why don't you just say thank you?" I asked him, my voice rising in something like panic. Then, spinning back around to the bachelor, I said, "Whether or not I'm with someone is an extremely personal question. I didn't ask *you* whether or not *you* were with someone. You're not wearing a wedding ring, but I didn't say, 'Excuse me, sir, are you single, or divorced, or God forbid maybe even married but not wearing a ring in the hopes of misleading trusting young women?' So what's your excuse? What do you care if I'm single, or if I'm married, or if I came *this* close to getting married but didn't, and had to mail back all the lovely presents, some to Buffalo, New York, even?"

Perhaps I wasn't ready to start dating again.

"Look, I'm just trying to see a movie here." The bachelor was now backing into the aisle, hands raised in surrender. "No hard feelings. It's pretty obvious you have stuff to work out."

After he walked away, I closed my eyes and imagined myself as a little girl skipping through a field of wildflowers, the sun warming my skin. When my breathing returned to normal, I opened my eyes and picked a piece of popcorn off my vintage black-and-white Lilli Ann suit with raspberry silk lining and three-quarter-length sleeves. Whatever. The suit was tweed bouclé, so debris actually blended in.

As the house lights went down, the collective sound of several hundred people switching their cell phones to vibrate filled the cavernous space. I scrambled around beneath my feet but couldn't find my purse because the beige cardigan's neurologist lover had arrived and piled her own plastic-wrapped dry cleaning on the floor in front of us. Plus groceries. Smelled like fish. Brain food. Anyway, it didn't matter about my phone. It was unlikely ever to ring again. Everyone I knew thought I was out of my mind.

The red velvet curtains parted with a swoosh, and the Orpheum's magnificent Wurlitzer organ began playing the overture to Alfred Hitchcock's *Vertigo*.

I took a deep breath and let the music wash over me, the haunting low harp, the ominous two-note falling motif.

Then, apparently unable to stop myself, I leaned across the first woman, her lover, and the bald man and whispered to the blonde in the robin's-egg blue dress, "Is it really that obvious? About my stuff?"

She chewed on some licorice and considered. "It's not like you're an exception to the rule. You love and lose, and then you love and lose all over again. It's all there in the movie. Haven't you seen it before?"

Twelve times, to be exact.

How I came to be sitting three rows up from the back in a restored former vaudeville theater in downtown Los Angeles where Judy Garland once sang as one of the Gumm Sisters, watching (for the thirteenth time, no less) doomed lovers Scottie (Jimmy Stewart) and Judy/Madeleine (Kim Novak) run circles around one another may require some explanation.

My name is Cece Caruso.

I am approximately forty years old.

I am Italian, named after my fat aunt Cecilia.

My family consists of cops, beauticians, and the people who love them.

I am a former beauty queen, strictly small-time, who married once, early and badly.

I was blessed with a second chance at love, but as you may have surmised, I recently blew that, too.

That is why I made the decision to pour myself into my work (Freud—speaking of—called this sublimation), which consists of writing biographies of dead mystery authors.

Currently, I'm researching the auteur Alfred Hitchcock, the Master of Suspense, he of the portly silhouette and legendary perfectionism.

Pay attention now.

Alfred Hitchcock is the most recognizable director in the history of the cinema, with a career that encompassed fifty-three

*films, two long-running television series, and a magazine that still
bears his name.*

That's what I've got so far.

The sum total of eight months of research.

You'd think a person could do a little better.

Hitchcock was, after all, a man who infected the world
with his deepest neuroses and darkest obsessions, a man whose
stated aim was to leave not a dry seat in the house, a man who
liked to introduce himself to new acquaintances as "Hitch—
without the cock."

Okay, I did know this: he liked practical jokes.

Practical jokes, expensive red wine, dark suits, and Dover
sole he had flown in from England and stored in his walk-in
freezer in Bel Air. Also cool blondes that got hot in taxicabs.

What he didn't like was sex (Had It Exactly Once) and
cops (Was Locked in a Jail Cell as a Boy as Punishment for
Naughty Behavior). Or so he said.

Ask him a question, and he'd toss you a red herring.

Look for a person, and he'd offer you a persona.

Perhaps you see my problem.

Hitch's movies are equally dissembling, all reflective sur-
faces, switchbacks, and spirals: Janet Leigh's blood swirling
down the drain in *Psycho*; Tippi Hedren's lingerie circling her
ankles like shackles in *Marnie*; Jimmy Stewart's corkscrew iris
and Kim Novak's coiled chignon in *Vertigo*.

Oh, but what the man could do with a chignon. A chignon,
a glimpse of white neck, and a tailored suit. If Hitch couldn't
undress his leading ladies, he'd fetishize every detail of their
dress.

Some of them rebelled.

Tallulah Bankhead, the star of *Lifeboat*—who came to Hollywood to sleep with Gary Cooper, which a person could well understand—refused to wear panties, leaving Hitch to moan, "I don't know if I should consult wardrobe, makeup, or hairdressing!"

Kim Novak—Hitch's second choice for the role of Judy/Madeleine after Vera Miles had the temerity to get pregnant by her husband, Gordon Scott, the movies' eleventh Tarzan—wouldn't wear a brassiere, but he showed her. *Vertigo* is the only one of his love stories to end with the leading lady's death.

"I'm not buying it," said the beige cardigan, gathering up her dry cleaning as the lights came up. "Is this yours?" She handed me my purse, which had gotten mixed up with her things.

"Thanks." It was Lucite, from the fifties, with a tortoise-shell handle that didn't quite close. I'd gotten it cheap, like most of my vintage wardrobe.

"Of course you're not buying it," said the neurologist girl-friend. "Vertigo is not psychological in origin. It's a problem relating to disequilibrium. Calcium buildup in the inner ear. Makes you feel dizzy, light-headed, and faint."

"Sounds like love to me," said the blonde in the robin's-egg blue dress, stepping over them.

"Actually, overuse of antidepressants," the neurologist inter-jected. She handed me her business card. "I see it a lot in my practice, this being L.A. and all."

I mulled that one over in the parking lot, waiting for my turn at the ticket kiosk. Then I got rear-ended. Well, you could barely call it that. More like a tap.

"Hey!" I said, leaning out the window.

Bachelor Number One leaned his head out his window. He had one dimple, which made him appear rakish as opposed to cherubic. "Hey."

"Look, I'm sorry about before," I said.

"I'm sorry about now," he said, "which makes us even."

I put the car in park and met him at my rear bumper, which looked fine.

"It looks terrible," I said, snapping pictures with my cell phone. "I'll have to take it in."

"Absolutely."

"We should probably exchange numbers," I said.

"Good idea."

I followed him back to his shiny black car, which was a total mess inside. I like that in a man. Schizophrenia. Keeps you on your toes.

The bachelor scrawled his number on the back of a Chinese menu he found in his back seat, and I scrawled mine on a parking ticket he pulled out of the glove compartment, dated two years earlier.

I drove away feeling dizzy, lightheaded, and faint.

It wasn't love, though.

I didn't believe in love at first sight.

I did, however, believe in déjà vu.

Which turned out to be one hell of a problem.

Chapter 2

It was three in the morning when I caught him staring at me with those narrow, flinty eyes.

Suppressing the urge to scream, I grabbed for the phone on my nightstand and dialed 911.

When the operator finally came on and asked if it was an emergency, I hemmed and hawed for a minute. "Suppose not," I finally admitted, flopping back down onto the bed. "But I would like to get my hands on a dart gun and a net."

She sighed, and asked if I was from around here. Like I was supposed to know that the steroidal rat on the fence outside my window was an opossum.

As it turns out, the opossum is nature's own Dustbuster, ridding the world of rotten fruit, slugs, and cockroaches. Poor things are virtually helpless. They can't run fast or bite hard. The only thing they can do when threatened is play dead by entering a temporary near-coma. They sometimes do this when they are scavenging roadkill only to become roadkill themselves. The operator suggested I shoo him away with a broom.

After hanging up, I tiptoed back to the window and peered out at him.

He didn't really look like the result of nuclear fallout.

He had nice pink paws.

He was cousins with the kangaroo.

And I had no idea where the broom was.

I shut the curtains and went back to sleep. I dreamed I was a stewardess on Quantas, serving shrimp on the barbie to the helpless passengers.

The cell phone woke me up at eleven.

I bolted upright.

My first call since the ill-fated un-honeymoon.

Buster, my teacup poodle, sensing something important was happening, was jumping up and down by my Lucite purse, which was sitting on the living room couch where I'd left it the night before. I dove for the purse, knocked it over, grabbed the ringing phone.

"Hello?" Calm, cool, and collected, that was me.

"Hi—just wanted to confirm our hike."

What hike? I had no idea to whom I was speaking. Plus I'd thrown away the baggy gray sweatpants. I suppose I could wear shorts. But then I'd have to shave my legs.

"Beachwood Canyon," he went on without taking a breath, "By the stables, around five."

"I'm sorry, I don't think you—"

"See you then. Bye."

I studied the phone for a minute, then reached back into

my purse and pulled out another phone that looked exactly like the first one.

I rubbed my eyes and frowned.

The hot pink cell phone in my left hand belonged to me. I recognized the scratches.

The other one was brand-new. It must've made its way into my purse last night.

Strange.

Well, the theater had been packed. I'd bumped into dozens of people. My purse had a broken handle and pretty much hung open. The phone could've fallen in at any time. Could've belonged to anybody. But my money was on somebody from the third row up from the back.

The neurologist or her beige cardigan girlfriend?

The blonde in the robin's-egg blue dress?

The bald boyfriend?

Bachelor Number One? He didn't look like the hot pink cell phone type, but you never knew.

One way to find out.

Received calls.

My son-in-law, Vincent, had given me a lesson on received calls the day I'd bought the phone. The other lesson had been on the phonebook, but by that point my eyes had glazed over, the unfortunate result being I couldn't program somebody's phone number if my life depended on it. I stuck with received calls. My philosophy was if I didn't know your number by heart, or you hadn't been one of my previous ten callers, I probably didn't need to talk to you. During the tutorial, Vincent had also shown me how to work the camera. We took pictures of my daughter Annie making vegan avocado ice cream (no animal products included!). Then, sadly, we had to eat it.

Anyway, I'd simply check the list here, return the call, find out whose phone this was, and give the thing back. It would be my good deed for the day.

Unfortunately, the number was private.

I tossed a pillow against the arm of the couch, lay down, and scrolled down the rest of the list. Private, private, private—all of them were private. Too bad.

Dialed calls was my next option. Dialed calls I'd figured out all by myself. These were all to the same number. Ten calls in a row. That seemed a bit obsessive. But at least the number wasn't private. I got the machine of somebody named Anita. I went to high school with an Anita. She had a tremendous overbite. I left a convoluted message.

Last chance. 411. Calling information was a rip-off at $1.49 plus airtime, but it was cheaper than the cost of a new phone.

Unfortunately, I had no luck at the Orpheum, either. Nobody had reported a missing phone.

Oh, well. I'd given it my best shot.

Mimi the cat jumped into my lap and started purring. She didn't want to cuddle. She wanted brunch. She and Buster had spent all of last week with my septuagenarian neighbors, Lois and Marlene, who'd spoiled them with one-pound bricks of cheddar cheese and nightly performances from their late, unlamented burlesque act. The pets weren't going to be happy to return to their special senior diet. And I'd used up the last of it before leaving on my trip.

I scratched Mimi's tummy. "Okay, I can take a hint." When

did I start talking to animals? It was a bad sign. "I'll be back in twenty minutes."

I swiped a washcloth across my face, shoved my hair into a bandana, pulled on jeans, grabbed my keys, and headed out the door.

Unfortunately, there was a car blocking my driveway.

A Porsche 911 Turbo with a license plate reading BYEBYE.

Well, I supposed I'd put it off long enough.

Time to meet the new neighbor.

Chapter *3*

The new neighbor's house was hidden behind a tightly clipped eight-foot hedge. Maybe it was the New Jersey in me, but I liked a well-tended front lawn passersby could see. Not that I did much mowing myself. Everybody in L.A. has a gardener. Mine is named Javier. Javier is an excellent source of information. Last week he told me that the trick to coiling a hose is to first spin it like a jump rope to work out the curls. Also, that the world's largest tree is a ficus in India, which covers five hundred and fifty acres.

There was a yellowed touch pad bolted to one of the concrete pillars on either side of the new neighbor's weathered wooden gate. I pushed the button, smoothed down my hair, and waited. When nobody answered, I pushed it one more time, then peered through the two-inch gap between pillar and gate.

The front and back doors were lined up on the same axis and both made of glass. I could see straight through to the backyard, which was quite glamorous, with lacy wisteria and lush bougainvillea. Also, I could hear a fountain. And somebody hammering. While he was at it, he should probably fix that gap. An intruder could easily slip a hand in there and unlock the gate. Well, if he were of delicate proportions. Or a she.

I locked eyes with a sunburned woman standing in the doorway.

"Hello?" She took off her glasses. "Can I help you? Please don't be selling something. If you are, I don't want it."

"I'm not selling anything," I said.

"Fine. Hold on."

I stepped back as she approached, her heels crunching on the gravel.

The gate swung open at about forty miles per hour and whacked her on the shoulder.

"Ouch!" she cried, dropping her clipboard. I bent down to get it at the same time she did, and we bumped heads. She scrutinized me, like she was a facialist and I was a client with big pores. It was unnerving.

"Hi. I'm Cece, your neighbor. Right next door?"

"Stupid hinge is loose again. Jilly Rosendahl." She was in her thirties, short, blond, overweight, aggrieved. She smelled like she'd been eating corn chips. "Do you have a problem with stray cats in your backyard?"

"No," I replied. "I have an opossum."

She made a face. "These two mangy cats have been hanging out on my superexpensive pool furniture and shedding all over it. I *hate* cats. I'm not feeding them, but they seem to think they live here."

"I wouldn't worry about it. Unless you're allergic."

She thought about that for a minute. "I am. Deathly allergic."

Just then a young man covered in tattoos appeared at her side. He shoved a piece of paper under her nose. "Sign, and then I can fax it over."

"My nephew," she explained, taking the pen out of his hand. "Note for the teacher. He's always in trouble. Anyway, what can I do for you, Cece?"

"First, I wanted to welcome you to the neighborhood—"

"Yeah, and?" she interrupted.

Nice. "And to see if you could move your car." I pointed to my driveway. "I need to get to the store."

"Let me see if it's convenient. I think my guys are in the middle of something. . . ." Her voice trailed off as she walked toward the foyer, a flick of her wrist indicating that I was to follow. Why she needed her guys to move her car for her was not explained, nor was who her guys were, nor why exactly she had guys. Good thing I'm not the curious type.

The foyer was dominated by a gargantuan oak table that looked like it should have knights gathered around it, feasting on platters of roasted animal parts and tankards of ale.

"Isn't it gorgeous?" Jilly asked. "It used to belong to Cher."

She could barely squeeze around it. She had to get up on tiptoes. As she passed, she stuck her nose into a bouquet of long-stemmed red roses arranged in a crystal vase and inhaled. Then she disappeared down the hall.

Pretty flowers.

Oh, look.

There was a note clipped to one of those little plastic pitchforks.

I will not read the note, I told myself. *I will not read the note.*

I was about to read the note when the hammering started again, putting me back on the path of righteousness. It was followed by a sudden burst of laughter, then somebody cranking up the music. Hip-hop.

Jilly materialized with a muscular guy who looked straight out of central casting. He was blond and wearing a tool belt. "Take 'em, Connor," she said, tossing him a set of keys. To me, she explained, "Connor's moving his truck and Decker's van around the corner, then he's going to pull my car in. The Porsche, I mean. That one's mine."

"BYEBYE," I said. "Right?"

She studied my pores again.

I fidgeted.

"I saw you looking," she smirked. "It's okay."

"What's okay?"

"They're yours."

"What's mine?"

She looked over at the flowers. "They got delivered here yesterday by accident. You should take them with you when you go, hint, hint." She drummed her long nails on her clipboard. "Sorry if that sounds rude, but we're working here. Paying the rent, you know what I'm saying?"

I was about to reach for the flowers when Jilly shoved the clipboard under her arm, scooted the vase over, grabbed a pile of water-stained letters wedged underneath, and handed them to me.

"I'm talking about the letters, *of course*. A person can't trust the post office." She shook her head. "I tell that to my guys at least once a day. FedEx is the only way to go. What the—? Is this *chewing gum*? You gotta be kidding me!"

Like a woman possessed, Jilly went after a grayish lump on Cher's former oak table. "You know the way out, right, Cece? Decker, Ellroy, get in here *now*!"

I took my letters—a bill from the gas company and assorted junk—and got out while the getting was good.

Connor, sitting pretty in Decker's van, gave me a wave as I headed up to Santa Monica Boulevard. New friends always raised a person's spirits.

So did Petco, which was decorated for the season with a grim reaper–themed birdbath at the entrance filled with complimentary goblin-shaped pet treats, and orange-and-black streamers hanging from the ceiling. I browsed through the costumes, wondering if Buster would consent to dressing up as Minnie Mouse. They were all out of Mickey.

Within minutes, my cart was overflowing with things I didn't need. That happened to me a lot. Once, I'd made it as far as the checkout counter with a $249 cooled and heated pet bed to keep my dog active and healthy in all seasons. Since I'd last visited, Petco had added to their inventory. There was now an athletic gear section with doggie jogging shorts, doggie hoodies, and tiny doggie water bottles. The food section had expanded, too. My eye went straight to a pile of plastic-wrapped sausages, the stuff of Buster's dreams.

"Just slice and serve," said the clerk. "They're made by Dick Van Patten. One-hundred-percent holistic. He makes them for tigers, cheetahs, and polar bears, too." I tossed a couple in my cart, mostly because I used to have a crush on Willie Aames, who played Dick Van Patten's middle son, Tommy Bradford, on *Eight Is Enough*.

I shuddered as I passed the parakeet cage. It happens to

people who've seen *The Birds* too many times. Poor Tippi Hedren. Legend has it she'd rejected Hitch's advances and he'd punished her by having real birds attack her instead of mechanical ones. The hairdresser smeared her with anchovies and ground meat to attract them, and at one point the birds were even tied to her clothes with long nylon threads, the better to get them biting and flapping in her face. These parakeets looked pretty harmless, though, with their bright blue and green feathers. A little boy tapped on the cage, trying to get them to pay attention, but they were too busy nibbling on each other's beaks.

"Are they kissing?" he asked the clerk, who was walking by with an armful of chew toys.

"Passing seeds," the clerk replied, " which is the ornithological way of showing love. Birds are monogamous. Until death us do part, and all that cool stuff? They're also extremely altruistic. It goes against Darwin's theory of natural selection, but science can't explain everything."

"What goes around comes around," the boy said.

The clerk nodded sagely. "You can't hide from karma. It'll get you in the end." He dumped the toys into a cardboard box, took my cart, and wheeled it over to an empty register. "I'll open up and take you over here, hon."

After I got home, I fed the pets, then checked my home phone and the matching pink cell phones.

No messages for anybody.

I wasn't expecting to hear from Bridget, my second best friend. Her vintage clothing store was going through an IRS audit. She was probably busy staying out of the big house.

But I was surprised not to have heard from my best friend,

Lael. A master baker, she'd been designing a Taj Mahal–themed wedding cake when I'd left. I was dying to know how the sugar-paste elephants had come out.

And what were my daughter and son-in-law up to? Probably playing with little Alexander and baby Radha. Having fun. Bonding. Eating barley and seitan casseroles.

They were disappointed in me, all of them. They didn't understand how I could hurt Gambino. That was my ex-fiancé's last name. His first name was Peter, but I called him Gambino. They said that was the whole problem.

That I was afraid of intimacy.

That I'd broken his heart.

I said I wanted to save him from more of the same.

They said that wasn't my call to make.

Was karma going to get me in the end?

Maybe I could still turn it around.

"Buster!" I called out, dumping an entire Dick Van Patten sausage into his already empty bowl. "Dessert!"

He was going to need the energy. After his nap, we were going for a hike.

Chapter 4

I'd always believed you could catch more flies with honey than vinegar.

My dog, however, was a cynic. He shook himself awake, appraised my manic smile, then lay back down with a grunt.

Undeterred, I headed for the closest bottle of Tylenol and, shaking it like a maraca, cried, "Vet!"

True to form, he made a beeline for the door. It could have been the pleasant drive down Melrose Avenue, past all the nice restaurant smells. But I suspected Munchausen's. Buster was one weird dog. He liked the pills. The weigh-in. Having his temperature taken. I would pay dearly for deceiving him.

Undeterred, I shoved the collapsible water bowl and a bottle of Evian into my bag, and we were off.

Lael lived in Beachwood Canyon so I knew the way: King's Road to Fountain, Fountain to Vine, crest the hill, right on Franklin, left on Beachwood. From there it was a straight shot up, past the swaying palms, the noble sycamores, and the usual crowd of crackpot tourists who positioned themselves in the middle of the road, hoping to get an unimpeded view of the Hollywood sign.

I wondered if they were disappointed. The thing didn't look forty-five feet high from down here. And they all had such expensive cameras. I'm a big fan of disposables. Disposable everything. Cameras. Plates. Dresses. Few people realize that paper dresses were huge in the sixties. They were sold at stationery stores with matching tablecloths to women of capricious temperament, like myself. And diapers. Disposable diapers were another thing my daughter and I didn't see eye to eye on. But I was no longer dwelling on the negative because today was a happy day.

I patted the hot pink cell phone of unknown origin, which I'd plugged into my charger for double brownie points. Yes, today was the happy day I was going to turn around my karma and work out with my dog and then go home and make a big pot of pasta carbonara for both of us because the heavy cream was about to go bad and it's wrong to be wasteful. Plus we'll have exercised.

Twenty minutes later I pulled into the dirt lot just below the Hollyridge trailhead. The rendezvous was clearly underway. There were two cars parked there, both new-looking BMWs with fancy rims. Not that I had anything to be ashamed of. I'd washed the Camry a month ago.

Buster scrambled out behind me, kicking up the dust with abandon. Looked like there were no hard feelings about the vet.

"Slow down," I said as he took off up ahead, where the trail started to fork to the right. The top of Beachwood was home to the Sunset Ranch, known for its "taco rides," which involved renting a horse to ride over the hill into the San Fernando Valley for Mexican food and then riding back, sloshed on margaritas, for the mere cost of eighty-five dollars. For some reason, it had never appealed to me. I peered over the wooden railing at the red stables below. Tonight's dinner crowd must've already taken off. Nobody here but us chickens.

Buster had found a pile of horse dung, and was running gleeful circles around it, like it was a birthday present. I let him have his moment, then put on his leash and pulled him away, past the sign warning against mountain lions. We didn't scare easy, Buster and I.

We walked for a while in contented silence. Communing with nature. Eschewing our usual frenzy. It had been one of the driest years on record so the foliage was brown and crispy, but still beautiful in a cowboy-kicking-the-tumbleweeds kind of way. And the view! You could see all the way past Hollywood to the Wilshire corridor. Well, I think it was the Wilshire corridor. I was never much good at geography. In any case, there it was, across the open space of the canyon, silhouetted against the low-slung haze, a heroic expanse of skyscrapers filled with people in itchy suits huddled over blinking computer monitors in tiny, airless cubicles.

It was hot.

Really hot.

Even at five-thirty in the evening the sun was merciless. I wiped the sweat pooling under my baseball hat, then poured a little Evian on Buster's head. Where were these people? I hadn't seen a soul since we'd gotten here. I'd eliminated the neurologist and her girlfriend. They seemed like hybrid vehicle types. I was betting on the blonde in the robin's-egg blue dress. The caller hadn't sounded like the bald boyfriend, though. Maybe she was cheating on him. I hoped so. He didn't appreciate her.

I trudged onward.

As we rounded the next turn, I realized that the only sound I could hear was the dirt crunching under my feet. That, and the sound of my own breathing.

"Hello!" I called, suddenly eager to leave. Nature makes me nervous. I like retail establishments. Retail establishments with air-conditioning.

Just then, Buster started barking like a madman. "What is it?" I asked. "Did you see somebody?"

He took off like a shot, the leash stinging as it pulled out of my grasp.

"Slow down!" I yelled, going after him full speed. "Where are you going?"

I had no idea Buster could move like greased lightning. It took me a solid two minutes to catch up to him, which I could do only because he'd stopped and sprawled belly up in the middle of the path, ready for a beer and a show on Animal Planet from the looks of it.

Crouching down, I scratched his tummy, then pulled out the dish and poured him some water, which he slurped up greedily. Shielding my eyes against the sun, I looked up to where the path zigzagged across the hillside. Now *this* was where you stood if you wanted to get a really good shot of the Hollywood sign. I reached in my bag for the phone. Then I flipped open the top and waited for the image to come into focus.

This wasn't the original Hollywood sign, of course, which had fallen into disrepair soon after it was erected in the twenties to advertise the Hollywoodland housing tract. This was the new and improved sign, courtesy of Hugh Hefner, who saved the day when he organized an "adopt a letter" party for concerned celebrities at the Playboy Mansion in 1978. Alice Cooper, you may be interested to know, paid $28,000 to refurbish the third *O*.

I got some great shots. Now where to store them? As phonebook entries? As screensavers? As wallpaper? The blonde might enjoy that. I knew she liked old movies. But this was way too complicated for me. Vincent had never gotten to wallpaper. I pushed a few buttons at random, then shut the phone. Why was I wasting my time? The blonde wasn't getting her phone back today. She wasn't even here. Nobody was here. Buster was starting to growl at me.

"Don't worry." I picked him up. "We're leaving."

He squirmed out of my arms, hit the dirt on all fours, and starting pulling me along, ears perked up.

"Where are you taking me now?" I asked, though I could see we were headed exactly where I didn't want to go, which was farther away from the car. My armpits were soaked and I was getting a chill. My bag was thumping uncomfortably against my hipbone. "Face it, Buster," I said. "We are not outdoors people."

Then I heard some scuffling in the dry leaves.

"Hello?" I whipped my head in the direction of the sound, which seemed to come from higher up the hillside.

"Hello? Can you hear me? I've got your cell phone!" I pulled the phone out of my bag again.

More scuffling, then muffled voices. I took a slug of Evian and squinted toward the far ridge.

I could make out two people now, just behind a trash can. They looked like they were embracing. They broke apart for a moment, then the voices got louder, and I heard one of them, the man, say, "It wasn't supposed to happen. Not like this."

Looked like trouble in paradise. They could get past it. They had so much in common. Well, their taste in cars. And both of them liked the great outdoors. Relationships have been built on less.

Now they were wrapped in each other's arms. A reconciliation? A minute passed. Two. I averted my gaze. Get a room, people.

Then she yelled, "I've had enough of this! Let go of me!"

She was done with this guy. I was done, too. I piled some rocks in the middle of the trail and balanced the cell phone on top of it—my version of a flashing red arrow. Picking up Buster's leash, I started back toward the car.

Then, much louder this time, she said, "Let go of me!"

Something in her tone made me stop. I turned around.

"You're not listening to me!" she said.

But I was. I was a good listener. Such a good listener that every time I went to a restaurant I made it my business to eavesdrop on the conversations on either side of me. It was the biographer in me. We are unnaturally fascinated by other people's stuff.

"Is everything okay?" I called out. "Miss? Do you remember me, from the Orpheum?" I couldn't see her face. But maybe it wasn't who I thought it was.

"Get your hands off me!" the woman demanded. "This fucking instant!"

This wasn't a lovers' quarrel.

"Let go of her!" I cried.

He didn't.

"I said let go!"

He didn't.

"Then I'm coming up there!" Like hell I was. People who got in the middle of this kind of thing wound up getting shot. Or worse.

"Somebody help me!" she screamed.

I broke into a run, hoping I'd magically transform into a superhero by the time I got to where they were. I craned my neck upward. They were close to the edge now, still tangled in each other's arms. It was at least thirty feet down. The sound of branches cracking under their feet reverberated across the canyon.

The sweat was pouring off my face now, the panic rising in my chest. Buster was barking loudly.

"Please!" The woman was struggling to pull herself free. "I'm begging you!"

Oh, God. I couldn't think. Everything was happening too fast.

"I'm calling 911!" I finally shouted.

But to my horror, I realized that I'd left her cell phone on the trail at least a quarter of a mile in the opposite direction.

I had to go back.

I had to get to the phone and call 911 so somebody would come and get her down and haul him off to jail.

But it was too late for that.

Because it was at precisely that moment—when I was feeling hot and scared and sorrier for myself than you can imagine—that a man I didn't know pushed a woman I didn't know off the edge of a mountain.

Her body hit the ground, somewhere out of my sightline, with an obscene thud.

Chapter 5

I ran faster than I knew I could, my chest burning with every breath.

Her cell phone was lying just where I'd left it, on top of a pile of rocks like some sort of lunatic offering to the gods. I stared at it in surprise, hands pressed to my knees.

It was ringing.

So I picked it up.

That was how it started.

"Hello?" My voice sounded strange. It was the rush of blood, the adrenaline.

"I'm glad you answered." A man's voice. Hoarse. Distant.

"I don't know who this is," I said, trying to catch my breath. "But I can't talk."

"No need to be rude." He cleared his throat. "I'm sure you've got a minute."

"I don't," I repeated, frantic now. "I have to hang up. I have to call 911."

"You don't have to do anything of the sort," he said. "It doesn't matter anymore."

I was quiet for a moment. Then I said, "What do you mean it doesn't matter?"

"You know exactly what I mean."

My legs started to give way.

I shook my head.

Buster began to wail.

"You don't know what you're talking about," I said. "I have to hang up."

"See for yourself," he said matter-of-factly. "Go back to where you saw her fall."

I hung up the phone and dialed 911.

Call failed.

No reception.

I tucked Buster under my arm and started to run in the other direction. I ran fast, then faster. I was stumbling over my own feet. The ground was rushing up to meet the sky. The birds' cries were deafening. My head was pounding. I was dizzy. But I kept running.

The phone rang.

I stopped, looked at the display.

Private.

I picked it up, listened.

"What, no hello?"

I didn't reply.

"You're breathing hard," he said. "You must be close. No reason to rush, though. A park ranger is with the body."

The body.

Please, no.

"I'm sure you can see the ranger by now. Or can you?"

I couldn't see a thing. "Look, I don't know who you are, and I don't care." I bent over. I needed air. "I've got reception now. I'm hanging up and calling the police."

"They're already on their way."

He was right. I could hear sirens now. They sounded close.

"Who is this?" I looked around. "Where are you?"

"Don't worry about that." His voice was eerily calm. "I want you to relax. Have some water if you want. There's time. You have to be ready. You've got an important job to do."

My legs were aching. My head was throbbing. I had to think. I couldn't think. I put Buster down. He howled to be picked up. This was madness.

"You listen to me," I said. "This conversation is over."

"No, Cece. This conversation is just beginning."

The shock was physical, like a punch to the gut. "How do you know my name?"

Silence.

"Answer me!"

"Listen carefully, Cece. When you get to the police, you're going to tell them what you saw. A woman jogging by herself on the path above you. She was distracted, she fell. End of story. It was a horrible accident. That's what you're going to tell them."

"Like hell I am!" I hung up the phone and threw it into my bag.

I could see them now—two uniforms and the park ranger. The cop car was parked sideways on the trail, sirens blaring. Thank God.

"Hello!" I cried. "Over here!"

One of the uniforms looked up. "Stop right there, Miss! Not another step. This is a crime scene."

"Don't you think I know that?" The words tumbled out of my mouth, one on top of another. I stopped, took a breath, spoke as slowly as I could. "I saw it happen."

At that, the other uniform signaled for me to approach, cautioning me to watch where I was stepping.

I could see her now, face down in the dirt. She had long blond hair and was wearing a blue tracksuit and one black running shoe. The other shoe was lying maybe ten feet away from her body. It must've come loose during the fall. The contents of her purse were scattered everywhere—wallet, lipstick, keys, tissue, change.

"Is she dead?" I whispered.

The taller of the two cops was pulling a notepad out of his back pocket. "Looks like it happened on impact. Can we get your name?"

The cell phone started to ring.

"Do you want to get it?" the cop asked. "We might be awhile."

"No," I said, shoving the phone deep into the recesses of my bag. "He'll go away if I don't answer. I don't have to answer if I don't want to."

The uniforms exchanged glances. They were both young, straight out of the academy, hair cut too short.

"I'm Officer Lavery," said the tall one. "This is my partner, Officer Bell."

Bell smiled. He was short, with a peach fuzz mustache. He looked all of sixteen.

"And you are?" Lavery asked.

"Cece Caruso." I spelled it for them.

"Okay, Ms. Caruso," Lavery said. "Why don't you sit down on this boulder here while we wrap it up with the ranger?" He brushed the rock off with his sleeve. "It'll be just a minute."

I sat down. Kicked some pebbles. Gave Buster a stick to chew on. The sun was going down. The wind was picking up. Day was turning into night. The temperature would drop at least fifteen degrees in the next half hour. That was how it was in the desert.

A small piece of paper blew toward me.

I bent down to pick it up.

A driver's license.

It must have fallen out of the dead woman's wallet.

I checked for her name.

Anita Colby.

It took a minute to sink in.

Anita was the name of the person I'd left a message for yesterday.

Dialed calls.

So Anita wasn't the owner of the phone. She was the person the owner of the phone had called ten times in a row. The object of someone's obsession.

How dearly that had cost her.

I looked back at the license. Anita had brown eyes, blond hair, measured five foot ten inches tall, weighed one hundred and forty-five pounds.

She was barely thirty years old.

The phone.

It was ringing again.

I should've thrown it against the rocks.

I should've tossed it into the gorge.

I should've ground it underfoot.

I pulled it out of my bag and let it keep ringing. After the ringing stopped, I looked at the display.

Two messages now.

I glanced over to where the cops were standing. They were shaking hands with the ranger, saying their good-byes.

It couldn't hurt to play the messages. Just to listen.

"Okay, Ms. Caruso," Officer Bell called. "We're ready for you."

I nodded, stood up, and started walking in their direction, the phone pressed to my ear. Officer Bell held my gaze, smiling, as I heard a muffled click, then the sound of a voice.

I don't make empty threats, Cece. If you're not going to do as I asked, you're going to pay a very steep price.

The voice was cold as ice, hard as a stone.

"Miss Caruso?" Bell asked, touching my shoulder. "You okay? You might want to sit back down. We're waiting for the detectives anyway."

"Detectives?" My voice rose in pitch. "Why detectives? Do you have some reason to assume this wasn't an accident?"

"That's what you're supposed to tell us," said Lavery, giving his partner a sidelong glance. "Isn't it? But finish with your call first."

One more message.

I listened with a mounting sense of dread.

I don't like the game you're playing. You've left me no choice. I'm going to kill you—

I pulled the phone away from my ear and stared at it, utterly bewildered. Then I opened my hand and watched it spiral to the ground.

Officer Lavery sprang to attention. "Let me get that for you." He opened and shut the phone a couple times, saw the screen light up, and handed it back to me.

"Bad news?" asked Bell.

"That kind of day," Lavery said, nodding.

"I don't—yes, bad news," I stammered.

Bad and impossible.

Because the voice making death threats wasn't cold as ice, nor hard as a stone.

The voice wasn't his.

It was mine.

And then everything went white.

Chapter 6

"She's coming to," someone said. It was a woman's voice. "Glory be."

"You're not supposed to be so snarky," someone else said. Another woman. "Remember?"

Then my face was wet all over. I hoped it was Buster.

"What happened?" I murmured, trying to sit up. My head felt like it was about to explode.

I don't like the game you're playing. You've left me no choice. I'm going to kill you, Anita. And they'll call it justifiable homicide.

A confession before the fact.

The words had come out of my mouth.

It was crazy.

Impossible.

I didn't believe it.

But everyone else would.

"Shock," said Officer Bell, shaking his head. "Dead bodies do that to people. Glad to have you back with us." He was smiling now. "Listen, you don't have to be embarrassed. We see this kind of thing every day. People passing out, getting sick. Our own techs, even."

A woman in a razor-sharp black suit and pin-straight black hair glared at him. She was a looker, but mean, you could tell.

"I'm Detective Collins," she said, "and this is my partner Detective McQueen." I looked up at another attractive woman, this one with long, blond curls. Her suit was navy blue and she wore a scarf at her neck, like a stewardess. Then I leaned over and threw up.

"See what I mean?" said Bell.

Detective Collins stepped back, mindful of her heels, while Officers Bell and Lavery helped me to my feet. I wiped my mouth on my sleeve. Somebody handed me a water bottle and I took a drink, but my hand was so shaky the water wound up all over my T-shirt.

"Sorry," I said. "This whole thing is kind of overwhelming."

A mysterious cell phone turns up in my purse.

It leads me to the scene of a crime.

A woman is killed.

And I have to choose: tell a lie, or take the fall.

It was one hell of a set-up.

Detective Collins looked down at her watch. "Listen, why don't we just take your statement and send you on your way."

I closed my eyes for a minute. I didn't know what to do. I needed to go somewhere quiet and lie down. Sort things out.

Time.

I needed to buy some time.

"Ms. Caruso? Did you hear me?" Collins asked.

"It was an accident," I said softly.

"What was that?" asked Officer Bell. "I can barely hear you."

Detective Collins glared at him again. "We could use you down there, Officer." She waved her hand. "Make sure there aren't any more hikers headed up this way."

"It was an accident," I said, louder this time.

"Go on." She was staring at me now.

"The woman was jogging. I heard her footsteps, I looked up, and that was when I saw her trip and fall."

"Are you sure?" asked Officer Lavery, wrinkling his brow. "That there was nobody else up there?"

"Would you two please just go now!" snapped Detective Collins.

"I'm sure," I said, chewing on my lip. "She was alone."

"End of story?" Detective McQueen asked, gazing at me from under her long blond curls.

"Yeah," I said, feeling utterly defeated. "The end."

"Okay," said her partner, slipping a pad of paper into the pocket of her jacket. "Then we're done with you. For now."

"It would be wise not to make any travel plans," said McQueen.

"Nice touch," said Collins, whipping her black hair off her face. "You hear that on TV?"

"I'm not going anywhere," I said, getting up. "I just had a vacation. "

"I'm absolutely dying to get out of town," said McQueen. "I hope you were somewhere pretty."

"The Caribbean. It was beautiful." I shut my eyes for a

minute, saw the brilliant blue of the water, smelled the salt in the air. "More beautiful than you can imagine."

At sunset, the sky would be streaked with pink and orange and purple, fading minute by minute until there was an endless expanse of black and the twinkling of thousands of tiny stars. Most evenings, I'd sit on the deck, looking up, thinking. One night, an older woman came out with a big blanket and settled herself down next to me. Her name was Ronnie. We'd started talking. She'd been married for fifty-six years and had lost her husband two years earlier. She couldn't believe a girl like me was all alone. I was so pretty, she'd said. But I wouldn't be young forever. I told her a little about Gambino.

That he was the finest man I'd ever known.

That he'd never been married before because he'd been waiting for the right woman.

That he deserved someone who believed in true love.

That I wasn't sure I was that person anymore.

Ronnie had given me a sad smile.

"Sometimes you don't know what kind of woman you are," she'd said, "until you put yourself to the test."

It was dark now, but there were no twinkling stars. The two officers escorted me to my car. Buster crawled into the back seat and fell asleep. I sat there with the headlights on, staring through my dusty windshield.

I knew what kind of woman I was.

I was the kind of woman who wanted somebody else to fix it.

Mr. Gomez fixed my pipes.

Bachelor Number One was going to fix my broken heart.

And Gambino—Gambino was going to fix this.

He was a detective.

He'd know exactly what to do.

With sudden fury, I ripped open my bag and dug through the powdery bits of tissue, the unpaid parking tickets, the nail files, the coins, and the broken aspirin tablets until I finally found the hot pink cell phone. I pulled it out and dialed Gambino's number, but when I heard his voice on the machine, I hung up.

I couldn't call Gambino.

Not today.

Not ever.

I hurled the phone into the back seat.

Damn it.

I was on my own now.

I had to fix this myself.

But could I?

For Anita?

For me?

Chapter 7

The next morning I opened the front door and found Javier the gardener and Connor from next door standing side by side on my stoop.

"Morning gentlemen," I said. "Look like rain to you? We could certainly use it."

"Do you know this man?" Javier asked, running his fingers menacingly over the serrated edge of his trowel. "I find him lurking."

"I wanted to know if I could borrow a lemon from your garden," Connor said. "For Jilly's tea."

Javier looked horrified. "This is not the time to pick lemons."

"I didn't know that," Connor shrugged.

"You must wait at least one month before harvesting," Javier said. "And please. Do not pull. You do not want the stem end of the fruit to tear. This promotes deterioration." He shook his head.

"Okay, then," I said, closing the door behind me. "So I'll just be on my way."

Neither of them budged.

"I have this appointment." I tapped my watch. "Really soon."

Still no sign of movement.

"Listen, Javier," I said.

"Yes?" He narrowed his eyes.

"Can you check the Brugmansia? It's drooping again. Maybe it needs to be staked."

"It droops because you must cut back, but you do not want to cut back. I tell you the same thing every time, but you do not listen to me." Glowering one last time at Connor, he stomped into the backyard.

"Sorry," I said. "Javier's kind of protective."

"Beautiful woman like you," Connor said. "I understand."

"Was there something else you needed?" I bent down to pick up my *L.A. Times*, my *New York Times*, and a Thai take-out menu Javier had kindly watered for me.

Connor tugged at the bottom of his T-shirt like a kid. Which he was. "Cup of coffee?"

"Isn't there coffee at Jilly's?"

"Jilly's got coffee."

I gave him a look. "One cup. Then I really have to go."

I opened the front door, tossed the newspapers onto the entry hall table, and showed Connor into the living room, which was in much better shape than normal. Normal was a pile of sticky plates on the coffee table, magazines and pillows scattered across the floor, cat hairs stuck to the maroon velvet couch. Connor kicked off his shoes, stretched out on my white synthetic fur chaise, and grinned.

"Don't be shy," I said, heading into the kitchen. "Just make yourself at home."

"Are you going to take your coat off?" he called out.

"I am not," I said. "How do you like it, by the way?"

"You toying with me?" he asked.

"The coffee is what I meant."

"Cream and sugar."

I opened the refrigerator, sniffed the heavy cream, and tossed it into the trash. I was out of sugar, so that took care of that.

I set two steaming mugs of black coffee down on the table. Connor rose from the chaise and sat down on the couch next to me.

"No coasters?" he asked.

"Life's too short," I replied. "So. Are you this fresh with Jilly?"

"Jilly's my boss," he said. "And I like my job."

"Which is?"

"I help Jilly with things that come up."

"What kinds of things?"

"You wouldn't believe it." He took a sip of coffee. "She's in entertainment."

"That's a broad category," I said. "Does she run some kind of escort service? That'd explain the guys. Who's Decker, by the way?"

"Computer specialist."

"I get it." I put my cup down. "You're all CIA, right? Jilly's got a sunburn because your last assignment was in the Bahamas where you helped extradite a drug kingpin who was trying to bring a thousand kilos of cocaine into Miami."

Connor laughed. "You're good. Usually it takes at least a couple of months before our cover is blown. Now we'll have to infiltrate another average American suburb."

"I hate to break it to you," I said, "but West Hollywood is not your average American suburb. Stroll up to the boulevard next Monday. Hundreds of thousands are expected for the Halloween parade, at least fifty thousand of whom are going to be dressed as Dolly Parton."

"My mom loves Dolly Parton."

"How about you?"

Connor smiled. "I love my mom."

The kid was now officially Bachelor Number Two.

"So what do you do?" he asked.

"I'm sort of in entertainment, too."

"Let me guess. You manage wrestlers?"

"That's a good idea," I said. "I should manage wrestlers. I wonder if Andre the Giant is happy with his representation."

"Andre the Giant is dead."

"Dead people need representation, too."

Connor frowned. "How's that?"

"They have legacies. The truth has to get sorted out from the lie. You know, the story isn't over just because somebody dies."

He looked confused. "What exactly are we talking about here?"

Anita Colby. I was going to fix it. The story wasn't over yet.

"I don't know," I said. "I'm a writer. That's what I meant by entertainment. I write about dead people. I'm struggling with one of them right now. Alfred Hitchcock, the film director?"

"Good evening," Connor intoned lugubriously.

"That's him," I said.

"I remember the night I first saw *Psycho*. It was this time of year. Late October. A dark and stormy night."

"Listen, Connor, I might have mentioned I have an—"

"Don't you know it's impolite to interrupt?" Connor settled deeper into the couch. He cleared his throat. "It was a first date. She was a psych major and hated it. Said Marion Crane blinked when she was supposed to be dead."

"That's partially true," I said. "Hitch's wife caught the mistake during the editing, and they did the best they could. But it still looks like an involuntary twitch. The other problem is that Marion's pupils are still contracted after she's stabbed. Hitch received several letters from ophthalmologists informing him that the pupils of a corpse dilate after death. From then on, he used belladonna drops to achieve the proper dead-eye effect."

"May I continue?"

I held up my hands. "Don't let me stop you." Mimi the cat jumped onto my lap. She loved a good story.

"I took the freeway home so we wouldn't have to talk," said Connor. "It worked. We drove in total silence, desperate for the evening to be over with. There was this car driving next to us. She noticed it first. 'Connor,' she whispered. 'Look over to your left. That man is staring at us.' I looked over at the car in the next lane. The windows were kind of fogged up, he must've had the heater on, but you could see the guy's face and it was true, he was staring right at us. 'Maybe he thinks he recognizes us from somewhere,' I said. 'Forget about it.' But he kept staring. He was going seventy miles per hour on the freeway at midnight and never took his eyes off of us. 'I'm scared,' she said. 'Get off the freeway. Do it right now.' But before I could exit, she started to scream. 'Help! Oh, my God!' I looked over at the guy and saw something that chilled me to the bone. He'd taken his hands off the wheel and placed them on either side of his face and spun it around on its axis, and where his face used to be was a hideous, bloody—"

This was taking way too long. I stood up, dumping Mimi onto the floor. "It was a mask, right? On sideways? Happy Halloween."

"Guess you've heard the story." Connor rose to his feet, reached into his pocket, and pulled out his cell. "Sorry," he said, checking the display. "Jilly. Probably needs me to get something." He pulled on his shoes.

"I've got to be going myself." I checked my watch. Ten o'clock. Perfect timing.

"California Charlie's," Connor said into the phone, and hung up.

"Is that CIA for 'Yes, I'll bring back a loaf of bread and quart of milk?'" I shut the front door behind us.

"Damn," he said, heading toward Decker's truck. "Now I'll have to kill you."

He was a sweet guy, but he didn't exactly have a way with words.

Chapter 8

My mother always taught me to dress for the occasion. She also taught me that girls should be seen and not heard, except when they are belting the theme song from *Cats* in the hopes of parlaying a humble Miss Asbury Park victory into the infinitely more glorious Miss New Jersey title, in which case they should go for it like there's no tomorrow. Which goes to show you shouldn't always listen to your mother.

I decided on my little-black-dress-except-it's-navy, with the low square neck and elbow-length eyelet sleeves, and a white silk scarf in my long brown hair. Plus an armful of gold bangles and navy blue patent leather peep-toed slingbacks with white rope platforms. Little Bo-Peep meets Jackie O meets Mata Hari. Weird, perhaps, but calculated to appeal to a broad range of possible marks.

The phone store was a ten-minute walk from my house.

I was the only customer, not that anyone was in a hurry to

assist me. If I'd actually wanted to buy something I might've been annoyed, but I wanted information and that required patience and cunning. After what seemed like an eternity, the young Indian man behind the counter gave me a smile that radiated intelligence, so I eliminated him. Ditto a girl in a business suit who had the smell of a management trainee, possibly with a college degree. That left the pot-bellied teenager with the dull look in his eyes and the enormous Afro. It was the largest Afro I'd ever seen, especially on someone white. It must've measured a foot in every direction. I wondered what happened when he tried to get into a car. He probably took the bus.

The kid was tidying up the display area. The stretchy cords were tangled, and the phones were in the wrong cradles. I watched from a distance for a while, then sidled up to him and ran my fingers over the phones.

"Uh-oh," he mumbled, glancing back at the girl in the business suit, who smiled at him with fake good cheer like they teach you in company seminars on motivation and team development. Not that I'd ever been to one, but I used my imagination.

"Welcome?" he said, phrasing it as a question. He did not appear to be a people person.

I smiled encouragingly.

"I'm George," the kid continued haltingly, "and I'd be happy to assist you with your telecommunications needs today." He tugged on his hair. "Today or any day. Any day that I'm here, I mean. Mondays through Thursdays, and half-day Sundays." He rubbed his nose. "So are you looking for something special?"

"Yes, George," I replied. "I'd like a phone with all the bells and whistles. My friend Donatella got one here last week, and I want one just like hers. Now was it this one?" I picked up a $675 model. "Or was it that one?" A $235 number with clean lines, available in pink, silver, or blue. "Or maybe this one?" A $65 option suitable only for someone who wanted to maintain a low profile, but needed to check in regularly with his parole officer.

For the next half hour I ran George ragged. At approximately eleven-fifteen, the Indian guy and the suit asked him if he'd be okay while they went to the back to unload a shipment that had just arrived. That was most likely George's job, but they knew better than to get stuck with me.

When the coast was clear, I pounced. "On another topic, before I settle on one of the phones."

George looked unhappy.

I reached into my bag and pulled out the hot pink cell phone. "Donatella and I were out to dinner last night. Cambodian food." I shook my head. "Never again. Too spicy."

George tugged at his hair again.

"On my way back to the car, I found this phone lying in a puddle in the street. I want to do the right thing and get it back to its owner, only I don't know how to find him. It's a Motorola. I see the model right over there."

"The Razr." George took it out of my hand and stroked it tenderly. "Expertly crafted, ultra-thin, MPEG4 video play-back, Bluetooth technology, precision-cut keyboard, minimal-ist styling, metal finish."

"Wow. You really know your inventory." I reached up to tuck a loose strand of hair behind the scarf, and the brace-lets slid down my bare forearm, tinkling melodiously. "So," I said. "Do you think you could just look this Razr up in your big data bank thing over there and give me the name on the account? I would be so appreciative."

George shook his head with genuine regret. "I'm sorry. I'm not allowed to do that."

"I don't think it would be such a big deal." I tried to keep the desperation out of my voice. "And then we can finish up my purchase, make your boss happy, and everybody can go their merry way."

"I could lose my job," George said.

"Well, I don't want you to lose your job," I said, chastened. "Of course not. That'd be bad karma. What comes around goes around."

"Amen to that."

"But then how am I going to do the right thing here?"

"Let me think." He scrunched up his face. Then a ray of sunlight broke through the storm clouds. "By George, I've got it!"

Everybody's a comedian.

George picked the hot pink cell phone up off the counter and dialed a number. The store phone immediately started to ring. He ambled over to the other side of the front desk, picked up the receiver, and turned it around so I could see the display.

"There it is," he said.

"The number of the cell phone," I said. "Now what?"

"Now you go to the reverse directory and look it up. Only costs $4.50."

"Can you do that for me?"

He shook his head. "Against store policy. Just go home to

your computer and do it. It's easy. Anybody can look it up."
Then George looked me up. And down. Now I was the one
tugging the hair.

"Anybody can do it," he repeated. "I mean, anybody who
knows even the slightest thing about computers." He paused
meaningfully. "Which we all do these days, right?" Another
pause. "Of course if you're in a rush, I *could* show you a
BlackBerry. That's probably what Donatella got. In fact, I think
I remember Gupta, he's the store manager, selling it to her.
She's tall, right? Louis Vuitton handbag, I believe. Matching
wallet? Yeah." George nodded. "That was Donatella. The
thing is, if you had a BlackBerry like Donatella, you wouldn't
have to wait until you got home. You wouldn't even have to be
good with computers. You could find out the person's name
right here, right now, and I'd show you exactly how to do it.
One, two, three, you'd be out of here. And we've got a promo-
tion going. If you get a three-year contract, the phone itself is
half price."

The dull look in George's eyes was obviously due to
allergies.

By twelve noon, I was the proud owner of a BlackBerry.

By twelve-ten, as per George's instructions, I was typing
in my AmEx number and waiting to discover the name of
the person who'd purchased the hot pink cell phone that had
taken over my life.

The person so obsessed with Anita Colby that she'd called
her ten times in a row. And maybe even killed her.

What a surprise.

Cece Caruso was her name.

Chapter 9

It poured the whole walk home.

Gambino once told me that sudden October rain marked the tail end of a hurricane. It would fall fast and furious for a while, then die down just as quickly.

He knew about things like that.

That lightning is three times hotter than the surface of the sun.

That the average person falls asleep in seven minutes.

That I fall asleep in less than four. He said he'd timed me, even though he already knew I wasn't average.

When I got home, I realized I'd forgotten my key. It was that kind of day. Week. Okay, year. I reached into the flowerpot by the front door, pulled out the spare key, shook off the dirt, and let myself in.

Stopping to pull a fresh towel out of the hall cupboard, I went into the bedroom, where I peeled off my little-black-dress-except-it's-a-sodden-dishrag and tugged on a pair of blue jeans and a T-shirt. I was about to put on a pot of coffee when I noticed that the light on my phone machine was blinking.

I froze.

The lady detectives.

They'd figured out my statement was a lie.

Then I remembered that the cops don't call first. They just show up with handcuffs and a warrant.

However, it turned out the message was from Bachelor Number One.

His name was Ben McAllister and he wanted to see me.

Unfortunately, all I wanted to do was go to sleep for the next hundred years, with a forest of briars around my house that no one could penetrate without facing certain death in the thorns. Maybe Javier could arrange that.

The doorbell rang.

I looked through the peephole.

Bachelor Number Two. Connor. This was getting confusing.

"Hi," I said.

"Can I come in for a second?" He had an anxious look on his face.

"Sure," I said, opening the door.

He bypassed the white chaise this time and took a seat on the couch.

I sat down opposite him and waited.

He rubbed his hands on his jeans.

"Would you like something to drink?" I asked.

"Nope," he said, kicking one shoe with the other.

"Hungry?"

"I had lunch a little while ago." He was staring at the floor. "Nice of you to offer."

"What?" I asked sharply.

"Is there anything you want to tell me?" He finally looked up.

"Not really." I rose to my feet. "Actually, there is. I want you to go home so I can take a nice, hot bath in peace."

"The cops were here," he said.

I was right. They don't call. They just show up.

"What on earth are you talking about?" I went into the kitchen and pulled out the coffee pot, poured the old coffee into the sink, rinsed out the pot, and filled it with fresh water.

"They were asking all kinds of questions about you." Connor followed me into the kitchen.

"Asking who?" I washed this morning's grounds out of the filter and spooned in enough for a full pot.

"Jilly, me, the guys. I saw them at your door a little before they came over, then when they didn't get an answer, they went to the back and looked around for a while. "

"Since when do you keep tabs on who comes and goes at my house, Connor?"

Ignoring my question, he said, "They rang our bell, wanted to know if we'd seen you today, or if we'd noticed anything suspicious about your activities, stuff like that."

"And Jilly ratted me out, right? Said I was a master criminal whose presence on the block was bringing down property values?"

"Not exactly."

"What then?"

"She used the word 'strange.'"

"Strange?" I slammed down the coffee pot and hit the on switch. "I was being facetious."

"She said you don't even seem to live here."

"That's ridiculous. I've been away. In the Caribbean."

"On vacation?"

"On my honeymoon."

His mouth fell open. "Are you *married*?"

I sighed.

"Is that a yes or a no?"

"It's a no. I'm not married. I went on my honeymoon by myself, okay? It's a long story."

"Can I tell Jilly?"

I stared at him. "Tell her whatever you want. She's not going to care. She hates me."

"That isn't exactly true."

"I don't get it. I'm a good neighbor. I'm friendly. I don't complain about loud parties or barking dogs. Okay, so I could've gone over there with a Bundt cake when she moved in, but the truth of the matter is, I don't own a Bundt pan!" I collapsed onto the kitchen chair.

Connor crouched down in front of me so we were eye to eye.

"What is it?" I asked wearily.

"What's up with your tennis shoes?"

Nothing was up with them. I'd worn them to the hiking trail. They'd gotten filthy, and I'd kicked them off before coming inside. I got up, pushed him out of the way, ran to the front door, threw it open. My tennis shoes were exactly where I'd left them the day before.

"Look!" I said, picking them up. "They're just ordinary,

messed-up tennis shoes. A little wet, maybe. Why are you asking about them?"

"Because the cops were taking pictures of them."

Of course they were. They'd found footprints up by the crime scene. They wanted to compare them to my shoes. How easy I'd made it for them. They hadn't even needed a search warrant. And they were going to get a match.

Whoever set me up knew exactly what kind of tennis shoes I wore.

Whoever set me up had been watching me.

God.

"You have to leave now, Connor," I said. "I have somewhere I have to be."

"I thought you wanted to take a bath."

"I changed my mind."

"Don't you ever sit still?"

"It's important to stay active."

"Are you going to be okay?" he asked. "You need anything?"

"How about a new identity? You think your CIA buddies can arrange something?"

"Is it that bad?"

"I'm kidding," I said. "Really. I'll see you later. Please?"

I waited a few minutes, then peeked out the stained-glass window in the living room to make sure he was gone.

Ten minutes later, I was parked in front of the Andalusia Apartments at 1475 Havenhurst Avenue.

According to her driver's license, the dead woman's last known address.

Chapter 10

With its red tiled roof, carved wooden balustrades, and ornate, star-shaped fountain, the Andalusia was one of the most beautiful courtyard complexes built in West Hollywood in the twenties.

As I walked across the rain-slicked brick auto court, I imagined the starlet who might have lived here back then. Going to the studio every day, hoping to catch Louis B. Mayer's eye. Living on tinned peas. And then, one day, running up the tiled staircase, elated, because it had finally happened: she was going to be cast opposite Clark Gable, and every night for the rest of her life she'd be living it up at Mogambo's, or the Brown Derby, or Chasen's.

I wondered if Anita had been a dreamer, too. Dreamers usually get the short end of the stick.

Suddenly, the French doors on the second floor loggia flew open and a young woman with a cap of neon yellow hair cried, "Here, kitty, kitty! Here, kitty, kitty!"

Something black crossed my path.

"Excuse me," she called down to me, "can you grab him? He can't be outside. It's October!"

"Come to Cece," I murmured, bending down to pick up the four-legged vagabond. "There, now. Mommy's coming."

The woman came tearing down the stairs. She was barefoot, clad in tight black leggings and a Metallica T-shirt, and tiny, like her cat.

"Hello, my love." She scooped the furry creature out of my arms. "Thank you so much. You know, the shelters declare a moratorium on black cat adoptions this time of year. The Satanists and all." She actually looked at me for the first time, "Oh! Hi! I mean, oh, God, what can I say?"

"Excuse me?" I said.

She shook her head, her hair shimmying like fringe. "Life's a bitch and then you die. At least Charley here has nine lives, don't you, baby? Anyway, I can't get over it." She opened her eyes wide, then peeled off her eyelashes. "Sorry. Didn't get a chance to take them off last night." She tucked them inside the pocket of her leggings. "Can you?"

"Can I what?"

"Get over it. You heard, right? That's why you're here, isn't it?"

Ah. She thought I was a friend of Anita's. Paying my respects. "Yes. That's why I'm here."

She nodded, pursing her lips. I guess it was still my turn.

"It was so unfair," I said.

"Unfair is right." She sat down on the edge of the fountain and patted the roughly cut white stone. "It's not wet. You can sit."

"Thanks," I said, taking a seat next to her.

"What's so awful is I was just getting to know her. Anita was great. I could tell her anything. And vice versa."

I nodded. "A girl needs someone to confide in."

"Damn straight," she said, stroking Charley's fur. "Especially in this town. I'm from Ohio, and let me tell you, the people out here are total freaks. But she wasn't like that."

"No," I agreed.

"She was from the Midwest, for chrissakes! And after all that shit with her ex. And then the credit cards. And then the bank. She was just getting out from under, taking her life back, you know?" She shook her head. "But what am I telling you for? You were so close. Like Siamese twins."

Siamese twins? "You really think so?"

She looked puzzled. "Well, of course. You came over, like, every night and sat in her apartment right over there, drinking your cranberry martinis or whatever, talking girl talk. I was a little jealous, to be honest."

I'd never been to Anita Colby's apartment before. I'd never even had a cranberry martini. She was lying. But why?

"But I'm kind of busy most nights anyway," she went on. "I'm in a band. Kiki Madu? I'm the only one who's not Japanese. It's not like I've ever been much of a girl's girl anyway. I have four brothers."

Maybe she wasn't lying.

Maybe they'd planted someone who looked like me as part of the set-up.

Or they'd picked me because I looked like somebody who was already close to Anita.

"I have two brothers," I said. "Richie and James Jr."

She smiled. "They teach you to catch a ball and all that?"

"Oh, yeah. It was great." My brothers had never wanted the slightest thing to do with me. I was the alien with big hair.

"Yeah," she said. "I miss home."

"Poor Anita," I said, reaching over to scratch Charley behind the ears, "never getting to go home."

"Never getting to see her mom again."

"Awful."

"And that dreadful ex."

"Hoo boy," I said, looking right at her. "Worked at that insurance company, wore those dreadful ties. What a controlling—"

"Yikes," she said, bending down. She pulled one of her eyelashes off a moss-covered brick. "Slippery little buggers. No, not him. He must be another ex I didn't hear about. No, I meant the one who works at the used car dealership. Out in Bakersfield? That's the creep I meant."

"Oh, *him*, " I said. "*He* was in a class by himself."

"Those letters he wrote," she said.

"They were something all right."

"Anyway, I should go," she said, standing up. She had a tattoo on each ankle. A fairy and Betty Boop. "I only came down to get Charley. I've got some people waiting up in my apartment, and they must be done with their coffee by now. Two detectives, can you believe it? Knockouts. They look like they should have their own cop show or something."

Whoops.

I leapt to my feet and started for the exit.

She wheeled around. "Actually, do you want to come up

and talk to them? I mean, you knew Anita a lot better than I did. You might be able to help."

"Help? With what exactly?"

"The case."

"I heard it was an accident," I said, trying to keep the edge out of my voice. "That she fell."

"I don't know about that. They're talking murder."

Jesus.

"At least that's what I'm hearing. But maybe I'm wrong. The whole thing's kind of like freaking me out, to be perfectly honest." She shivered dramatically.

I pulled out my brand-new BlackBerry and pretended to check my messages. "Oh, man. I was hoping this wouldn't— listen, I've gotta run." I looked at my watch. "I'd like to help, but I've got this work thing, and I've got less than half an hour to get downtown."

"Yeah. I know. I'm supposed to go to rehearsal, but these cops say they need like an hour of my time. They've got a whole list of questions. Not that I'm about to feel sorry for myself. Not after what just happened to my friend."

I watched her go back up the stairs with Charley and close the French doors.

When the coast was clear, I broke into Anita Colby's apartment.

Chapter 11

Breaking in may be overstating it a bit. The door to Anita's apartment was ajar, so I pushed the rubbed brass knob and let myself in.

Another person might have wondered why the door to a recent murder victim's apartment wasn't sealed with police tape, much less bolted nine ways to Sunday, but another person probably wouldn't have been in this particular situation to begin with, so there's no point going down that road. Closing the door behind me, I slipped out of my ballet flats and put them in my purse. Then I tiptoed into the living room.

It looked like a movie set.

There were Oriental rugs on the dark hardwood floors, a folding peacock screen that made me think of Gloria Swanson, a persimmon satin chaise, a plum crushed-velvet settee, embossed leather ottomans, and hanging Moroccan lanterns with panes of multicolored glass. Two wrought-iron cande-labras flanked either side of a baby grand piano, over which hung a portrait of a dark-haired woman in an antique gold frame.

I wanted the name of the set decorator.

Not that he or she would have been happy to see fried eggs on the coffee table with a cigarette stubbed out in them.

Or the half-empty wineglass with the dead fly floating in it.

Or the bouquet of white flowers, which must've looked beautiful once, but were now browned at the edges.

The kitchen was an unfortunate seventies redo with dark wood paneling, harvest gold linoleum, and fruit-themed wall-paper. The refrigerator, however, was a brand-new Sub-Zero. Inside was beer, sour cream, lox, whole milk, bologna, diet soda, and plain nonfat yogurt. The pantry contained bagels, refried beans, tortilla chips, Slim Jims, calcium supplements, and chai tea bags.

Call me psychic, but I'd say Anita Colby had a boyfriend.

The telephone and answering machine were in the nook just outside the kitchen door. The red light was blinking.

Five messages.

I sat down on the little tufted stool and hit play.

Hi, it's me. I've got to leave a little sooner than I thought. I'll call you next week, when I'm settled. Don't worry about your stuff. It's in good hands. You can come get it whenever you want.

Cryptic.

Next message.

It's Tuesday at 6:00 p.m. I'm at Musso's. Good thing they

make a decent martini because I've been fucking waiting here for at least a fucking hour! Where are you? Screw you. I'm done waiting. I'd be lying if I said you were worth it.

Nice.

Third message.

Hi, Anita. It's Cece Caruso.

Oh, God.

Last night I was at the movies by myself. I don't like to go to the movies by myself, but I'm on my own these days, if you know what I mean. Anyway, I really need you to call me. (323) 555–6480. I'm getting pretty frustrated.

Well, that certainly confirmed it. I was out of my mind. Couldn't have sounded more unhinged if I'd tried. Like it would have killed me to have said, "Hello, I don't know you, but I found a cell phone and you, Anita, are one of the calls dialed, so here I am, calling you now, to find out who the phone might belong to because I'm a Good Samaritan, which is the opposite of a murderer, in case you are listening to this, Detectives McQueen and Collins." No, that would've made life too easy.

Fourth call.

Hi, babe. Are you okay? How'd it go? Give me a call. Bye. Love you.

So the creep cooling his heels at Musso's, a famous old Hollywood watering hole I happened to love, had called early Tuesday evening. The woman with Anita's stuff had to have called sometime before then. I'd called early Wednesday. This fourth person could have called Wednesday during the day, Wednesday night, or any time today. How did what go? The hike? Not well, obviously.

Fifth call.

Anita?

A man's voice. Not the creep. Someone else. There was static on the line.

Anita? Pick up. It's—

More static. I couldn't make out the name.

I'm in Coldwater. Bad reception. Can you hear me? I'll bet you're listening. Anyways, in answer to your question, yes, I'll have what you asked for with me, and I expect you to hold up your end of our . . .

Static again.

I suppose I deserve the shit raining down on me. But . . . you're a piece of—

Whatever Anita was a piece of got lost somewhere over Coldwater Canyon. But the message got me thinking. I had no idea why Anita had been killed. Love gone bad had been my default motive, but according to Gambino, it's not always love. Sometimes it's money.

Blackmail would certainly be one way to pay for a Sub-Zero.

I moved down the hall to the bedroom, which looked like somebody had taken the entire contents of Bloomingdale's and dumped it on the floor.

Anita? Or somebody else?

Cops don't make that kind of mess.

The bed was unmade. White sheets, high thread count, half ripped off the mattress. I hoped the last night of Anita's life had been filled with wild sex, not bad dreams.

There was nothing much underneath the bed. A stained T-shirt. Dust balls. A jump rope.

I rose to my feet.

Aha.

A desk.

Desks are important places.

Desks are where people keep things.

This one was ersatz Chippendale, with ornate legs, fret-work, and gold leaf. The surface was covered with pages torn out of magazines. There were pictures of watches on most of them. Expensive watches. Gold Rolexes and Omegas and Cartier tank watches modeled by beautiful tennis players with impressive serves. Maybe the boyfriend who liked bedsheet-ripping sex and Slim Jims was the generous sort.

The desk had only one drawer. I slid it open. Then I closed it with my elbow. I was out of my mind. I needed gloves. The last thing I needed to do was leave fingerprints.

Back in the kitchen, I opened the cabinet under the sink and found a dozen pairs of rubber gloves, all white. Anita must've liked a clean kitchen. I slid a pair on. They were too big, but I wasn't complaining.

The last time I'd worn white gloves was junior prom. They were silk, full-length, and crushed slightly at the wrist. My gown was red chiffon, with a matching shawl. I'd wanted to wear lavender, but my mother talked me out of it, claiming that psychologists had proven that the majority of men do not like the purple family.

I took a seat at the desk and resumed the search.

Inside the drawer was a stack of take-out menus: Thai, Vietnamese, Cambodian, Indian, Brazilian.

Then there were catalogs: Bliss Spa, Harry & David, Robert Redford's Sundance catalog, where you could buy a high mountain earflap hat, a vintage Tyrolean sled, or a set of peace-sign coffee mugs.

A huge pile of credit-card solicitations. Anita must've been a pack rat.

Some change-of-address forms. Maybe she was planning to move.

At last. Her Filofax.

I flipped it open to the week of October 22.

And there it was.

Wednesday, October 26th, 5:00 p.m.

It was marked with the letter *B*.

That was no help.

B for Beachwood Canyon?

Or *B* for the bastard who killed her?

Shit.

I looked up.

Someone was at the front door.

Diving into the Bloomingdale's pile was an option, but I worried about suffocation.

There were footsteps in the hallway now.

I dashed into the closet, pulled the accordion doors shut, and squeezed my eyes shut.

This was the scary part of the movie.

Like when the heroine decides to get out of the car along the deserted highway even though everybody knows the psycho killer is waiting for her behind a bush with a hatchet.

Or when the beautiful lady detectives who are supposed to be upstairs drinking coffee come wandering down the hallway to catch the falsely accused killer as she tries to abscond with clues as to the real killer's identity, while wearing the dead woman's rubber gloves.

Or worse yet, when the guy being blackmailed breaks into the person's apartment to destroy the evidence against him but winds up killing an innocent, barefoot bystander with big brown hair and a pageant-worthy smile.

The footsteps were in the bedroom now.

Something was clawing at the doors to the closet.

I held my breath. It was only a matter of time. I looked around wildly. Could you impale someone with a hanger?

"Charley?"

I heard meowing.

"Come here, you bad boy. Let's go back upstairs. I can't have you wandering around the dead lady's apartment."

His nails scratched against the wooden floor as she swooped him up.

"But first, let's grab that bottle of Chardonnay out of her fridge. She can't drink it anymore, can she? No reason it should go to waste."

That made two times Charley had crossed my path in one day. Like I needed more bad luck.

I waited until I heard them close the front door, then I made a run for it.

Back at home, I had another message from Bachelor Number One.

Who happened to be named Ben.

Which starts with a *B*.

Ben had been at the theater that night. He could've easily dropped the phone in my purse. He could've set this whole thing up.

But *B* could just as easily stand for bald.

Or blonde in a robin's-egg blue dress, for that matter.

Before I drove myself completely crazy, I returned Ben's call and suggested we meet for dinner the following night at Musso's. The idea was to kill two birds with one stone. Plus I remembered how delicious their pork chops were.

What I forgot, however, was that multitasking is not for the faint of heart.

Chapter 12

Neither is babysitting for two children under the age of four.

"Higher!" Alexander shrieked. "Faster!"

"Okay," I said. "Be careful what you wish for!" Panting for air, sweat dripping into my eyes, I gave him a shove. As the swing ascended, rusty metal poles quaking, Alexander kicked his heels together and his light-up tennis shoes shot into the sky like tiny rockets to Mars.

"Whee!" he cried. "Again! "

Hitchcock had a theory about swings. Swings are the gateway drug. By age five, you're already craving the adrenaline rush. Then come roller coasters and haunted houses and before you know it you're an unregenerate addict, sitting in a dark movie theater, heart pounding, as Marion Crane gets stabbed to death in the shower of the Bates Motel.

"Bet you can't fly like Spiderman," Alexander said to the boy on the swing next to him, who was dragging his feet in the sand, enthralled by something he'd found in his nose. "I can! I can fly!"

"With great power comes great responsibility," I said.

"I'm 'sponsible!"

"Of course you are." I grabbed hold of the swing to slow him down, then unhooked the safety chain. "Which is why we've got to stop and take care of your sister now."

"We left her at the gas station." He wriggled out of his seat and ran toward the giant steel mesh octopus that sprayed water every fifteen seconds.

I glanced over at Radha, asleep in her stroller. Her little chest moved up and down, as regular as the waves at sea. I pulled up her blanket and tucked it under her chin. "Why would we have left this angel at the gas station?"

Alexander was now hanging upside down from one of the octopus's tentacles. "Because she's full of gas, of course!"

The kid on the swing guffawed appreciatively.

At nine o'clock this morning, I'd gone over to Annie and Vincent's sprawling house in Topanga Canyon to pick up the children. We'd arranged it over a month ago, back when I was still a beloved member of the family. It was a very important day for all of us. Alexander's mother—with whom Vincent had been involved prior to meeting Annie—had pulled another disappearing act, only this time she'd had the sense to relinquish her maternal rights before taking off.

Today was the day Annie and Vincent were due to appear in court so that Annie could sign the adoption papers. Today was the day Alexander would officially become her son. But she'd been his mother from the moment he'd first given her one of his beautiful, crooked smiles. And I'd been his grandmother. Despite being in the full flower of my youth, I might add.

Now Alexander was digging in the sand with a yellow Bob the Builder shovel someone had left behind.

"I'm going to China," he said.

"That's wonderful, honey. I'll just be over here, okay?" I pushed Radha's stroller onto the curb and over to an unoccupied bench. "Stay where I can see you, please."

I hated to wake a sleeping baby, but she needed changing. I opened Annie's diaper bag, which was the size and heft of a carry-on, and dug through the toys and snacks and changes of clothes until I found the fully biodegradable aloe vera–infused baby wipes; a clean, fair trade white cloth diaper; and the hundred-percent-recycled changing pad.

Radha was light as a feather. "Hello, angel," I whispered into her little pink ear. She had Vincent's ears, slightly pointed at the top. But those were Annie's lips and Annie's nose. And Annie's unearthly cry. I remembered it well.

"Uh-oh, you woke up the baby," said Alexander, ambling over with the kid from the swing in tow. "She doesn't like it when you do that."

"Uh-oh," opined his new friend.

The howling intensified.

"Sometimes," Alexander continued, "she screams for a whole hour. Mommy and Daddy get very sad."

"I never get sad," I said.

Radha squirmed and shrieked, her face turning the color of a pomegranate. But not counting the small amount of blood I drew when I poked myself with the diaper pin, she was no match for me.

"I'm going to give her a bottle now," I announced.

"The hot rod hates milk," Alexander said.

Hot Rod was Gambino's nickname for Radha. It'd stuck.

Alexander's friend tapped me on the shoulder. He looked like Alfalfa from the Little Rascals. "The ice cream truck is here. Can I have a snow cone?"

There was something missing from this picture. "Where's your mommy, little boy?" I asked, hoisting the still-crying baby onto my shoulder.

Alfalfa spun around, then turned back to me and shrugged his shoulders. "She went home."

I plugged the baby's mouth with a pacifier. Then I knelt down in front of the little boy. "What do you mean she went home?"

"Look around," Alfalfa said. "No mommies here."

It was true. We were the only people left in the park. The dark clouds had driven everyone away. Even the ice cream man had turned on his creepy music and was decamping for sunnier climes. I felt a droplet hit my nose. Then, without warning, it started to pour.

"Head for cover, boys!" I tucked Radha into her stroller and pointed toward the small brick building by the parking lot in which the senior center and park office were housed.

Hooting and whooping in delight, the boys ran across the soggy grass. I pulled down the stroller's hood and followed, instantly regretting it as the spokes of the wheels quickly filled with mud and wet leaves, then locked up entirely so that I had to pick the thing up and run with it the rest of the way. By some miracle, though, the bouncing had soothed the baby, and by the time I put her down under the pergola she was sleeping contentedly, dry as a whistle, which was more than I could say for the rest of us.

After shaking ourselves off, we went into the office, which smelled like freshly brewed coffee and cinnamon rolls. But there was nobody seated behind the front desk. Maybe they were all taking their break. At times like these, I always wondered why I hadn't become a civil servant.

"Hello!" I called out, peering down the hall. "Anybody back there? I've got a lost kid here."

"I have to go to the bathroom," Alfalfa said, squeezing his legs together. "Also my feet are wet."

"Can you hold it in for a minute?" I asked. "Until we see about your mom?"

"Okay." He uncrossed his legs and went over to a little blue table in the corner of the waiting area, picked up a copy of *Highlights*, and started reading it upside down.

"Do you know your phone number?" I asked.

"Yes," he replied. "It has a three in it."

"I have to go to the bathroom, too," said Alexander.

"Honey, please just hold it while I think for a minute. Hello! Hello!"

Still no answer.

"Stay here, boys," I said, "while I go back there and look for somebody."

Pushing the stroller determinedly in front of me, I walked behind the desk and into the corridor, my wet sneakers slapping the cheap linoleum. All the doors were shut. I banged on them successively, but to no avail.

Back in the waiting area, both boys were on the verge of tears.

"No need to worry." I smiled hysterically. "Let's go to the bathroom, then we'll figure out what to do."

That's when they really started to cry. That woke up the baby, who joined them in a rousing three-part harmony.

Just as we were heading out, a hatchet-faced woman with freckles came storming in, a uniformed cop behind her.

"That's the one!" shouted the hatchet face. "She's the one who snatched my son!"

I stepped back, incredulous. "What?"

"You should take those other children into protective custody." She grabbed Alfalfa by the collar and pulled him toward her. "Are you hurt, Freddy? Why are you crying?"

"He's crying because you abandoned him in the park! And don't even think about going near my grandkids! Sir," I said, turning to the policeman, "this child was left in the park, and we came here hoping to reunite him with his mother."

"I'm sure this has all been a simple misunderstanding," the cop said. "Can I see your driver's license, Miss?"

I shot a triumphant look at the hatchet face, dug around in my purse, and handed it to him.

"Anita Colby," he read. "1475 Havenhurst. Is that your current address, Ms. Colby?"

Pride goeth before a fall.

"Uh, that's not the right one." I grabbed Anita's license out of his hand and shoved it back in my purse, digging deeper until I found my own. "Here it is. Cece Caruso. Just look at the picture." I pulled my wet, straggly hair back off my face. "See? It's me. Okay, so maybe I've gained a couple of pounds."

The cop sat us all down, then turned away while he punched my driver's license number into his handheld computer. After a couple of minutes, he said, "I think we've got a situation here."

"A situation?" I asked meekly.

"Seems you're wanted for questioning in another matter." He paused a beat. "The Anita Colby matter?"

I swallowed hard.

"I'm supposed to let you know, Ms. Caruso, that you are expected at the twenty-eighth precinct Sunday morning at 9:00 a.m. for a sit-down with Detectives McQueen and Collins. I'm assuming their names are ringing a bell?"

I nodded.

"That's this Sunday. The day after tomorrow. I apologize in advance if it interferes with your worship schedule. You with me?"

I nodded again.

"I'd like to suggest you bring a lawyer. That's just my advice. I'm only telling you because you seem like a nice person. And you've got grandkids and all. My grandma's back in Oregon. She raised me." He started tearing up. "Anyway, you can go now."

"That's it?" asked Freddy's mom in disbelief.

"You okay, kid?" the cop asked Freddy. "Lady didn't try to snatch you, did she?"

"Nope," Freddy replied. "But she wouldn't buy me a snow cone, neither."

"Remember to drive safely," the cop said. "Precious cargo, ladies."

Freddy stuck out his tongue at me in parting.

I reciprocated because I'm that kind of person.

Chapter 13

The children slept the whole way home, but Alexander perked up the moment he saw Vincent and Annie.

"Grandma got in trouble with the police!" he yelled, leaping into his father's open arms. "We'll miss her when she goes to jail!"

Annie stared at me. "Mom? What is he talking about?"

"Just a little misunderstanding. Do you have any of your special Kombucha tea, sweetie?"

Kombucha tea is the vilest substance known to man, but Annie was a devotee and I was still trying to worm my way back into her good graces.

"You don't have to go overboard," she said. "I'm over it. Your relationship with Gambino, I mean. If you say it wasn't meant to be, it wasn't meant to be."

"Thank you," I said. "In which case I'd love coffee."

She went to the freezer and pulled out a bag of organic beans. "As long as you're really sure."

"I am."

She waited until the grinder was done whirring. "Absolutely sure?"

"Yup."

"So what's this little misunderstanding with the police?"

"Unpaid parking ticket. How'd it go with the judge?"

Annie smiled and the room lit up like the Fourth of July. She was that kind of person. If she was happy, you couldn't help but be happy, too.

"Like clockwork," she said.

"I'm giving them their baths now." Vincent had come in with a naked child in each arm. "Say goodnight, Alexander."

"Goodnight, Alexander," said Alexander. It was part of their routine.

"Vincent," I said suddenly.

He turned around. "Yeah?"

I grabbed my purse and pulled out the hot pink cell phone from hell. "Can you do me a favor? Because you were so nice when I first got my phone. Thanks to you, I love received calls."

"I'm glad," he said patiently.

"Unfortunately, we never got through all the camera stuff. So I'm wondering if you have a minute to show me how to retrieve these photos I took the other day. I was on a hike and got some really beautiful nature shots. I'd love to show them to you and Annie. Maybe make Christmas cards with them. I was thinking a nice collage."

"Since when do you make Christmas cards?" Annie looked dubious.

"I *love* art."

"Christmas cards aren't art. They're crafts. You hate crafts."

"I crocheted that oven mitt."

Annie put her hands on her hips. "When you were nine."

"Enough," said Vincent. "I'd be happy to show you when I'm done giving the kids their baths."

Annie sidled up to her husband and slipped the phone into the back pocket of his jeans. "There goes the rest of our evening."

"I heard that," I said.

"How about I sit here for a minute, then," Vincent said, handing me the baby and walking over to his computer, "and just e-mail them to you? Then you can peruse them at your leisure."

"Works for me," I said, counting Radha's beautiful toes. Ten.

Annie poured our drinks and sat down.

"I'm just so relieved," she said, exhaling. "You know, I used to be worried about what would happen if Roxana ever did come back."

Roxana was Alexander's biological mother. "I know."

"But that's all over now."

"Yeah?"

"Yeah. Because I'm the one Alexander goes to for a hug when he falls down. And I'm the one who tucks him in at night. And I'm the one who knows his favorite color is green."

She was still trying to convince herself. I could hear it in her voice.

"Did I ever tell you, Mom, that he's the only kid in his whole school who knows the names of all the knights of the round table?"

"You told me," I said. "He's an amazing child. And so are you," I said, kissing the baby. "You, too," I said to Annie.

And so she was. When I first left my ex and we came out to Los Angeles, I was a wreck. Annie got herself up for school every day, made her own lunches, did her homework, got herself ready for bed. All I had the energy for was gin rummy. I used to play with my grandmother when I was little. Gin rummy made me feel safe. So Annie played with me every night for six months. After that, she said it was time to pull myself together. The first thing we did was go to the nursery together and pick out two tiny citrus trees, an orange and a lemon. We had a little ceremony and planted them next to each other in the backyard. The sour with the sweet, she'd said.

"Speaking of knights, how's Lael?" Lael had made a cake for Alexander's last birthday party that was shaped like a jousting tent, with banners and flags and a solid peanut butter knight. One boy in his class couldn't attend because of life-threatening allergies. "Have you made up with her yet?"

"No. "

"That's crazy."

"All done," said Vincent.

"What a day," said Annie. "Am I right?"

"What a day," her husband echoed. He dropped the phone back into my purse and took the baby. "Almost out of juice."

"The baby?" I asked.

Vincent smiled. "Your phone."

"Mom. About Lael."

"I'm going to call her soon." I drained the rest of my coffee and stood up. "I've just been so busy since I came back from the cruise."

"With what? The book? How is it going?"

"You're sweet to ask," I said. "It's going great."

I do not believe a parent owes a child the unvarnished truth. Annie needed to get involved in another one of my crises like she needed a hole in the head.

"I've got to run," I said. "Congratulations to you both."

As I was leaving, my daughter gave me a hug and pressed one of her famous carob and tofu loaves into my hands. The thing weighed at least ten pounds. As I sprinted to the car, I dropped it, then my purse, and finally my brand-new BlackBerry, which bounced once, then rolled out into oncoming traffic, where a Hummer going double the speed limit pulverized it. And I hadn't even filled out the warranty.

The carob and tofu loaf, however, survived intact.

What a day is right.

Chapter 14

It had been only a short rain, but Pacific Coast Highway was still bumper-to-bumper. The forty-five-minute drive home took close to two hours.

After finally pulling into the driveway, I lurched out of the car, ran across the lawn, whipped open the front door, stripped off my damp things, and made a mad dash for the bedroom. I had half an hour tops to clean myself up and get to my five o'clock appointment.

Thirteen minutes later, I was buttoning the top button of my suit and feeling pretty good when I caught a glimpse of myself in the hall mirror.

Never apply red lipstick in a hurry.

I suppose this was how Pat Hitchcock must've felt when she walked into the bathroom first thing in the morning and realized that while she was sleeping her father had smeared her face with Cherries in the Snow. What a hoot. During the filming of

Strangers on a Train, Hitch sent her up on the Ferris wheel in the amusement park, then turned off the machine. He planned to leave her hanging overnight, but the joke got cut short when she freaked out and he took pity on her.

I ran down the hall as fast as a person can in high heels and a pencil skirt, and scrounged around in the bathroom cupboard for some makeup remover. Naturally I couldn't find any, so I used a few drops of Frizz-Ease. It's all the same stuff. At least that's my theory.

It took exactly seven minutes to toss on Buster's leash, walk him up and down the block once, and let myself back into the house. Transferring the contents of my blue shoulder bag with fringe into my red-and-plum woven clutch with the Bakelite handle took an additional thirty seconds. After that, I plugged the hot pink cell phone into the charger by my bed and hightailed it out to the eighteen-by-eighteen space in my backyard formerly known as the garage.

It was now known as the office.

My office.

I loved the sound of those words.

I'd never expected to have an office of my own, much less to be a published author. No one else had expected it either, least of all my ex. He was the one who published books—endlessly footnoted, profoundly dull tomes on James Fenimore Cooper that nobody read voluntarily (like Cooper's own novels, it might be said)—but books nonetheless. I was the waitress. That was just the way it was.

I sat down at my Lucite desk.

For once, you could see straight down to the floor.

There were no piles of paper stacked vertiginously on top,

no index cards, no newspaper clippings, no legal pads, no random jottings. In frustration, I'd shoved those utterly useless things into a shoebox.

No, there was only one thing on the desk. That was a ten-inch collectible Madame Alexander *Rear Window* doll clad in a miniature version of the filmy peignoir Lisa (Grace Kelly) pulls out of her Mark Cross overnight bag, much to the consternation of Jeff (Jimmy Stewart), symbolically emasculated in his wheelchair, who compensated by keeping a huge tele-photo lens on his lap, even while he was sleeping.

The doll was supposed to inspire me to think outside the shoebox.

So far it wasn't working.

But that was a problem for another day.

I turned on the computer. I had thirteen e-mails, most with enticing subject lines like "Save up to 75% in the BIG SALE!" and "casino welcome conditions." I scrolled down to Vincent's message, mentally crossed my fingers, and opened the attachment.

Seven pictures popped up on the screen.

A dry hillside.

Scattered leaves.

An abandoned truck parked on the trail.

The Hollywood sign.

The Hollywood sign again.

More dead leaves.

Dirt.

Shit.

I pressed delete.

I'd been hoping there'd be at least a shadowy glimpse of a

person I could show to one of my CIA friends next door who'd blow it up with their know-how and expensive equipment and boom, I'd have the identity of the killer.

Unfortunately, it wasn't going to be that easy.

I went back into the house. It was 4:40 p.m. now. I had just enough time to check my machine.

There were two messages.

Hi, there, Ms. Caruso. Sy here. Glad you called the other day. I couldn't tell from your message if you had or hadn't gotten the dossier. We mailed it out last week in a big, fat manila envelope. It should've gotten to you days ago. Give me a call back if it hasn't shown up. We appreciate your business, as you know.

What dossier?

What manila envelope?

Who was Sy?

The number was private, so I couldn't call him back.

The other message was from Detective McQueen. Apparently, she'd heard about the incident at the park with Alfalfa. She snickered unattractively. Then she said she wanted to make sure that the beat cop had told me about Sunday's conversation. She dragged the word out so it sounded like "all-day interrogation without food or water in an overheated room with one-way mirrors." But maybe that was me.

My last moments at home were spent scurrying around looking for my own cell phone, which appeared to be AWOL. I called it from the home phone, but didn't hear it ringing. Maybe it was somewhere in my car. If not, I was going to have to go back and see my friend George with the Afro. Or maybe I would live without a cell phone. What good had a cell phone ever done me? Why should I be reachable at all times and in all places? Thus far, it had only led to heartache.

I flew out the front door.

Jilly's Porsche was blocking my driveway again.

Shit. I didn't have time to go next door and hear another one of Connor's endless stories. I got into the car and pulled on my seat belt. I could *just* make it out if I didn't mind mashing my grass a little bit. Javier could replace it with some sod next week. Or rip the whole thing out. Lawns were ecologically unsound anyway.

As I backed out of the driveway, my neck craned at an unnatural angle, I caught a glimpse of a car in the rearview mirror. A familiar car. A '68 Mustang, black with red interior.

It was Gambino's car.

The car he'd dreamed of when he still lived in Buffalo, the car he'd promised himself if he ever had the money.

It was going too fast for me to make out the driver. But I swear I saw Gambino's square jaw. His close-cropped hair. His wire-rimmed glasses. The little crinkles around his eyes that appeared whenever he was concentrating hard on something, or laughing at something funny somebody had said.

Maybe it was a trick of the light.

Had to be.

Because I wasn't ready to admit it was wishful thinking.

Chapter 15

They tried, you had to give them that. The walls were painted a soothing shade of blue, a jasmine-scented candle was placed discreetly in the corner, and Barry Manilow was crooning an inoffensive tune. But the room still radiated waves of anxiety.

The window slid open with a creak.

"Welcome," said a woman with thick, horn-rimmed glasses and an advanced case of rosacea. "You're here for a five o'clock, aren't you? You look a little edgy."

"I'm fine—"

"Take a deep breath. All the doctors are running behind. We had a fire drill at three. Do you need tissues? Take some. Please. They're complimentary."

She gestured to a hamper filled with enough pocket packs for everyone in greater Los Angeles suffering from a serotonin deficiency.

"I think there may be some confusion," I said. "I'm giving the lecture on Hitchcock and the problem of identity. Your series on psychoanalysis and the arts? I'm not a patient."

My accountant, Mr. Keshigian, was the patient here. Given his creative approach to the tax code, I was surprised he could make do with biweekly sessions. The man had nerves of steel. Medication also helped. Anyway, he'd gotten me this gig. He was always finding me odd jobs. He worried about how I was going to manage in my impending old age, which was sweet, but rather rude when you thought about it. In any case, five hundred dollars was five hundred dollars.

"Ah, Dr. Caruso." The receptionist clapped her hands in glee. "We've been expecting you. Oh, they're going to love your sexy little suit! Red symbolizes defloration, you know. Time to shake things up around here!"

"Actually, I'm not a—"

"They're not quite ready for you in the lecture hall, Dr. Caruso. Did you get some tissues? Maybe you're sensitive to the sudden change in weather? Okay, then! Just make yourself comfortable. It'll be a minute."

There was one couch, and it was covered with an Oriental carpet. I didn't know if I should take a seat on it, or lie down and start talking. I sat down. But there was no escape. Staring down at me was a blown-up photograph of Sigmund Freud, puffing on his favorite phallic symbol. Averting my gaze, I noticed a small bronze statue of a four-breasted Sphinx that had been repurposed as an ashtray. Poor thing couldn't breathe. She was being smothered by too many breasts. Fine. So I have mother issues. But what kind of mother won't let her daughter wear purple to the prom and makes her wear red, the color of defloration? When I wound up pregnant at seventeen, who made me get married to the wrong guy? My mother. My father was already dead. Not that the poor man wasn't rolling in his grave—her words, not mine.

I got myself a packet of Kleenex and blew my nose. Then I buried myself in the latest issue of the *Journal of the American Psychoanalytic Society*. It had an oral fixation theme. There were articles on mouth-based aggression, nail-biting, and Freud and high cholesterol. Turns out that prior to 1924, most Americans had toast and coffee for breakfast. Then Edward Bernays, applying his Uncle Sigmund's ideas about the unconscious to the new field of public relations, convinced people that bacon and eggs constituted the true all-American breakfast. I liked the cartoon on the back page: "An analyst says to a ginger-bread man lying on his couch, 'I am afraid you are sufferink from vat ve call zee Edible Complex.'"

"Dr. Caruso?"

I leapt to my feet. "Actually, I'm not—"

"I'd like to introduce our director, Dr. Rachel Heilmann."

Now that the receptionist had emerged from behind the counter, I could see she didn't have rosacea. She was just hot. Her upper lip was dotted with perspiration and her blouse was soaked under the arms. Probably menopause. She was also wearing an apron, which struck me as odd. Maybe it was a trigger for free association. Apron, kitchen, pancakes, syrup, viscous, tangle, sticky, mess, mother. It all comes back to Mommy. Ask Norman Bates.

Dr. Heilmann was not wearing an apron but rather a caftan and a strand of African beads.

"So nice to meet you, Dr. Caruso." She extended her hand.

"Likewise, but you should know, I'm not—"

"Cranky and overheated?" interjected the receptionist. "And what if I am?"

"All right, Elsa," said Dr. Heilmann, clearly exasperated. "I get the message. You may go ahead and turn on the air."

"Thank you," the receptionist said, heading back to her desk. "Age discrimination suit in the works," she muttered as she passed me. "But I've been instructed not to comment."

Dr. Heilmann linked her arm through mine and led me into a stuffy room filled with other women wearing caftans and African beads and a couple of men with beards and corduroy jackets. They looked like they'd all taken their clothing cues from the same Woody Allen movies.

"Ladies and gentlemen," said Dr. Heilmann, taking her place on the stage, "a few announcements first. Our seminar this Saturday on couples therapy is canceled. Dr. Gruber has sprained his ankle and will be undergoing physical therapy. And where are my runners for the 5K? Remember, we are supporting our sister society in Detroit. Motown," she chuckled. "Finally, I twisted Elsa's arm—figuratively speaking, of course—and she has made us her famous zucchini muffins to have with our coffee after the talk. Yes, that's a bribe, so don't go anywhere. And now I'd like you to join me in welcoming our guest speaker, Dr. Cece Caruso."

The shrinks applauded politely.

"Dr. Caruso, as I'm sure you know, is an expert on artistes such as Dashiell Hammett, Agatha Christie, and, of course, Alfred Hitchcock. She was educated—I'm sorry, Dr. Caruso, where did you receive your doctorate? I'm afraid I don't have that in my notes. We psychoanalysts tend to be a bit anal about the back story."

I gave up. "Harvard University."

Dr. Heilmann beamed. "Harvard University. Very good. My alma mater. Of course, you all know that Harvard never gave Dr. Freud an honorary degree. They were assured by Erik Erikson that there was no chance he would accept. So in 1936 they offered the degree to his arch-nemesis, Carl Jung!"

She waited until the cries of outrage died down.

"And now, ladies and gentleman, I give you—figuratively speaking, of course—Dr. Cece Caruso!"

I took the podium. Figuratively speaking, of course. Not that Dr. Caruso wasn't capable of hoisting something that weighed a mere eighty pounds. She worked out.

Hitch loved dirty jokes, so I started with one. "A psychiatrist was conducting a group therapy session with four young mothers and their small children. 'You all have obsessions,' he said. To the first mother he said, 'You are obsessed with eating. You even named your daughter Candy.' To the second mother he said, 'Your obsession is money. You even named your child Penny.' To the third mother he said, 'Your obsession is alcohol, and your child's name is Brandy.' At this point, the fourth mother got up, took her little boy by the hand and whispered, 'Come on, Dick, we're going home.'"

They liked it.

Hitchcock has long been a favorite of shrinks, and no wonder. His films depict all manner of psychic phantasmagoria: hypnosis, concussions, nightmares, hallucinations. Take Scottie's attacks of vertigo in the film of the same name. Hitchcock had us experience them along with Scottie by having the camera track away from the subject and zoom toward it at the same time. Film scholars have long interpreted this dual camera movement as emblematic of Scottie's mental instability. But the truth is that here and elsewhere, Hitchcock was less interested in psychological extremes than he was in extreme visuals.

This goes back as far his earliest experiences in silent film, where visual style always outranked narrative logic. Indeed, many of his most memorable scenes abandon narrative logic entirely (think of Cary Grant being chased by the crop duster in *North by Northwest*). Or rely upon a single striking image to tell an entire story (as in *Strangers on a Train*, where the murder is seen through the lens of the victim's glasses).

This is not to say that Hitchcock was a formalist with no interest in human psychology. Quite the contrary. What fascinated him in particular, however, was the question of identity: false identity, mistaken identity, split personality, and, above all, the figure of the doppelgänger, or double.

Innocent young Charlie and murderous Uncle Charlie in *Shadow of a Doubt*.

Bruno and Guy, in *Strangers on a Train*, who swap murders.

Norman Bates and his mother in *Psycho*.

Roger Thornhill and his imaginary alter-ego, George Kaplan, in *North by Northwest*.

Suddenly, Dr. Heilmann's hand shot up. "What does Hitchcock have to say about feminine identity?"

A good question.

What is discussed again and again in the Hitchcock literature is the "wrong man" theme: the innocent man mistaken for his guilty double. But what is in fact more interesting is the extent to which all of Hitchcock's heroines are the "wrong" women—that is, women who have sacrificed their identities to fulfill someone else's desire.

In *Shadow of a Doubt*, young Charlie's mother says, "You know how it is. You sort of forget you're you. You're your husband's wife."

In *Vertigo*, Judy pleads with Scotty, hell-bent on transforming her into someone else, "Couldn't you like me, just the way I am?"

Hitchcock is the Master of Suspense, yes.

But he is also a poet of feminine loss.

The suspense isn't merely about whether or not the bomb will go off, or someone will get away with murder. The suspense is about whether or not, once lost, a woman's identity can ever again be found.

That's when it hit me.

What about my identity?

I hadn't been alone since I was seventeen. Who was I without a man? Without a PhD? Without a BlackBerry?

And then the room started spinning. I reached out and clutched the podium.

Dr. Heilmann was immediately at my side. "You don't look very well, my dear."

"I—I don't think I had any food today," I stammered.

"Eating disorder?" asked a chubby woman wearing eight strands of beads, but I might have been seeing double. "Can cause amenorrhea and later osteoporosis in perimenopausal women."

"Are you talking about me?" I said too loudly. "I may be a grandmother, but I'm barely forty!"

Suddenly, the shrinks were surrounding me en masse.

"Have you been experiencing extreme degrees of stress?"

"Have there been any major changes in the close relationships in your life?"

"Have you taken on any new responsibilities, either in the personal or professional arena?"

"Do you feel trapped, and that you have nowhere to turn?"

After two of Elsa's zucchini muffins, three cups of hot coffee, and a promise from Dr. Heilmann to consider how I might benefit from psychoanalysis, they finally let me leave.

As I drove down Wilshire Boulevard toward Hollywood—because, no, this very long day wasn't even *close* to being over—I felt multiple sets of eyes upon me: Dr. Heilmann's, Dr. Freud's, my mother's, my daughter's, Alfalfa's, the hatchet face's, Detective Collins's, Detective McQueen's, the person with the voice that was cold as ice and hard as a stone—you pick.

I suppose I was being paranoid.

But like the saying goes, just because you're paranoid doesn't mean you're not being watched.

Chapter 16

Musso & Frank is the oldest restaurant in Hollywood, a wood-paneled shrine to the finer pleasures of tobacco, red meat, and booze. Back in the day you couldn't go there without bumping into somebody who was somebody, or somebody who used to be somebody, or somebody who was going to become somebody, and I'm not talking about the waiters.

Charlie Chaplin, Rudolph Valentino, and Douglas Fairbanks would race each other down Hollywood Boulevard on horseback, the loser picking up the tab. F. Scott Fitzgerald, Dorothy Parker, and Raymond Chandler, good citizens all, walked over from the Writer's Guild, located on nearby Cherokee. William Faulkner held court in one of the high-backed red-leather booths, which were almost as picturesque as a green lawn in Mississippi, not to mention they let you mix your own mint juleps.

Nowadays, Musso's is frequented by the sort of people

enamored of Hollywood history, as well as those who like meals that start with jellied consommé and end with Postum.

I walked up to the bar and found a seat. The bartender appeared with a discreet clearing of the throat. He was about eighty. He'd probably mixed drinks for Faulkner himself.

"Madame would like?"

I ordered a mint julep, then had a look around.

There was a redhead at the far end of the bar drinking alone, always a bad sign.

A plumpish guy with a goatee in a motorcycle jacket, also alone, sucking down a glass of beer.

A woman next to me who looked exactly like the woman next to her, if you added twenty years of sun damage and an equal number of pounds. They were nursing matching tumblers of vodka and bickering affectionately, the way mothers and daughters do on television, even though this was real life.

The bartender set down my drink.

I took a sip. "Delicious. Thank you."

"Thank *you*, Madame."

He wiped down the counter, polished a few glasses. I popped some nuts in my mouth and glanced at my watch. Ben wasn't coming for ten more minutes. The mother was asking the daughter about a date she'd recently had. The daughter was telling the mother to mind her own business. I stared at the empty place on the third finger of my left hand where my engagement ring used to be. Then I put my hand in my lap and sighed.

"Madame would like another?"

I was supposed to be killing birds here. "Not yet. But I would like to ask you a question."

He was good. I barely saw him cringe.

I leaned forward, lowering my voice. "Was there a guy here a few days ago, waiting for someone, kind of sitting around, acting hostile?"

"Yes, Madame. Now would you excuse me?"

He went to pour a drink for the redhead. Miss Lonelyhearts. When he was finished, he came back over to where I was sitting.

"Will there be anything else, Madame?"

"What exactly did he look like?"

The bartender gave me a knowing smile. "Every night they look different. Some are young, some are old. Some come alone, some with friends. See the gentleman over there?" He shifted his head in the direction of the guy with the goatee. We watched him pick something out of his teeth with a toothpick. "That gentleman will be making a fuss shortly. One spots them early in the evening. One tries to slow them down, but more often than not they are determined to self-destruct. Ready for that mint julep now, Madame?"

It would've been rude to say no.

Then I heard a voice behind me. "You started without me."

I wheeled around in my chair.

"*B* is for Ben," I said. "How are you?"

He was wearing a dark suit, crisp white shirt, and expensive loafers with tassels. Gucci, if I had to call it. He was taller than I'd remembered, and older—late forties, say. And sexier.

"*C* is for Cece," he said. "I'm good."

Time would be the judge of that.

He slid into the seat next to mine and took off his jacket. "How about you?"

"How about me what?"

"Are you good, Cece?"

I crossed my legs. Dr. Heilmann would undoubtedly have a few things to say about that. I uncrossed them again. "I like to think so."

"Maybe that's an unfair question. Good is relative."

"Actually, I believe in black and white."

"Yet you're wearing red."

I decided not to mention it was the color of defloration.

The bartender appeared in front of us. "For the gentleman?"

"I'll take a gimlet."

There was a six-pack of beer in Anita's Sub-Zero. Budweiser. "I would've pegged you for a beer drinker, Ben."

He grinned. "I've been known to enjoy a beer now and then."

"Let me guess," I said. "Budweiser, right? No pretentious foreign stuff, just good, all-American beer, the kind you grew up drinking in your little house on the prairie."

"I grew up in a split level on a cul-de-sac in Tarzana," Ben said. "Never even seen a prairie. And I haven't had a Bud since I was fifteen and had to pay the kid down the block to buy it for me."

Just as the bartender set down his gimlet, Ben's phone started to ring. He pulled it out of his jacket pocket and turned down the volume without checking to see who had called. Smooth. I studied his hands. They were big and strong. The right size for pushing a woman off the side of a mountain.

I stepped down from my seat. "Will you excuse me for a minute?"

"Sure."

"Which way to the ladies' room?" I asked the bartender, overenunciating and blinking animatedly so he'd get the hint.

"If Madame takes this aisle and then—"

I grabbed his arm and pulled him down to the end of the bar. "Is that him?" I whispered, shooting a glance back at Ben. "The one I asked you about, sitting at the bar waiting for someone a couple of nights ago?"

"Madame, I—"

The goatee cleared his throat. "What does a guy have to do to get another beer around here? Looks like I'm shit out of luck. Bartender's preoccupied. Yeah, I'll take a piece of that, too, if you don't mind."

Here was the fuss, right on schedule.

Ben looked up. "Watch your mouth, buddy." I could see the muscles in his back tensing through his white shirt.

"It's okay, Ben," I said.

"Cece," Ben said, eyes glued to the goatee, "just go ahead to the ladies' room. We're fine, here."

"Go ahead to the ladies' room," said the goatee in a singsong voice.

Ben got up from his seat.

So did the goatee.

I didn't want any more blood on my hands. "Ben, let's just go to our table." I walked back over and reached for his arm.

"Listen to Mommy," said the goatee.

Ben was on him in a flash, yanking him out of his seat by the collar. I backed away. Miss Lonelyhearts tossed a ten on the bar and left. The mother and daughter with the matching drinks looked resigned—barflies, obviously. The bartender braced himself.

"I think you owe a couple of people here apologies," Ben said.

The room went silent. Everybody knew the goatee wasn't going down easy.

"Nah," he said, jerking himself free, "I don't think—"

Then the daughter pushed back her tumbler of vodka and let out a huge belch. The kind that wins contests.

"Miriam!" Her mother was shaking her head. "Did I raise you in a barn?"

The tension dissipated pretty fast after that.

"Okay, already." The goatee looked down at his silver-tipped cowboy boots. "So I've got a little drinking problem."

After inhaling deeply, he rolled his head around a few times, cracked his knuckles, and started apologizing—to Ben, to me, to the bartender, and to his mother, who'd raised him right but couldn't stop him from getting mixed up with a bad bunch in high school. Ben accepted his apology on behalf of the group, then helped him pay his tab, including a twenty for the bartender. After that, he escorted the goatee out the back door.

When Ben returned, the mother and daughter started clapping. Ben turned red, which was unexpected for a sexy guy in Gucci loafers.

"I hate fights," he said.

"My father was a cop," I said. "My brothers, too. They all felt the same way."

The next thing I knew I was kissing him on the cheek. The next thing after that we were sitting very close to each other in a small corner of a large booth.

The waiter came over and handed us menus.

I ordered cream of mushroom soup, pork chops with extra applesauce, and mashed potatoes. Ben ordered Caesar salad with anchovies and spaghetti Italienne. In homage to me, he said. Before I got carried away again, I reminded myself I was on a mission.

"So," I said, putting my napkin in my lap, "how exactly did you wind up at the Orpheum that night?"

Turned out Bachelor Number One was a Hollywood agent. And a Hitchcock buff. *Vertigo* was his favorite movie.

"What do you like so much about it?" I asked.

This was a test.

He stopped with the fork midway to his mouth. "The beauty of the shots. The brilliance of the reveal two thirds of the way through the film. The unsettling notion that love is always perverse. Scottie transforms Judy into Madeleine just like Hitch remade all his leading ladies. That's what makes it his most self-reflexive film. And the saddest. Hitch understood his own obsessions, but couldn't get beyond them."

"Salt, please?" Our fingers touched as he handed me the shaker. I felt a definite spark. "But you're wrong about one thing."

"What?"

"The most personal of Hitch's films was actually *Rear Window*."

"How so?"

"It's all about an immobilized man sitting in the dark, spying on his neighbors. It's the perfect allegory of why we go to the movies: to watch people do things we can only fantasize about." I guess my *Rear Window* homage doll hadn't been a waste after all.

"Okay," he said. "I'll give you that round. But I'll bet you didn't know that Hitch cast Raymond Burr as the killer because he looked exactly like the evil supermogul David O. Selznick?"

"Common knowledge. Hitch hated Selznick going back as far as *Rebecca*."

"Not to mention for what he did to Robert Walker."

Robert Walker had given a chilling performance as the dough-faced killer Bruno Anthony in *Strangers on a Train*. He'd died at age thirty-two, eight months after the movie was released. "I'm impressed. I have absolutely no idea what Selznick did to Robert Walker."

Ben put down his fork. "He stole his wife, Phyllis, changed her name to Jennifer Jones, and made her a star. Walker never got over losing her."

"Ouch," I said. "Love hurts."

Bachelor Number One gave me a smoldering look. "It doesn't have to."

The rest of the evening was a blur of witty repartee, strong cocktails, and sexual tension.

And then we were standing in the parking lot. The light was dim. It was late, and the attendants had gone home. I reached into my bag for my keys. I wondered when I was going to see Ben again. He'd passed the test. He'd ordered spaghetti. I loved his shoes.

"Cece?"

I smiled. "I'm sorry, I was distracted for a second."

He waited for me to look at him. "Do I have your full attention now?"

I stood up straight. "Yes."

"I asked if you wanted to know what I was really doing at the Orpheum that night?"

It was at that point that I remembered I was a terrible judge of character.

"What you were really doing at the Orpheum that night," I repeated, putting the key into the lock. "I'm listening." When I heard the click, I opened the car door and started to get in.

He put his hand on my shoulder and turned me around. "Give me the keys, Cece."

"I'm fine."

"You shouldn't be driving."

"I said I was fine."

"I don't know about that." He took the keys out of my hand. "I wouldn't want anything to happen to you."

I felt the blood rush to my face. "You still haven't said what you were doing at the theater."

He flashed a grin. His teeth looked sharp. "I was hoping to bump into you. Come on. Don't you recognize my voice?"

It was him after all.

He'd dropped the hot pink cell phone in my purse.

He'd called me on the trail.

He'd killed Anita.

And he was framing me for it.

But why?

Why me?

I wrenched my keys out of his grasp. "You picked the wrong person to fool with." My voice was quavering. "I'm leaving. And don't try to stop me."

"You're frightened."

I shook my head. "You don't frighten me, Ben."

"But I don't understand. I thought we made a connection that day."

"You're sick." He sounded like Bruno Anthony from *Strangers on a Train*. What, had he memorized the lines?

"Cece, I don't know what you're talking about. This isn't how you sounded the other day. Crazy, I mean."

"At the Orpheum? I most certainly did sound crazy that day. I wouldn't even let you sit down next to me. Ask the lady in the beige cardigan."

"I'm not talking about the Orpheum. I'm talking about the radio."

"The what?"

"You were being interviewed on KPCC. We talked about Hitch's marriage. I can't believe you don't remember."

Oh, God.

I did remember.

I was a guest on one of the afternoon programs. Some listener had called in. It must've been Ben. He and I had had a long talk about how much Alma Hitchcock had sacrificed to support her husband. Sublimating her career to his. Overlooking his infatuations with his actresses. Alma had admired her husband. Respected him. Built a life with him. They'd worked side by side each and every day until he'd died, and he'd valued her opinion over anyone else's. That was love. The whole time this caller and I were talking I was thinking I could never be the kind of wife Alma was. Or any kind of wife. Two days later, I broke it off with Gambino.

So maybe Ben wasn't who I thought he was.

Maybe I'd jumped to conclusions.

But he'd given me ample reason.

I got into the car and slammed the door behind me. As I tore out of the parking lot, I saw his eyes in the rearview mirror.

They didn't look angry.

They looked sad.

And that wasn't even the end of the evening.

As I pulled into my driveway, Connor came striding across my front lawn.

"Hi," he said, opening the car door for me. "Have you been drinking?"

"Of course not." Three Advil and a glass of water would take care of it. I started up the path, then stopped, confused. "Why is my house all lit up? Why is my front door open?"

"No need to panic," he said. "That's a nice suit, by the way. You look great in red."

"I'm not panicking," I said, panicking.

"Good. Because it's nothing serious." He took my hand. "Just a little break-in."

And I knew exactly what they were looking for.

Chapter 17

I raced inside, Connor at my heels.

"Slow down," he said. "Let me make you some coffee."

"I don't want any coffee." I headed straight for my bedroom, stumbling a bit as my shoe caught on the edge of the rug.

"You could hurt yourself that way," said Connor, steadying me. "The last thing you need right now is to be on crutches."

"Stop being so overprotective." I continued down the hall. "Where are my animals?"

"Next door. We can go get them whenever you want."

"Jilly hates cats," I said. "She's deathly allergic, remember?"

"She's out tonight. She won't be back until morning. I hope you're not mad. I brought them over because there was a lot of confusion with the cops and everything."

I stopped dead in my tracks. "What were the cops doing here?"

Connor looked surprised I was asking. "Attempting to apprehend a criminal, I would imagine."

"Very funny."

"Sorry," he said, pushing his blond hair out of his eyes.

"Look, I'm extremely confused. What exactly happened here?"

"When I got home, there was a cruiser parked outside your house, lights on and everything. I was at the movies. One of those torture porn things. I'm the perfect demographic, males aged eighteen to twenty-seven. But bad acting always ruins it for me. It had a great opening scene, though."

I cut him off before he launched into a plot synopsis. "So the cops were here when you got home."

"Yes, ma'am."

"And you didn't call them."

"Nope."

"Then who did?"

"I don't know. Maybe they were driving by and noticed the open door."

"This is crazy," I said. "Why would the door be open? The lock hasn't been jimmied. There are no broken windows. Nothing's missing—look around you!"

The TV was sitting right in front of his nose. Not that anyone would want a TV dating back to the year America found out Bobby Ewing wasn't really dead on *Dallas*.

"And?"

"And, so, I don't know," I said. "Maybe the cops wanted something so they broke in themselves! It's happened before!"

"Come on, Cece. You're starting to sound crazy."

I didn't answer. I was standing in front of the outlet by my bed, staring at the place where the hot pink cell phone that had ruined my life used to be.

I'd plugged it into the charger before I'd left for my lecture.

And now it was gone.

The phone that was registered in my name.

The phone that had been used to harass Anita.

The phone that had a message in its mailbox—from none other than me—threatening Anita's life.

I sat down on the edge of the bed. "I'm not crazy."

"It's okay," he said. "I know you're not."

He sat down next to me, pushed aside the comforter, and put his arm around my shoulders. I leaned into him without thinking. It felt good. But I wasn't looking for a man anymore. I had work to do. I straightened up. "So about these cops."

"Yeah?"

"Two women?"

"Yeah."

"Good-looking?"

"You jealous?" He looked happy for the first time all evening.

"Just answer the question."

"Not really. They were kind of butch, actually. Short hair, no makeup. I think they were into each other. They gave me this." He reached into his pocket and handed me a slip of paper. "That's the phone number of the precinct house. You're supposed to call once you know what's missing. They can't do a full report without it. But they said it was unlikely you'd recover anything. You should go through your insurance company. Anyway, that's what they said."

I stood up, crumbled the slip of paper into a ball, and tossed it into the trash.

"What'd you do that for?"

"I have a photographic memory. Let's go next door, okay?"

Chapter 18

It was after midnight, but Jilly's place was a hive of activity. Maybe the drones preferred it when the Queen Bee was in absentia.

"Hey, man," said Connor to two guys who were heading out the door, arms weighed down with cardboard boxes.

"Hey, man," they said. "See you tomorrow. Don't forget those cables."

"No problem," Connor said.

We squeezed around the oak table formerly belonging to Cher and went into the living room, where the nephew with the tattoos up and down his arms and another guy with tattoos up and down his arms were sprawled on a huge black leather couch with pagers and BlackBerrys and various other electronic devices I couldn't identify surrounding them like sacred talismans. The television was on, but the sound was off.

"Hey, man," said Connor.

"Hey," they responded in unison. Both were wearing rapper-style baggy shorts and house slippers.

"What's on?" Connor asked.

"Reality show," said the nephew.

"Reality bites," said the other one.

They thought that was really funny.

Connor threw his arm around my shoulder. "This is Cece, our neighbor."

"Terence." The nephew extended his hand.

"Ellroy," said the other one. "From what I hear, you lead an exciting life, Cece."

"Nice to meet you." I glanced at Connor, who shrugged his shoulders.

"Ellroy's our smart-ass," he said.

Terence smiled. "Every family needs one."

"You're our dropout," said Ellroy, much to Terence's amusement.

One of the devices started ringing, then another. Terence picked them both up, put one to each ear, said, "Hey," listened, then handed one of them to Connor, saying, "She's got eyes everywhere." He handed the other one to Ellroy, who promptly hung up, saying, "I answered those questions an hour ago. I can't help it if she's got early-onset Alzheimer's." Connor listened for a few minutes, making faces all the while. Then he said, "Your wish is my command," and hung up.

"So you guys are in entertainment?" I asked.

They looked at each other and cracked up.

"We entertain each other," said Terence, getting up, "that's for sure. Anybody need a soda?"

"Actually, I need to get my pets and go," I said, "but if it's okay, I'd like to use the rest room first."

"Sure," said Connor. "It's just down the hall."

I headed the way he pointed, but unfortunately I'm bad with directions.

The first room I came upon looked like the bad guy's lair in a James Bond movie. There were lights blinking, terminals humming, aluminum attaché cases everywhere.

"Uh, excuse me? Can I help you?" A Latino kid with problem skin pulled off his headphones, and the giant computer screen he was sitting in front of went black.

"Looks like I overshot the bathroom. Sorry."

He waited until I left before returning to his cyber-plotting.

Further down the hall, I was bushwhacked by the scent of corn chips. Looked like I'd found Jilly's bedroom. The door was open so I peeked in.

The bed was covered by a pink patchwork quilt with a stuffed Daisy Duck in a pink pinafore propped up against a pink gingham pillow. The dresser was covered with dozens upon dozens of miniature perfume bottles. Plus an industrial-sized bottle of patchouli, which cures dandruff and is also used as an anointing oil in tantric sexual practices. I read that someplace. There were French doors leading out to the pool, draped with pink eyelet curtains with pink lace ruffles at the bottom. I walked over to have a closer look. Jilly had strung fairy lights all over the palms and yuccas. It was magical, in a gruesome sort of way.

Then I heard something rustling outside. I was about to freak out when I remembered the house was full of people. No danger could come to a person in a house filled with people. Slowly, carefully, I took a step closer to the open window just opposite Jilly's bed.

There, perched ignobly on the fence between our houses, was my opossum.

His back was turned.

Perhaps he didn't like corn chips.

I stared at him for a moment. And that was when I discovered something very disconcerting.

From the very spot where I was standing, I could see not only my opossum on the fence, but the entirety of my bedroom.

My curtains were open. My lights were ablaze. My clothes were strewn across the floor. I could even see through my bedroom directly into my turquoise-tiled bathroom. The place where I take off all my clothes at least once a day.

"Hey, man," said Ellroy. "This isn't cool. What are you doing in Jilly's bedroom?"

I spun around guiltily. "What am I doing in Jilly's bedroom?"

He took a step closer to me. "Yeah, that's what I asked."

A loud meow came from under the bed.

"I was looking for my cat, of course." I got down on my knees, yanked up the dust ruffle, and grabbed Mimi by the tail. "And here she is, none the worse for wear." I pulled her out for Ellroy's inspection.

"Jilly's going to be pissed," he said. "She hates cats."

"That shouldn't be encouraged."

Ellroy looked nonplussed. Some smart-ass. "Did you find the bathroom?"

"Yeah. You've got a leak under the sink. Did you know that can lead to toxic mold?"

"Shit. Jilly's going to go ballistic. Do you know a good plumber?"

"No," I said, smiling.

"There you are, Cece," said Connor. "I've got your dog."

I took Buster's leash. "We have to go home now."

As we were squeezing back around Cher's table, something occurred to me. I asked Connor if it was possible that there was a piece of mail he'd missed giving me the other day.

"You missing something in particular?"

"Maybe," I said. "Maybe something like a big, fat manila envelope. The kind you put a dossier into?"

Terence pulled a large envelope out from under a flyer advertising cheap flights to South America. "What about this?"

"I think that belongs to Jilly." Connor took the envelope out of Terence's hands.

"No, man," said Ellroy. "Look."

It was clearly addressed to Ms. Cece Caruso.

"My mistake," Connor said. "Take it."

Once I was back inside my house, I dead-bolted the front door and pushed three of my dining room chairs up against it. Then I sat at the kitchen table and picked up the manila envelope. The return address read, "Gersh Investigations."

Hands shaking, I ripped it open and spilled the contents onto the table. Inside were dozens of photographs of a tall blond woman who was starting to look very familiar.

Anita Colby.

Anita smiling.

Anita frowning.

Anita walking down the street.

Anita getting into a car.

She had the kind of grace you could see even in a still photograph.

There was also a packet of smaller envelopes tied up with a pale blue ribbon. The letters from her ex, I was guessing.

And an invoice made out to Cece Caruso in the amount of twelve hundred dollars.

Looked like I wasn't just your average stalker.

I'd been so obsessed I'd hired a P.I.

Later that night, as I sat in the chair in my bedroom, the lights off and the curtains drawn, I wondered what would have happened if I'd hadn't gone back for the cell phone that day.

What if I'd just kept running toward Anita's body?

Maybe she would have been alive when I got there.

Officer Lavery said she'd died on impact. But maybe she'd lived for a few minutes.

Maybe I could have held her hand. Talked to her. Listened. I was such a good listener.

But I hadn't run to Anita. I'd run away from her dead body, and when I'd come upon the ringing phone, I'd given in to my curiosity.

What if I hadn't given in?

What if I hadn't said, "Hello?"

Chapter 19

The next morning, I got up at the crack of dawn, showered, dressed, and ate a well-balanced breakfast.

After washing and putting away the dishes, I opened the freezer, took out a gallon tub of vanilla ice cream, removed the top, and extracted six hundred and eighty dollars in wilted twenties.

Then I went into the bathroom, opened the medicine cabinet, and pulled out a can of Solarcaine Aloe Extra spray, for non-stinging sunburn relief. I unscrewed the bottom and pulled out a roll of twenty ten-dollar bills.

In the living room, I thumbed through my CD collection, and found *The Judds: Greatest Hits*. The case opened with a click, and out came six crisp hundreds.

Next, I unzipped one of the seat cushions on the maroon velvet couch, stuck my hand inside the foam rubber, and slid out seventy-six five-dollar bills, which added up to the tidy sum of three hundred and eighty dollars.

The ficus plant next to the couch yielded a Ziploc bag containing two hundred dollars in fifties.

I keep my tool kit in the basement. After finding a Phillips head screwdriver, I headed into Annie's old bedroom and in two minutes flat I'd removed the switch plate by the window, pulled out the little box I'd ordered a decade ago from the back of a magazine, and removed a stack of bills held together with a fat rubber band.

Seven hundred and ninety five dollars to be precise, bringing the grand total up to two thousand eight hundred and fifty-five bucks.

It was more than enough to get out of town.

I closed the curtains, hit the lights, locked up, threw my suitcases into the trunk, dropped the pets off at the ladies' house—staying just long enough to request they cool it with the cheddar cheese—and made my getaway.

My first stop was the office of Dr. Barbara Rudes, lesbian neurologist.

That would be *B* is for Barbara Rudes.

She'd given me her card that night at the Orpheum, and by some miracle I'd come across it again when I was packing. As luck would have it, she ran an open clinic on Saturdays. Her receptionist told me to show up early if I didn't want to wait.

Out of sheer laziness, I pulled into the overpriced lot opposite Cedars-Sinai Medical Center only to have it hit me that I had to be extremely careful about money now. But I didn't want to waste time moving the car to the municipal lot two blocks over, so I promised myself I'd skip lunch.

As I approached the building, a swarm of men in hoodies descended upon me, cameras clicking, until one of them informed the group that I was a nobody, which would have been insulting if it weren't true, not to mention I was supposed to be going underground. He did open the door for me, proving that chivalry is not dead, even among the paparazzi.

The receptionist asked me to sign in.

I picked the very first name to pop into my head.

Mrs. Cece Gambino.

Then I sat down on a chair to fill out the medical history. Cece Caruso's was pretty boring, but Cece Gambino suffered from a host of hideous ailments, including migraines, insomnia, and vertigo. I figured that was my best shot at getting in before the beefy guy sitting next to me, who was reading the Bible and appeared to be in the pink of health. The only glitch came when the receptionist asked for my insurance card, which I pretended to have forgotten at home, reassuring her that I'd be paying in cash.

After about fifteen minutes, the beefy guy's beeper went off. He stood up, tucked his book into his pocket, and straightened his shirt. Then the door to the inner sanctum opened and out came a world-famous former teen pop star wearing dark glasses and what appeared to be a nightie. The beefy guy helped her on with her coat, took her arm, and led her out to the vultures.

My turn.

After a twenty-minute wait in the exam room, I heard some shuffling outside the door, then some pages turning. Finally Dr. B is for Barbara Rudes entered with a grim look on her face.

"I'm feeling better," I said. "The room stopped spinning."

"I don't usually cure people that quickly," she said. "What about the migraines?"

"Amazing. Vanished like that." I snapped my fingers. "Magnesium supplements. Plus I've been doing a lot of exercise. Hiking in particular." I looked her in the eye. "On all the wonderful trails we have here in Southern California."

"Is there something else I can help you with, then?" she asked. "Because I'm pretty busy today."

I wasn't letting her off that easy. "Is hiking something you enjoy, Dr. Rudes?"

"Yes," she replied, "not that I have much time for leisure activities."

"That's a real pity."

"It is," she agreed, warming to the theme. "I should probably join a club or something. Is that what you're suggesting? Get out into nature, away from the office once in a while? Physician, heal thyself?"

"Yes. Exactly. Hobbies are very therapeutic." As opposed to murder.

She looked down at my high-heeled gladiator sandals. "Tsk, tsk. You don't wear those shoes when you hike, do you?"

"Of course not. I don't want to get bunions. I wear tennis shoes. They're very muddy from the other day. I left footprints in the wrong places, if you know what I'm saying."

She ran her finger up and down the edge of my file. "You might consider hanging out in the right places, then." Then she smiled coyly.

So that's how it was.

You didn't have to hit me over the head.

Cross B is for Barbara Rudes off the list.

"Time to 'fess up," I said. "I'm not here because you're a legend in neurology circles."

She slammed down my file on the sink before I could finish. "I'm such an idiot. This is unbelievable. It was Chantal. She sent you, didn't she?"

"Who's Chantal?"

"My girlfriend. She's the jealous type. Did she pay you? She usually pays handsomely."

"Chantal," I said. "Beige cardigan, a little edgy? Speaking of Chantal—"

"You know the way out." The doctor opened the door.

"Wait," I said, hopping off the exam table. "Don't you remember me? From the other night at the Orpheum? We were watching *Vertigo*. You, me, and Chantal. Also a blond woman in a robin's-egg blue dress, and a bald man. Third row up from the back. You gave me your card."

"Oh, God," Dr. Rudes said. "Of course I remember you. Chantal told me about the little scene you made. We could run an MRI, but I suspect the trouble has no organic cause. You need a psychiatrist, not a neurologist."

"Barbara," I said.

"Yes?"

"Did you happen to notice anybody with a hot pink cell phone that night?"

"No offense, but do you know how crazy you sound?"

"Have you ever heard the name Anita Colby?"

"No."

"Do you think Chantal knows anybody named Anita Colby?"

"I'm sure she does." She sighed. "To tell you the truth, I work too hard to have the time or energy to pursue multiple relationships, much less hobbies, but Chantal is voracious.

That's the only word for it. Nothing and nobody satisfies her! She assuages her guilt by attributing the same behavior to me, but it's projection, pure and simple."

And she'd looked so beige and mousy.

"You have one more minute," Dr. Rudes said. "There are sick people waiting."

Think.

I'd put my purse under my seat next to Chantal's shopping bags. When the lights came up, she was the one who handed it back to me. She could easily have slipped the cell phone into it. Was she the person who'd pretended to be me and hired the P.I.? The one who'd purchased the phone in my name? The one who'd sipped specialty cocktails with Anita at her apartment in the Andalusia?

"Cranberry martinis," I blurted out.

"I'm sorry. I don't date patients," Dr. Rudes said.

"I'm not asking you out," I clarified. "I'm married, remember?"

"Then you're just Chantal's type," she said. "And she adores Crantinis. With a twist of lime."

Bingo. "Where was Chantal the afternoon of Wednesday, October twenty-sixth?"

"I have no idea where Chantal is while I'm earning a living. She does a lot of shopping. She sees a life counselor. Takes Pilates classes. It's a lot of work being Chantal."

I'll bet.

"But in answer to your question"—Dr. Rudes pulled out her BlackBerry and fiddled with it—"Chantal spent the afternoon of October twenty-six getting microdermabrasion. I've already received the bill. And she looks like hell, if you want my opinion."

"Do you have before and after photos?" I could show them to the tiny girl with the cap of neon yellow hair and solve this whole thing like that.

"I do not. Let's go," she said, ushering me out the door.

Damn it.

"That'll be $195 for an office visit," chirped the receptionist.

"No charge for the lovely Mrs. Gambino," Dr. Rudes said.

The receptionist raised an eyebrow.

"Oh, stop it," said *B* is for Barbara. "Just order me my usual pork with mint leaves. And don't even *think* about getting Chantal on the phone."

Chapter 20

The next item on the agenda was a visit to On the Bias, Bridget's vintage clothing store. It was only a couple of blocks away, but at $2.75 every fifteen minutes, I wasn't leaving the car behind.

I found a spot right on Burton Way and deposited a couple of quarters in the meter. Then I tucked one of the suitcases under my arm, and pushed open the heavy celadon and gold door.

At the sound of the bell, Bridget's dachshund, Helmut, trotted out and gave me the once-over. Then he backed up a few steps, steeled himself, and made a flying leap for the hem of my baby blue swing coat.

He missed.

"We're not open," said an African-American woman who was not my friend Bridget but a smaller, younger, and quite possibly more officious version of the same.

She was wearing a black turtleneck minidress, her waist

cinched with a wide black leather belt covered in bronze studs. She scared me, which I suppose was the idea.

I put down my suitcase. "I'm not a customer."

"Indeed," she replied, rising from her chair.

"What's that supposed to mean?" A chip on the shoulder can feel like a boulder. I'd learned that from a fortune cookie.

"Nothing at all. Now if you don't mind . . ." She gestured to the stack of papers on her desk. "I have to get back to my correspondence."

"You go right ahead," I said. "Is Bridget around?"

She studied her perfect red nails. "I'm afraid Miss Sugarhill is indisposed."

"Can you tell her Cece is here?"

She frowned. "Cece who?"

"Cece Caruso."

"I've never heard of you," she said icily.

"Helmut knows me." And hates me, I did not add.

"Helmut is a dog."

"I'll bet Bridget doesn't know you talk like that."

On cue, the boss emerged from the back room, also wearing a black turtleneck minidress with a wide leather belt covered in bronze studs. She would've scared me, too, if I didn't know she liked to sleep in pj's with little sheep on them.

"Well, well, well." Bridget scooped up Helmut from the pink mohair chaise where he'd been busy grooming his privates. "Look who the cat dragged in."

"Bridget, shouldn't you be resting?" the woman asked, brows knit in concern. "Or shall I bring you a nice cappuccino?"

"A nice cappuccino?" Bridget pursed her lips. "Do you mean with chocolate sprinkles and extra foam?"

"Just the way you like it."

"Good idea," Bridget said. "And some of those liver treats for Helmut."

"I like mine with no foam," I said.

No response.

I tried again. "So. You must be Bridget's new intern." They rotated seasonally. Most of them followed up the experience with a visit to the psych ward.

"I prefer the term 'assistant,'" the woman said. "I'm Bernadette. As in *Song of*?"

I'd seen it. Jennifer Jones, speak of the devil, won an Oscar for her role as Bernadette, the young woman who has a vision of the Virgin Mary, played by an uncredited Linda Darnell, best known for her topless photos.

"Before you go," said Bridget to Bernadette.

"Yes?"

"Tell me about Cece's purse." She clapped her hands. "Quick!"

Bernadette straightened her spine. "1958–66. Bonnie Cashin for Coach, pink glove leather with gilded frame, no chips, skinny chain handle and signature Mexican striped cotton lining. Approximate value: $225.00."

"Open the purse, Cece," Bridget demanded. "Show us the lining."

There was almost three thousand dollars' cash in there. No way was I opening it.

"I have a headache," I said abruptly. "Can we go somewhere private and talk?"

Bridget looked at me curiously. "Okay."

I followed Bridget into the back, whispering, "I'm worried about you. Haven't you ever seen *All About Eve*?"

"Pish-tosh." Bridget picked a green Fortuny gown off the seat of an old leather chair before sitting down and rolling over to where I was standing. "It's you I've been worried about."

"You've got to be kidding."

"Yeah, well," said Bridget with a grin. "It sounded good. Sit down, Cece. You're making me nervous."

I perched on the edge of a hard chair. "So I wanted to talk to you about something."

"They're ready!" announced Bernadette.

Bridget rolled over to Bernadette, took the drinks, and shooed her away after explaining that I was the dear friend who had canceled my wedding at the last second like a crazy person.

My cappuccino was tepid.

"Nice and hot," Bridget said of hers, licking the foam from her lips. "Just the way I like it." She rolled back toward me, stopping an inch away from my face. "All right. I'm all ears."

"I'm taking a little trip," I began.

"Again?"

"This one is work-related."

"Speaking of work, you didn't ask me how the audit went." Bridget turned away. "I'm hurt."

"How did it go?" I knew better than to get exasperated.

She beamed. "Did you know that both Jimmy Hoffa and Amelia Earhart disappeared on their way to IRS audits?"

I stared at her blankly.

"It's a joke. My auditor had me in stitches. When he

wasn't complimenting my books, that is. I'm getting a refund! William says he's never met anyone as scrupulous as me."

"Probably doesn't get out much," I mumbled.

"What was that?"

"Nothing." I reached out and gripped the arms of her chair so she'd stop rolling. "About my trip."

"Yes."

"I don't know how long I'll be gone, but I'm planning on getting a lot done. It all depends on how fast I can work. Anyway, the thing is—" I heaved my suitcase onto the desk. "The thing is, part of the time I'm going to be in the middle of nowhere. No nail salons, no fancy restaurants, no ATMs, even. Which is what I wanted to talk to you about." I unzipped the suitcase and flipped it open.

"What is all this?" Bridget asked, gaping at the piles of clothing inside. "Is this—no! This isn't your Lanvin capelet, is it?"

It was. The rarest and most expensive vintage garment I'd ever owned.

"And this? What is this gorgeous thing all wrapped up in tissue?"

It was a black velvet Juliet cap covered with hand-embroidered flowers—irises, roses, hyacinths—and trimmed in the palest lavender silk.

"I found it at a garage sale in Evanston," I replied. "I hope you're proud of me. I practically snatched it out of the hands of a curator from the Chicago Art Institute. It's from the twenties. French. I wore it exactly once. With my lavender bias-cut dress, the one that looks like Jean Harlow, with the gold feather trim? You've seen that dress. It's at the bottom of the suitcase someplace."

"Oh, my God," Bridget said, no longer listening to me. "I love this!"

She'd grabbed a black, art deco evening bag with a lapis and canary yellow enameled clasp.

"And this!"

She dropped the bag and held up a muted olive green velveteen wrap from the seventies with an oversized white fur collar and fuchsia and tangerine paisley lining: Marlene Dietrich with a rock-and-roll twist.

"I'm glad you like it." My voice was quiet. "Because I might need you to sell some of this stuff for me."

"Sell it?" She looked aghast.

"Yes. In a hurry."

"But—"

"And then wire me the cash." I stopped. "Do you understand what I'm saying?"

Bridget frowned. "You're in trouble."

"Not exactly."

"I think we should get Gambino on the phone."

"No."

"Cece. He'd want to know. He'd want to help."

"It's not possible." I shook my head. "Okay?"

She shrugged her shoulders in resignation. "Fine."

"This may be overkill. I just wanted to be sure I could count on you if I needed to."

"You know you can."

"All right," I said, heading for the door. "Then I'm leaving."

"Wait!"

"What?"

"You almost forgot your coat." She helped me with it, then gave me a rare hug.

"Thanks," I said. "I mean it."

As I was walking out to the car, I felt something in the pocket that hadn't been there before.

Five hundred bucks and a Hershey bar.

I smiled as I pulled away from the curb.

There's no substitute for a true friend.

Chapter 21

One more stop, then I was flying the proverbial coop.

I'd never particularly noticed the two-story building, which was a block and a half east of West Hollywood City Hall and sorely in need of a paint job.

The lobby was your standard shabby affair. Stained linoleum tiles, peeling wallpaper, no directory. The only sign of life was an overflowing trash can.

I climbed the stairs to the second floor. The landing was covered in shag carpet of an indeterminate hue. There was a wood veneer console at the far end, and somebody named Phil had traced his name in the dust. I followed the sound of laughter down the hallway to the single open door.

A pretty brunette was sitting at the desk. Above her head was a sign that read DERMALUXE COSMOCEUTICALS.

"*Hasta luego,*" she said into the phone. "Can I help you, Miss?"

"I hope so."

"Great! You're in good hands." She whipped out a ther-
mometer. "We're not going to get an accurate reading on your
basal temperature, it's too late in the morning, but it'll give us
an idea of where to start. Ready?"

"No," I said, backing toward the door.

"Reluctance is perfectly natural. Skepticism, even. But do
you know how the system works? You pick a target date—say
your wedding—and we develop a custom skin-care regimen
based on your basal temperature and hormonal balance, keeping in mind the pheremonic boost caused by joyful expecta-
tion."

"I'm not exactly wedding material," I said.

"High school reunion, perhaps?"

"Actually, I'm looking for Gersh Investigations. Is it somewhere around here?"

"Gersh Investigations? Why didn't you say so?" The ther-
mometer went back into its case. "You've come to the right
place." She slid open the top drawer of her desk and sifted
through some papers. "Here it is." Out came a shiny plaque
that read GERSH INVESTIGATIONS. She studied it, frowned,
exhaled onto its surface, then rubbed it with her sleeve before
positioning it on her desk. "Um-hmm. Okay. Ready." She
cleared her throat. "Sy is out right now, but I'm going to give
him a call and get him over here, so don't move. He's in the
neighborhood. He never goes far." Her hand flew up to her
heart. "He's such a sweetheart. All his clients are like family
to him."

"Who said I was a client?" I asked.

"Whatever." She already had him on the phone. "Sy? Hi,

it's Esperanza, at the office. I have a woman here—yeah, tall, long curlyish hair, nicely dressed. White cropped pants, blue kind of twirly coat. What? Oh, sure." She looked up at me. "Are you Cece Caruso?"

I wasn't sure how to answer that. "I—"

"Yes," she said, jumping the gun, "it's her. Okay. I'll tell her. See you soon. No problem." She hung up. "He'll be here in a jiffy. Sit down." She gestured toward a plush chair in the corner. "Would you like a magazine while you wait?"

"I'm fine," I said.

"I know you're here to see Sy, but you might want to peek at one of our brochures." She pointed to the coffee table, where they were neatly fanned out. "We're launching at Cosmoprof in Bologna this spring. There are franchise opportunities. You'd be getting in on the ground floor."

"Thanks." I sat down and pulled the manila envelope out of my tote bag.

I was giving Sy exactly ten minutes.

So here's how I saw it.

Somebody showed up here, pretending to be me, most likely the same person who hung out with Anita those last weeks of her life, drinking cranberry martinis and talking girl talk. Maybe it was Chantal. Maybe it wasn't. Whoever it was hired Sy to follow Anita Colby, and possibly even to break into her apartment, which I know he must've done because how else would he have gotten his hands on a bunch of letters from Anita's crazy ex-boyfriend in Bakersfield? Anyway, the point was, once Sy saw me in the flesh, he'd realize that he'd been had. Then he'd be angry. And then we'd put our heads together to try and figure out where the imposter was hiding.

The false Cece.

She was the key to all of this.

"Here I am!" said a skinny little man who materialized out of thin air, like a rabbit being pulled from a hat.

"Sy?" I jumped to my feet.

"None other." He yanked up his gray trousers, which were several sizes too big.

"Have we met?" I demanded.

Maybe I was a little too intense. He opened his mouth and yawned nervously. "Sorry. Late night. Big stakeout." He tried to make eye contact with Esperanza, who was making a show of tidying up her desk. "Esperanza!"

"Yes?"

"Hold all calls."

"What about Big John?"

"You can put Big John through."

Sy ushered me into his office and took a seat behind an ugly desk with nothing on it except a plastic pumpkin filled with cellophane-wrapped mints and one of those pendulums that's supposed to prove Newton's theory of something or other. Sy smiled obsequiously. He had pearly white veneers, which had the odd effect of aging him.

"Well?" I asked.

"Have we met?" He wrinkled his brow. "That was the question, right?" He swung one of the silver balls and the horrible clacking began.

"That's right." I took off my coat, spun around, turned my head to give him both profile views. "You've never seen me before in your life, have you?"

"No," he replied.

Thank God. "Would you be willing to tell that to the police?"

"You in some kind of trouble?" Sy asked. "Because trouble is my business. It says that on my card."

"Of course I'm in trouble! Aren't all your clients in trouble?"

"You've got that right, sister. But I'm a little confused. Are we *supposed* to have met?"

"Yes. When you took the case. I mean, you met someone named Cece Caruso that day. Me. In theory."

He stared at me blankly.

"Didn't you?" I asked.

"No," he said. "You and I have spoken only on the phone, Ms. Caruso. We've never had a face-to-face until this very moment."

"Right," I said, sitting down.

"Now, *Marv*—him you've met in person. He was here the day you came in. Holding down the fort, so to speak. Esperanza was sick. Me, too. Bad oysters. But I doubt you're confusing me with Marv. He's a big guy. High blood pressure." Sy shook his head.

"Marv," I said. "Of course. And where is Marv right now?"

"Honolulu."

"Working on a case?"

"A tan."

"Can we call him?"

"Nope."

"Why?"

"He's on vacation. His first in eighteen years. No wonder he has trouble with his ticker. Stress kills."

It was then that I made the executive decision to go on the offensive. "Tell me, Sy, was it you or Marv who stole these from Anita Colby's apartment?" I pulled the stack of envelopes from the manila envelope and waved them menacingly. "I'm concerned about the illegality of that. I think it's imperative we get Marv into this discussion, and I mean now."

"Ms. Caruso, you've gotta take it easy. You've got some short-term memory loss here or something. You might want to see a doctor. I'm happy to recommend—"

"I'm under the care of an excellent neurologist already."

"Glad to hear it. Because Marv and I had nothing to do with getting those letters. You were the one who gave Marv those letters, to assist in the investigation. Don't you remember? After dropping your stuff all over the office, I might add. Marv said he'd never seen anybody so *verklempt*. You gotta relax, Ms. Caruso! We are *completely uninterested* in how you got your hands on those letters. Your business is your business, even if it is trouble, which is also *our* business, as I might have mentioned. But speaking of trouble, we do owe you an apology about something. Mea culpa," he said, raising his hands in the air. "Marv and I went out to Bakersfield like you asked, but All-America Auto was closed that day. So we never dealt definitively with the boyfriend question."

At that moment, the intercom buzzed.

"That'll be Big John," he said. "How ya doing, B.J.? Give me a minute." He put Big John on hold and walked around to the other side of his desk. "Good luck in all of your endeavors, Ms. Caruso. One last thing. About that $1200 invoice we sent you?"

I rose to my feet. "The check is in the mail."

Back in the reception area, Esperanza was watering a plant.

"Stop by anytime," she said. "You probably know you're normal to oily, but that's just the tip of the iceberg. It's best if you take your own temperature before you get out of bed or even speak, after a minimum of five hours' sleep. Have a great day."

I'd shoved my pink purse into my tote bag, buttoned up my coat, and was halfway through the door when Esperanza called me back.

"Sorry," she said, running back around to the other side of her desk. "I'm sure you've got someplace to be, but I don't want you to forget this again."

"What's this?" It looked like a business card.

"When you kind of lost it the other day, you know, dropped your purse and everything spilled out all over the place, you left this behind. Marv gave it to me and I completely forgot to stick it in the envelope I mailed you. Hope it's not too late."

I flipped over the card.

Cece Caruso had an appointment at Orchid Thai Massage in less than two hours.

Chapter 22

I pulled away from the curb like a bat out of hell, which turns out to be a bad idea in heavy traffic.

The accident sounded a lot worse than it looked. Despite partially caving in, my driver's side door still opened and closed. As for the other guy, his Chevy Nova suffered only a little chipped paint.

The bad news was he wanted to file a police report.

The good news was neither of us had a cell phone.

The bad news was I could see a pay phone at the end of the block.

The good news was he hadn't seen it yet.

I had to think fast.

The other guy's name was Lewis. Lewis took pride in fulfilling his civic duty. He'd voted in every presidential election since 1956. Plus, he'd just changed insurance companies and was eager to find out about his new coverage. I debated telling

Lewis that I was a suspect in a murder case in the process of fleeing the jurisdiction and therefore not exactly eager to alert the authorities, but I decided to skip the formalities and get right to the point.

I pulled four hundred bucks out of my purse.

When they say money talks, they're not lying.

After wishing Lewis a good day, I hopped back into my crippled Camry and headed west on Sunset, making four lights in a row.

It was half past noon now. I'd be fine assuming there were no more accidents.

I took it down to fifty-five, following Coldwater over the hill. After ten minutes or so, I started feeling nauseous. Maybe I needed food. I found the candy bar Bridget gave me and downed it in three bites. It had almonds, which made it lunch.

I felt better after that, and put on the radio. The relationship doctor was talking about people who couldn't commit, which made me feel nauseous again, so I switched to classic rock. Unfortunately, Bruce Springsteen was singing "Born to Run."

It seemed like a good idea to turn off the radio.

So this was life on the lam.

I tried to picture myself greeting each day peering through the slats of the blinds in miscellaneous anonymous motels. Eating at greasy spoons, where they always forgot to put the salad dressing on the side. Spending lonely nights at local dives shooting pool with petty criminals. What happened if I ran out of money before I got myself out of this mess? More to the point, would Coldwater ever end? Where the hell was I?

Uncharted territory, it would appear.

The San Fernando Valley, home to the multibillion-dollar porn industry and epicenter for much of ethnic Southern California. Not that you could tell. All I could see for miles in either direction were tract homes draped with last year's Christmas decorations.

I kept driving.

Thirty minutes of citrus trees.

Ten minutes of auto-parts shops.

Finally, I found it, a sun-baked storefront with peeling floral decals in the window and a faded sign reading ORCHID THAI MASSAGE.

As I pulled open the door, the sound of gong chimes filled the air. The waiting room was empty, except for a small dog in a rattan basket.

"Can I help you, Miss?" The man behind the desk stood up. He was huge, at least six foot four, and garbed in a flowing white suit.

I told him I was waiting for a friend who had an appointment at two o'clock.

He checked his book. "Ah. Cece Caruso."

"Yes. Lovely woman, isn't she?"

"I haven't met Miss Caruso yet," he said, opening and closing his fingers like a flytrap. "So I have no idea. But she's been coming regularly these past few weeks, so I'm certain she's starting to glow from within. Thai massage not only addresses soft-tissue disorders, chronic back pain, joint pain, and migraines, it also firms and tightens the skin." He peered at me. "You can forget about getting Botox after we're done with you."

"Cece looks fabulous for her age," I said through gritted teeth.

"I'm sure she does," he said. "Have a seat. It's almost two."

Whatever.

I went over to pet the dog, then sat down, wondering if I'd recognize Chantal in her Cece disguise. The way I remembered her, she looked nothing like me. But maybe I was flattering myself. Maybe I looked pretty good to myself, and beige, mousy, and in need of Botox to the rest of the world. It was kind of depressing.

Anyway, I didn't want to get too hung up on Chantal. That would be a mistake. Because it was quite possible she was innocent in all this and somebody else entirely was going to walk through that door, somebody I'd never laid eyes on before. Either way, I sat on the edge of my seat, ready to strike.

The minutes ticked by.

2:07.

I leaned back a little. Maybe she wasn't going to show.

I thumbed through a couple of magazines. The dog was snoring now.

I stared into space. She wasn't coming. But I wasn't beaten yet.

"Excuse me, is that a surveillance camera?" I pointed to a black object with a lens affixed to the molding over the door.

The man in the flowing white suit looked up. "A surveillance camera? Where?"

"Over there."

"Over where?"

I pointed again. "On the molding. Over the door."

"Oh, over there." He looked at it quizzically. "Yes, that's a surveillance camera. We get some unwanted traffic from time to time. You know, people looking for a massage parlor."

Cece had been coming here regularly.

There had to be footage of her in there.

How hard could it be to get my hands on it?

"How do you like that model?" I asked innocently. "I'm comparing brands for my house. I've had a couple of break-ins lately."

"I'm not sure," he said, picking up the phone. "It just arrived yesterday. We haven't even hooked it up yet."

But the red light was blinking.

"I see," the huge man said into the phone. "Consider it done. Good-bye." After hanging up, he stood up so abruptly his chair fell over backward. He came out from behind the desk and loomed before me like a national monument. "That was Miss Caruso on the phone. She's running late." He took my elbow and lifted me to my feet. "Instead of sitting here waiting for her, I'm going to lead you back to Tony. He's got twenty minutes to kill."

Tony? Tony didn't sound like a Thai name to me. And I didn't like the sound of the word "kill."

"That's very kind of you," I said. "But totally unnecessary."

"I insist," he said, pushing me through a curtain of multicolored beads. "Our business depends on word of mouth. You'd be helping us more than we'd be helping you. You like to help people, don't you?"

"But—"

He led me into a small, dark room that smelled of incense, and blocked the exit with his hulking physique. "I'm going to leave now. Tony will be in momentarily." Then he closed the door behind him.

I waited until I heard him walk away, then made a bee-line for the door, which was kind of pointless because anybody who goes to the movies could tell you that the door was going to be locked and I was going to be trapped in an incense-filled room in the San Fernando Valley for all of eternity, or at least as long as it took for the Stockholm syndrome to take effect, causing me to sympathize with my captors and not try to flee.

To my surprise, the knob turned easily.

Careful not to make any noise, I pushed it open and peered down the hall. I was expecting armed guards. Instead, I saw one small guy carrying a fresh white towel.

"Hi. I'm Tony." He was wearing a white T-shirt and baggy brown pants. "You here for the complimentary minimassage?"

The man had glasses on, for God's sake.

"Yes, that's me." I could really use a massage. And Freudian psychoanalysis. Combined with a drug regimen. It was official now.

Back in the room, Tony had me take off my coat and shoes and lie face down on a padded mat on the floor while he applied a hot, herbal compress to the back of my neck.

"How's that?" he asked.

"Mm. Wonderful."

"Do you know anything about Thai massage?"

I shook my head.

"It was developed by Jivaka Kumar Bhaccha, physician to Buddha, more than twenty-five hundred years ago in India."

If it was good enough for Buddha, it was good enough for me. I felt myself sinking deeper into the mat.

"From there, it made its way to Thailand, where the ayurvedic techniques and principles gradually became influenced by traditional Chinese medicine. For centuries, it was performed by monks as one component of Thai medicine. Did you notice the Wat Thai temple across the street? Cool roof, all fancy? I trained with the monks there after dropping out of med school. My mom was disappointed after all the money they'd put into my education, but my dad got it. "

"Too much information," I mumbled.

"What?" Without waiting for an answer, Tony told me to flip over onto my back and sit up. I scooted forward on the mat so he could lie down behind me. He raised his knees, then balanced a pillow on top of them. When he was in position, he had me do a kind of backward swan dive so that the small of my back was supported by the pillow, my head was resting on his pelvis, and my arms extended backward, palms up, until they reached the tops of his shoulders.

With his warm, strong hands, Tony pulled my shoulders back, intensifying the stretch.

I have never felt such bliss.

"The Bridge Pose," he said modestly. "Now for the Butterfly."

I lay down on my back, arms against my sides, and raised my knees up until they were at my shoulders. Then, with a small push from Tony, I lifted my back off the ground and extended my calves straight out over my head, toes pointing down. Tony ran around behind me, tucking his feet under my shoulder blades and squatting down so that we were pressed buttocks to buttocks. Then he grabbed the soles of my feet and tugged them gently toward the ground.

I couldn't speak. I was soaring heavenward. All my cares had evaporated. There were angels singing.

No, those were gong chimes.

The front door had opened.

Cece was here.

Oh, my God.

I had to get up.

I couldn't get up.

I was halfway into a somersault with Tony's hands wrapped around my feet.

"Tony?" My voice was muffled by my thighs, which were hovering an inch above my face.

"Shh." He pulled harder on my feet. "Give in to it."

I had no choice.

"Fire!" I cried.

Tony let go instantly. "I don't smell anything."

I flipped my legs back down and scrambled to standing. Then I threw on my coat, grabbed my shoes and bag, and pulled open the door, which banged loudly against the wall, upsetting a pile of freshly stacked white towels.

"Where are you going?" Tony cried.

I ran down the hallway and into the waiting room, just in time to hear the gong chime as a tall, dark-haired woman fled Thai Orchid Massage.

"I told her you were here," said the man in the flowing white suit. "And she just turned on her heel and left."

"Cece's full of surprises," I said, taking off after her.

Chapter 23

I didn't know a person could run that fast in spike heels.

She had on a great outfit, by the way: dark blue jeans tucked into high cognac suede boots, topped with a cropped, cream-colored jacket with three-quarter-length bell sleeves. And what looked like a real Chanel bag, the kind with the double gold-chain handles. At least my imposter recognized my superior taste in clothing.

"Stop!" I cried as she sprinted across the four lanes of Coldwater, dodging a big rig with aplomb. I was decidedly less graceful. I was also barefoot, and trying not to sever an artery on a piece of broken glass.

"Watch it!" The driver of the big rig leaned on his horn. "You crazy?"

It was a rhetorical question, so I didn't bother answering.

She was headed toward the rainbow-bright Wat Thai temple opposite, and I was stuck between lanes.

Car after car sped past me, the drivers screaming obsceni-ties in myriad foreign tongues.

She was through the ironwork gates now.

She was getting away.

"Give me a break!" I shouted at the top of my lungs as I braved an oncoming Mercedes, hopped the curb, and bolted down the sidewalk, racing past a long row of cypress trees and through the gates only to find myself in a swarm of at least five hundred people. Turns out weekends are the worst time to chase your doppelgänger through the Wat Thai Buddhist Temple of North Hollywood.

There was a band playing Thai pop in the middle of the courtyard, a mob of teenagers organizing a pickup basket-ball game, and vendors selling light-up good luck cats and Buddhist-themed amulets. The air was thick with the heady aroma of ginger, garlic, and fish sauce.

I stopped a woman in a white apron and asked her what was going on.

"Food fair," she replied, juggling a pile of Styrofoam plates. "Every weekend. Big deal on the Internet. Now nobody can find a place to park. You come to my stand and I give you free sample of *kanom krok*. Or maybe you prefer *som tum*?"

I had no idea what *kanom krok* was, but *som tum* was green papaya salad, which I loved. They do a good job at Palms Thai on Hollywood Boulevard, plus Thai Elvis, aka Kavee Thongprecha, performs Wednesday through Sundays in his platforms and shiny suits. But I digress.

Where the hell was Cece?

My instincts said go left, so I went right, stopping short to allow a procession of monks to pass. They looked splendid in their saffron-colored robes. Legend has it that Buddha was born in a grove of jackfruit trees, and the saffron represents the brilliant color of the pods inside. I learned that from the pamphlet the lead monk handed me.

"Welcome." He bowed.

"Thank you." I did the same.

"We appreciate the show of respect," he said, "but you need not remove your shoes unless you are going inside."

I clutched my gladiator sandals closer to my chest. "I am. Going inside."

I bowed one last time, then pushed my way past the elderly man hawking satellite TV systems to a shrine no bigger than a bus shelter. At the entrance were some grubby sneakers, a pair of stone lions, and an urn filled with sticks of burning incense. I dropped my shoes to the ground and tiptoed inside. Two people sat cross-legged before a statue of a female deity festooned with ropes of plastic pearls and colorful beads.

No evil twin here.

I backed out, sidestepping a chunk of grilled pork some-body must have dropped.

"Whoops!" I grabbed onto the door jamb.

The worshipers turned around.

"Peace," I said, bowing. "And love."

I got my shoes and headed in the other direction, past the giggling girls clustered around the sarong stand and their savvy mothers checking out rice cookers priced at a reason-able $39.99 to the far end of the courtyard where the temple stood.

With its peaked red roof and ornate gold trim, the Wat Thai temple was the first Thai Buddhist temple built in the

United States. It was guarded by a pair of gargantuan stone demons who looked like they'd been sculpted of marzipan. I ran up the stairs, setting down my shoes in between some wingtips and some brand-new Adidas. There were no boots in sight, but that didn't mean anything. The false Cece was hardly the pious type.

Inside was a huge gold Buddha surrounded by offerings of lit candles, fresh fruit, and silk flowers. People were praying, chatting with the monks, clipping dollar bills onto miniature paper trees. A nice man handed me a brochure about Buddhism's links to Christianity and a schedule of this month's events, written in Thai.

No evil twin here, either.

The clock was ticking.

I grabbed my shoes, ran down the stairs, and plunged back into the maelstrom, where I nearly tripped over a man who was on his hands and knees trying to get a low-angle shot of his wife's mango with sticky rice.

"By any chance, has either of you seen a woman with cascading brown hair and a cream-colored jacket?" I asked, trying to catch my breath.

"No." The wife handed her husband a plate of something square and gelatinous and studded with carbuncles. "Now take a picture of my sausage."

The food court was on the lower level.

I took the stairs two at a time.

It was chaos down there, with smoke rising from huge cast-iron pots, babies crying, lines snaking in every direction, and people with Styrofoam platters of grilled marinated pork, beef skewers, chicken larb, and caramelized plantains jostling one another for space at one of the picnic benches under the blue tent.

I blinked a couple of times. Looked right, left, in front of me, behind me.

Nothing.

Was she behind one of the stands, disguised as a Thai home cook?

Under a picnic bench, trying not to get kicked by people enjoying their curries?

Just as I was about to drop to my hands and knees, I saw her.

Standing no more than thirty feet away.

Looking nonchalant in the fried sweet potato line.

"Watch out!" I called as I dodged a family of four carrying bowls of duck noodle soup.

"Out of my way!" I said as I squeezed past a man in pressed chinos clutching last year's Zagat guide.

"So sorry!" I cried as I bumped into a woman balancing two plates of tiny fried dumplings, all thirty-six of which went flying in the air.

Nearly there now, I pushed past ancient grandmothers and cranky schoolchildren and desperate foodies until I was finally close enough to reach out and grab her skinny shoulder.

She turned around, stared at me, then starting screaming in Thai.

"Sorry," I said. "Wrong person."

"You wait," said an older man, clasping my wrist. "She says how dare you seek her autograph while she is on temple grounds?"

"I don't want her autograph," I said.

She started screaming in Thai again.

"She wants to know why you don't like her series," the older man said.

"What series?"

I felt something tug at the bottom of my coat.

"Air Hostess Wars," lisped a little girl in pigtails. "It's very violent."

Oh, God, there she was, heading up the stairs. The real fake Cece! There was no time to waste. "I love *Air Hostess Wars*! You look even more beautiful in person!"

The woman beamed. The older man released my wrist. I flew up the stairs. I was done with the victim stuff. I was going to think like a lion.

The lion senses her prey by vibration.

But it was hard to feel the vibrations with the Thai pop still playing.

The lion also uses her superior intellect.

Well.

The lion sometimes gets lucky.

I spied them outside a small office near the parking lot, splayed among the flip-flops and sneakers.

Her boots.

I think they were by Sergio Rossi.

My gladiator sandals hit the ground as I strode into the room.

Queen of the Jungle.

Never surrender.

Two young boys looked up from their instruments.

"Can I help you?" one of them asked. "We're trying to practice."

"The lady who just came in here," I said. "Where is she?"

The other boy put a finger up to his lip, and pointed to a closed door in the back of the room.

Stealthily, I made my way.

What was I going to say to her? What could she possibly say to me?

I threw open the door.

There was a vacuum cleaner inside.

The boys were beside themselves. Doubled over. Unable to breathe.

"Thanks, guys," I said as I left. "You've been great."

I sat down on the stoop. Fine. She'd outsmarted me this time. But she wasn't getting away with murder. That I would see to.

As for her fabulous cognac suede Sergio Rossi boots, they were a size 9 1/2, and I'd be damned if they didn't belong to me now.

Chapter 24

Bakersfield is halfway to Fresno, the raisin capital of the world. Undoubtedly it is other things as well, but I can't tell you what they are.

Those partial to the scenic route take Highway 1, which offers magnificent views of mountains on one side and crashing surf on the other. But I didn't have time for that kind of nonsense.

Long-haul truckers and persons tracking lovelorn used-car salesmen take the inland route.

That would be the 5.

Within half an hour, my ears were starting to pop. That's the other thing about the 5. It rises to an elevation of four thousand feet, then descends rapidly around the Tejon Pass. Every year there's a horrible accident with big rigs careening out of control and smashing into Camrys and other small, defenseless cars. But that's mostly in rainstorms.

Today the sun was shining brightly, not that I saw much of

it. For most of the trip I was trapped in between two trucks ferrying oranges. The worst part wasn't the absence of light or air but the fact that I didn't get to see any cows, always a highlight for city girls like myself. I managed to ditch the trucks at the juncture to the 99, which is the route the Joads took in *The Grapes of Wrath*. That humbled me. I stopped for trail mix at a roadside stand, and didn't toss the date nuggets out the window like I usually do.

Thirty miles later, I exited near Cal State Bakersfield and headed toward Oak Street, which may well be the happiest place on earth.

Never in my life have I seen as many balloons, banners, streamers, garlands, tinsel, and American flags billowing proudly in the breeze. Then there were the inflatables: ducks, clowns, tigers, bears. Apparently nothing says buy a car like an inflatable teddy bear riding a Harley. And the signs, neatly lettered on poster board, scrawled on chalkboards, or spelled out on LED monitors: FIRST TIME BUYERS OK! REPOSSESSIONS OK! BANKRUPTCY OK! Who knew a trip to Bakersfield could make you feel so good about yourself? Next time he freaked out on me, I was bringing my accountant Mr. Keshigian here.

Anita Colby's ex-boyfriend worked at All-America Auto, which was at the far end of the strip. It wasn't the fanciest of them, that was for sure. The sales office was a plywood shack festooned with a GOD BLESS AMERICA banner.

Three guys in leather jackets were out front, drinking coffee out of Styrofoam cups. They eyeballed me as I pulled into the lot, then engaged in a complex negotiation about who was going to get first crack at me. The one with the biggest gut must've won the coin toss because the other two hung back deferentially as he sidled up to my car and pulled the dented driver's side door open.

"That must've been some accident. Hope nobody was hurt," he said.

I smiled. "The ER doctor assured me they grow back fifty percent of the time."

He laughed nervously, then regained his composure.

"Lots of folks in the industry prize reliability, but I wouldn't have put you in a car like this." He shook his head. "You don't belong in a granny car. I see you in something young and sexy."

Flatterer.

"Hey!" He bugged his eyes out in feigned enthusiasm. "Do me a favor. We got this hot Mazda RX–8 in yesterday, and I'd love to see what you look like behind the wheel." He took my arm and steered me over to a small white car with gleaming white spokes on the wheels. The windshield was plastered with stickers: LOW MILEAGE, LUXURY, FULL POWER, ONE OWNER, SMART BUY, WE FINANCE.

"Very nice," I said noncommittally.

Noncommittal was not in this guy's vocabulary.

"The Motorsport Concept," he said, his voice trembling. "Leaner, meaner, and faster. That's right, I'm talking turbo. High power at sky-high revs. This is one of the top-ranking vehicles in its class, the only one that offers four doors and four seats without compromising its low-profile style or sports car–like performance. Take a seat." He whipped open the door.

I sat down and took a deep breath. Oh, that new car smell. It was so seductive. The smell of hope. The smell of optimism.

Somewhere in the distance I heard the Carpenters singing "We've Only Just Begun. "

"What do you think? Shall we give it a test drive?"

"Actually, I was hoping to talk to Jonathan," I said. "A friend recommended I see him. Said he'd give me a good deal."

He glanced back at his buddies. Their coffee finished, they were now munching on doughnuts.

"Jonathan," he said with regret. "I'll get him for you."

He brought me over to a short and powerfully built guy with thick black hair, a mustache, and a five o'clock shadow that probably started just after breakfast. He looked like ninety-five percent of my cousins—the females as well as the males.

"Mr. Tucci," he said. "This lady wants to see you. Don't let it go to your head, man."

So this was Jonathan Tucci.

Menacing? I hardly thought so. He was brushing crumbs off his leather jacket. But he'd written Anita the kind of letters that give a person nightmares. Said he loved her so much he couldn't breathe. That he couldn't live without her, and that he'd die before he saw her with another man. That if she wouldn't come back, he'd throw himself off a building and take her with him.

Anita hadn't gone to the police with the letters. She hadn't gotten a restraining order. She'd saved them, wrapped up in a blue ribbon, like love letters.

Maybe she'd known how to read between the lines.

"What can I do for you?" Jonathan Tucci asked. "You looking for a trade-in? If you are, I gotta tell you, your car isn't worth blue book, not with that kind of damage. What happened, somebody ram into you? You let me at 'em."

"That's awfully kind of you," I said. "But it was my fault. I was in kind of a hurry. Like I am today."

"One thing people never ought to be when they're buying a used car is in a hurry. But it's too nice a day to argue. See anything that strikes you?"

I scanned the lot. There were a lot of shiny pick-ups. "I'm looking for something reliable."

Jonathan smiled knowledgeably. "Bill tried to get you into something young and sexy, right? But I know from taking just one look at you that you don't need a car to validate you. You're a confident woman, and a confident woman needs a car that gets her from point A to point B, am I right or am I right?"

"You are right."

"I see you in . . . let me think for a second. Yeah, right over here, all right, yup, this is it. No doubt in my mind. A Plymouth Sundance!"

"I kind of like this Corolla."

He looked pained. "The Sundance has lower mileage and motorized seatbelts. It's the better deal at sixty-five hundred bucks out the door. What do you think? Shall we give it a test drive?"

"Sure."

"I've got to take it out of the lot, then you'll get your shot."

As we were buckling up, a police car pulled up on the opposite side of the street. I felt the blood rush to my face. But I had nothing to worry about. I wasn't even officially a fugitive yet. My appointment with Collins and McQueen wasn't until tomorrow morning. And I was innocent. More or less.

The cop got out of the car, slammed the door behind him,

and leaned against his door, arms crossed. He seemed to be looking straight at me, but it was hard to tell because of his sunglasses. How did I know he was an enemy? He could well be a friend. A friend trying to protect me from my own worst impulses. Not to mention the obsessed and possibly unstable Jonathan Tucci. How did I know Jonathan Tucci didn't have a police record? Maybe he was out on parole. Was I so stupid that I'd get into a Plymouth Sundance with a dangerous ex-con?

"Ready?" Jonathan Tucci asked, clicking the door locks.

Chapter 25

As we pulled out of the driveway, I sent one last imploring look the cop's way.

"Nice little residential area back here." Jonathan turned the corner. "Nice empty streets. You can put on some speed in a minute, see what it's like. Just don't crash into a wall or anything. I never checked on your insurance."

I wasn't the one with the death wish.

It was a modest neighborhood, mostly small, faded one-story houses with chain-link fences protecting the occasional snarling dog and rusted lawn chair. A couple of teenage boys rolled past us on skateboards, brushing their long hair to the side in unison.

"One more block and I'll pull over," Jonathan said. "By the way, I never did ask who sent you."

Might as well cut to the chase. "Anita Colby."

He turned his head. "Anita?"

Before I could respond, he looked in the rearview mirror, then sped up.

"What is it?" I turned around. There was a dark car with tinted windows coming up behind us.

"Nothing. Just this idiot tailgating me. Get a life!" he shouted out the window.

"I hate when people do that."

"No shit."

I looked in the passenger side mirror. Objects may be closer than they appeared, but this guy was practically on top of us. Jonathan hit the gas. The other guy did the same, coming close, then even closer. I felt a sudden jolt as the shoulder belt cut into my neck.

"Damn it!" Jonathan accelerated again, then swung a sharp left into the alley.

"What?" I asked.

"Didn't you feel that?"

"Of course I felt that." I grabbed for the door as we sped over a pothole. "What's happening?"

"We're being followed is what's happening!"

"What does he want?" I was trying to stay calm.

Jonathan maneuvered past recycling bins and trash cans, wrenching the wheel back and forth like this was Nascar. "You tell me."

"How am I supposed to know?"

He drove right over a clump of dead palm fronds somebody had dumped in the middle of the road. "You see what kind of suspension this car has? Best in class."

I clutched my seatbelt. If I bounced any higher, I was going to go through the roof.

"Figures it's trash day today," Jonathan muttered. "Better pray the truck doesn't come at us or we're goners. Oh, screw it. Hold on."

The other guy was still hot on our tail as we took a sharp right out of the alley and careened down a wide street, past a school with a bunch of kids playing four square on the yard.

Out of the corner of my eye, I saw a yellow bus start to pull away from the curb.

"Watch out!" I cried.

Jonathan veered to the left, passing the bus, then spun the wheel to the right. "I think we lost him," he said, wiping the sweat from his brow. "So you into the same shit as Anita, or what?"

But we hadn't lost him. He'd sideswiped the bus and was bearing down on us again.

"What shit exactly would that be?" I asked, my neck snapping forward as we flew over a speed bump. My purse toppled to the floor, and a thick wad of bills tumbled out.

Jonathan glanced at the money, then up at me. "Don't kid a kidder."

There was a dead-end street coming up on the right. Jonathan peered into the rearview mirror again and after hesitating a split second, turned down it, giving the car so much gas I thought we were going to crash into the freshly painted ranch house coming straight at us at eighty miles per hour.

"What are you doing?" I screamed.

At the last minute he slammed on the brakes. I lurched forward, then back, then forward again, hitting my head on the windshield. Apparently, this year and make of Sundance didn't have airbags.

"You okay?" He turned off the engine.

"I'm fine, no thanks to you." I rubbed my forehead. "But we're trapped. There's no way out."

"That's the idea. Look behind you." I wheeled around in my seat just in time to see the dark car idle for a minute at the other end of the cul de sac, then drive away.

I turned back around, incredulous. "How'd you know he'd do that?"

"Experience. Don't you think you should pick up your money?"

I unhooked my seatbelt, and bent down to retrieve the wad of bills. Jonathan watched me put it back in my purse.

"That's a lot of money," he said.

"I came here to buy a car."

"Maybe. I think you came here to talk about Anita and me. Does she know about your visit?"

He was a better actor than used car salesman. But maybe he wasn't acting. Still, how could he not know Anita was dead? It had made the *L.A. Times*. But this was Kern County. They had their own paper. "I don't think so. No."

"Listen," he said, leaning back in his seat. "I gotta be up front with you. I can't help. I'm sorry. I'm on the straight and narrow these days. Best thing for you to do is get out while you can. Make a clean break. An exit plan. That's what Anita did. When things got really bad, she was going to go to Gloria. You know her?"

I shook my head.

"Anita's sister. Lives here in town. Works at Hello Kitty. Gloria's great. Anyway, you've probably got somebody like Gloria in your life. Somebody you can trust. That's who you need to go to."

A tall man in an undershirt came out of the freshly painted ranch house. I thought pink was a poor choice, but this is America. He was carrying a baseball bat. His wife stood in the doorway, a phone in her hands.

"Is there something I can do for you?" he asked us. "If not, I strongly suggest you get the fuck off my lawn."

Jonathan started up the car and we drove back to the lot in silence. Instead of pulling up to the front, though, he stopped the car in the alley around the back. "Wait here. I have something for you." He disappeared inside.

Five minutes passed.

I'd barely had a chance to think these last few days. This was my chance. But it's hard to think on demand.

Okay.

I was looking for somebody who wanted Anita dead. I was also looking for somebody with the brains and resources to orchestrate a pretty complicated setup. I didn't know about his brains, but Jonathan Tucci was stuck in a dead-end job. If he'd had any resources, he'd surely have left All-America Auto a long time ago.

Which didn't necessarily mean he was one of the good guys.

I heard the crunching of tires on gravel. It was Jonathan driving my Camry, which now had Arizona plates where the California plates used to be.

I gathered up my things and got out of the Sundance.

"You're gonna need your money," he said, handing me my keys. "These plates should help, at least for a while. I put the old ones in the trunk."

"Thanks," I said. "I think."

"I gotta get back now," he said. "Maybe I can still make my quota for the week. It's tough because we don't have the inventory of some of the other dealers around here. Oh, well. A person does what a person can do."

I looked up. The sun was setting behind an old fence covered with layer upon layer of peeling paint. It reminded me of a laundry disaster I'd once had. It had been another long day. I was tired of thinking. I was ready to fall into bed.

"You have a place to stay?" he asked.

"I thought I'd try down the street." There were half a dozen dingy-looking motels, but I was going to the Marriott. Just for tonight. They had room service and I wanted a steak and HBO and a soft bed with cool, crisp sheets.

Jonathan shook his head. "Even if you plan on paying cash, you're going to have to leave a credit card. You don't want to leave a credit card, do you?"

"No," I admitted.

"Get back on the 99 heading toward Fresno. Get off at the next exit. Go to the E-Z Nights. Big sign. You can't miss it. I know the guy that works there. Jason. Tell him Jonny sent you. You say you're paying cash, that'll be good enough for him."

"Thank you," I said.

"You're a friend of Anita's," he said. "And pretty naïve, no offense. I don't think you get who you're dealing with. You want to make sure these people don't find you, and, if they do, that they don't recognize you."

Jonathan Tucci was helpful, but not very reassuring.

He reached out and touched my shoulder. "I never did ask you your name." But before I could answer, he said, "Never mind. It's better I don't know. Good luck."

I smiled.

"You remind me of Anita," he said, regret in his voice. "Just a little."

"Sounds like that's a compliment," I said.

"Yeah. I loved her. But it was a long time ago."

I nodded, then got into my Camry and drove away.

Chapter 26

Before getting onto the 99, I made a pit stop at a beauty supply store at the bottom of Oak Street. I tried my best to be anonymous, but the employees had some screwy ideas about good service. The clerk insisted upon accompanying me to aisle eight. The cashier swore up and down that I was a dead ringer for his cousin. The assistant manager appeared out of nowhere, urging me to apply for a frequent buyer card, which saves customers an average of thirty bucks a year. I mumbled something about my poor credit, then grabbed my purchases and slunk off.

By the time I got onto the freeway, paranoia had set in. Again.

First there was the red Pinto. I didn't like the look of the driver. He was wearing a fedora, like a hood in a film noir. He was sticking to me like glue.

Then there was the beat-up van I'd seen in the beauty supply store's parking lot. I'd noticed it because of the bumper sticker:

ROSES ARE RED, VIOLETS ARE BLUE, I'M SCHIZOPHRENIC AND SO
AM I. Could it be mere coincidence that this particular head
case was now driving in the lane next to mine?

I had to get a grip.

The whole world wasn't out to get me.

Just certain people in it.

Whose numbers appeared to be expanding rapidly.

I got off the 99 at the next exit, keeping my eye on the
rearview mirror as I took a sharp right onto Buck Owens
Boulevard.

*You want to make sure these people don't find you, and if they
do, that they don't recognize you.*

The words pounded against my skull like jackhammers. I
had to get to the motel. I had to peel off my sweaty clothes,
hide my money under the mattress, take the necessary security
measures.

But the E-Z Nights had obviously taken down the sign
Jonathan Tucci said I couldn't miss. I'd been up and down
Buck Owens twice now, and I still couldn't find it. The place
had probably gone out of business. Dive motels have small
profit margins.

I swung one last U-turn and headed back toward the freeway.

That was that.

I was going to the Marriott. I was going to pretend I'd lost
my wallet and that was why I had no credit cards or ID. It
was the obvious strategy. But that didn't mean it was going
to work. Let's face it. I was going to make a scene. The frightened receptionist was going to call the general manager, who
was going to call the security guard, who was going to call
the cops, who were going to haul me to the clink, where I

would be offered a hard pillow and a stale cheese sandwich, which would barely tide me over until the morning, when I was going to be escorted to Detectives McQueen and Collins at the twenty-eighth precinct, right on schedule.

And what about the security measures? They had to come first. The bad guys could get me even while in police custody. These things happen every day.

I slammed on the brakes, backed up, and pulled the Camry into the last establishment before the on-ramp to the 99.

BUCK OWENS' CRYSTAL PALACE. GREAT FOOD AND GREAT COUNTRY MUSIC TWELVE MONTHS A YEAR, FIVE DAYS A WEEK.

If it had a bathroom, it would do.

I parked behind a looming clump of saguaro cactus, yanked up my collar, and kept my head down all the way to the entrance.

The handles on the front door were shaped like guitars.

"Welcome," said the woman behind the desk, who had hair nearly as high as Marie Antoinette's. She was folding commemorative T-shirts.

"One for dinner." I glanced furtively in either direction, only then removing my sunglasses.

"We don't open until five."

Just like the sign out front said. "You're kidding me."

"Real sorry about that." She was almost to the bottom of the stack.

"Do you think I could just look around inside for a minute? I'm a huge country music fan." I walked over to the larger-than-life bronze statue of Merle Haggard and sighed appreciatively.

"Okay." She was tidying the commemorative pens now. "You want to visit the museum. Five dollars."

The museum appeared to be what they called the restaurant when it was closed. It was chock-full of memorabilia: Buck's first Fender guitar; a bejeweled jacket made by the famous rock 'n' roll tailor Nudie for Buck's third Japanese tour in 1973; the sheriff's uniform Buck wore when he costarred with Gavin McLeod and Tony Danza in the ABC Movie of the Week *Murder Can Hurt You*. The pièce de résistance was a Pontiac Granville convertible built for Elvis that Buck won in a poker game in Vegas in 1976, which was hanging sideways over the bar. And to think I only knew Buck as the guy who hosted *Hee Haw*. Not that he was my favorite member of the cast. That was Minnie Pearl, who wore those hats with the $1.98 price tags dangling from them.

The waitresses were setting the tables for dinner. I asked where the ladies room was, and they pointed me down to the far end of the bar.

I went inside, peeked underneath the stalls to make sure no one was there, and locked the door. Then I opened the bag from the beauty supply store, and laid the security measures out on the counter.

A kitchen timer.

Some plastic gloves.

A shower cap.

A hand towel.

A bottle of cream lightener.

A bottle of hydrogen peroxide.

I took a deep breath, then cracked my knuckles.

According to the cashier, this was serious business. There were no second chances. After applying the solution, my hair would go from dark brown to dark reddish brown to reddish brown to reddish orange to orange to orangey yellow to yellow to pale yellow to white—and, if I didn't rinse in time, to melted, then directly to bald.

I studied my reflection in the mirror. I loved my big, brown hair. After all these years, I knew exactly how to tame it into submission. It was bouncy and shiny instead of dry and cumulonimbus-like, thanks to recent advances made in the hair-care industry, which included the aforementioned Frizz-Ease.

I opened the bottle of lightener. It smelled like toxic waste.

I looked in the mirror again.

Straw isn't bouncy or shiny or sexy. Neither is cotton candy. Neither are bald spots.

I closed the bottle, gathered up my things, and headed back out to the woman in front.

"All done already?" she asked.

"Yes," I replied, putting my sunglasses back on. "My favorite was the picture of Buck with Marilu Henner. I love her. Anyway, I took one look in the bathroom mirror at this wretched mop and realized I need to get it done before coming back later tonight for karaoke. Is there a beauty parlor around here?"

She touched her sky-high teased locks and smiled. "In Bakersfield? We got a beauty parlor on every corner, honey."

Carmen from Carmen's Curl Up 'n' Dye kindly agreed to stay open an extra hour and bleach my hair after I promised her my high-heeled gladiator sandals and two hundred dollars for her trouble. I was hemorrhaging money now, but I supposed that was better than actually hemorrhaging.

Carmen was a large woman with soulful eyes and a taste for drama. Carmen likes her clients to sit facing away from the mirror while she does their hair so they get a surprise at the final moment before forking over the dough. And who doesn't love surprises?

Carmen draped a white cape around my shoulders and applied the solution with the quiet confidence that comes from experience, which made me feel better in spite of the nasty odor.

I started to relax.

I perused the edifying literature: *Star, US Weekly, In Touch, Hello!* and *Soap Opera Digest.*

That took ten minutes.

It took four times that long, however, for the bleach to oxidize the melanin molecules in my hair, removing the color in an irreversible chemical reaction. Which gave me time to think about the chemical reactions in *Vertigo.*

Poor Judy.

She falls desperately in love with Scottie, but he is still in love with the dead Madeleine. Caught in the grip of his obsession, he implores her to change her style of dress, her manner of speaking, and, finally, the color of her hair so that she more closely resembles his lost love object. The irony, of course, is that Judy and Madeleine are the same woman. Scottie has the woman he thought he wanted, but he prefers an apparition to flesh and blood.

Poor Kim Novak.

Never given her due as an actress, despite her unforgettable performance as the earthy shopgirl and the troubled ice queen Scottie manipulates her into becoming. But then Kim Novak was familiar with this kind of voluntary self-immolation. Her real name was Marilyn Pauline Novak, but the studio couldn't have another Marilyn, so they made her change her name to Kim. As for Hitch, he loathed her for resisting the transformation process all his leading ladies had to undergo.

"We're done!" said Carmen. "Ready to turn around?"

She whipped off my robe and spun me in the chair so that I was facing the mirror. Looking back at me was someone both familiar and utterly strange.

A Hitchcock blonde.

There was only one thing missing.

"Can you put it up?" I asked.

Carmen made a face. "How?"

"In a chignon."

"What's that, like a bun?" she asked.

The bun is to the chignon as Twinkies are to mille-feuilles.

"Yes," I replied. "Like a bun."

"Will can do." She whipped out the hairpins.

As I was paying, I caught another glimpse of myself in the mirror.

Déjà vu. That's what I was feeling.

"You're a love." Carmen buckled up her new gladiator sandals. "These are absolutely gorgeous. Xavier, my husband, is going to go ape shit."

I asked Carmen if she knew of a cheap motel in the immediate area.

"Try the E-Z Nights," she said, walking up and down the linoleum floor. "Like butter," she cooed.

"I've been looking for that place," I said, slipping into a pair of lime-green foam pedicure thongs Carmen had dredged up for me. "Where exactly is it?"

"End of the next block, just off the road. They took down the big sign because they're doing construction on Buck Owens. Even so, you can't miss it."

But some people miss things even when they're right under their nose.

Chapter 27

Now the rain was coming down in sheets. I'm not talking your ordinary hard rain. I'm talking torrential downpour. The kind that picks little children up off their feet and whirls them down storm drains.

I didn't have an umbrella, but Carmen was gracious enough to sell me a polyester scarf for the mere cost of twenty-five dollars. I covered my hair the best I could, then made a run for it.

It was dark now.

The windshield wipers were moving back and forth at a furious pace, but I still couldn't see more than a foot in front of me. I reached forward to wipe the condensation off the window, but that only made it worse.

This was a bad idea.

I hit the defogger button, which hadn't worked in at least five years.

I'd already had one accident today. The smart thing would be to pull over. Or give up entirely.

Just then something emerged from the haze.

A red neon sign.

I'd found the E-Z Nights.

The NO in front of VACANCY was sputtering inconclusively, which I was going to take as a YES. I pulled the car to a stop in front of a small cabin marked OFFICE and bolted inside.

The lobby was small, overheated, and overstuffed. Its contents included: a tile-top table covered with old *Life* magazines; a stained-glass lamp; a wingback chair; several hooked rugs; the overwhelming smell of cabbage; a grandfather clock mocking me with its relentless ticking; a desk, of course; and a bell, which I rung.

After getting no response, I sprinted back to the car and honked the horn several times. I waited less than a minute before backing out because, to be perfectly honest, I'd have rather slept in my dented car with the dysfunctional defogger than at the E-Z Nights. But then, all of a sudden, a tall figure emerged from the darkness and pressed his face to the window. He looked like he was melting. But that was just the rain. Or maybe my tortured state of mind.

The man gestured for me to roll down the window. I gave him an inch.

"Sorry," he said. "I was showing a guest to his room. Can I get your door for you?"

Something in his voice made me pause, but I didn't have the energy to figure out what. "Okay."

"Get under the umbrella."

I got under and we ran back to the office. He shut the door

behind him. Then he flipped the sign in the window from YES, WE'RE OPEN to COME BACK ANOTHER TIME.

"Don't you stay open all night?" I removed my scarf and tucked a loose strand of hair behind one ear.

"Well, there are no more vacancies. After you, I mean." With that, he clicked on the NO, and a burst of neon illuminated the night sky. "So there isn't any point, is there?"

"Guess not." I cleared my throat. "You must be Jason."

He pulled off his baseball cap. "Jason hasn't worked Saturdays in about a month now."

Of course he hasn't.

The man who was not Jason had close-cropped hair, a long straight line of a mouth, and eyes that darted back and forth like he was looking for something that wasn't there. He was wearing a pale blue shirt buttoned all the way to the top. But maybe he was more obliging than he looked.

"It'll be just you, then?" He plunged a No.2 pencil into an electric sharpener.

I spoke up so he could hear me. "That's right. Party of one."

"Doesn't sound like much of a party." He touched the point, which broke off. "Useless." Then he plunged the pencil back into the little hole. "How many nights did you say?"

"Just one. Two at the most."

"Either way is fine. It's a nice room, very private. $59.99 plus tax okay?"

"Sure."

"I'll just be needing a credit card to secure it."

"The thing is," I said, smiling, "I lost my wallet someplace earlier today."

He searched my face. "What're you smiling for, then?"

"I smile when I'm nervous."

"How are you going to pay if you lost your wallet?"

"Cash."

He shook his head. "I can't do anything for you."

I pulled a hundred-dollar bill out of my purse and placed it on the counter. "Any possibility you might change your mind?"

He pushed the money back at me. "No."

"Help me out here. It's pouring rain and I'm exhausted."

He narrowed his eyes. "It's not about helping or not helping. I can't do anything without a credit card."

I smoothed down my shirt. "Will a driver's license do?"

"Maybe."

I dug through my purse and laid the driver's license on the counter.

He studied it for a minute. "Anita Colby." He looked up at me. "Of Hollywood, California."

At least I had the hair now. "That's right."

"Originally from Arizona?"

"What?"

"Your plates."

"Right. Tucson. Dry heat. Which I really miss tonight."

He looked back down at the license, then at me. I held my breath. "You take a good picture, Anita."

I exhaled. "Thanks."

"You an actress?"

I shook my head.

"You remind me of somebody. Anyhow, just sign the book, and I'll show you to your room." He removed a key from the hook.

After I signed the register, we got my suitcases out of the trunk and headed down the path to the other side of the parking lot, stopping in front of a door with a tarnished number ten on it.

The man who was not Jason opened it, stepped inside, made a face. "Stuffy in here. The owner has Raynaud's disease. That's when your hands and feet turn blue. She has us set the thermostat on high. Most people don't like it, though. I can open this window here, let in some air."

I took the key out of his hand and laid it down on the flimsy wooden dresser. "That's okay. I like it warm."

"Your choice." He put one suitcase on the end of the bed and the other on a stand in the corner near the television. "No premium stations, I'm afraid." He walked over to the desk and opened the drawer. "A Bible, the yellow pages, and the current issue of *Bakotopia*. It's the local alternative weekly. You need anything else, dial zero."

"Thanks."

"Name's Roy, by the way."

After he left, I double-locked the door, peered through the blinds to make sure he'd gone, then sat down at the desk and looked at myself one more time in the mirror.

It was official.

I'd joined the sorority of the damned.

All of Hitchcock's blondes were lost souls: alcoholics, teases, frigid, kleptomaniacs, depressives. And I was one of them now. The kind of girl who has to touch up her roots every four weeks. But how long exactly could I afford to do that?

I opened my purse and dumped my cash on the desk. Then I got a pen and piece of paper out of the desk drawer.

Okay.

I'd started with two thousand eight hundred and fifty five dollars, to which Bridget had generously added five hundred. That made three thousand three hundred and fifty-five. But I'd paid close to ten dollars at the parking garage near Cedars-Sinai, and four hundred to Lewis, whose car I'd hit. Then there was the food at the Thai temple. I'd gotten a free sample of *kanom krok*, which turned out to be grilled coconut rice fritters topped with slivered scallions, and quite delicious. But I'd paid for my own beef satay and was still hungry when I was done with that, so I'd gotten a papaya salad and a Thai iced tea to wash it down. Before I'd left, I'd clipped a twenty to one of the little fake trees in the temple for the monks. Then there was the five dollars for trail mix, the five dollars to get into the Crystal Palace, the fifty at the beauty supply store, two hundred for Carmen, and twenty-five bucks for the polyester scarf she'd sold me, which was cunningly imprinted with penguins and something I'm sure I'll wear all the time. That made seven hundred and twenty, to which I was going to add one hundred and fifty for two nights here in paradise, meaning that if I wasn't touching Bridget's money, I had less than two thousand dollars left. At least my gas tank was full. Deduct another forty for that.

Exhausted, I kicked off my sopping wet pedicure thongs, stripped off my pants, shirt, and underwear, and slipped between the sheets. Only they weren't cool or crisp or even white because dead blondes don't stay in three-star hotels.

I sat up and reached for my suitcase, which was lying at the end of the bed. I got out my silk robe and wrapped myself in it. Then I padded over to the window, opened it, and sucked in a lungful of air.

The rain was deafening, spattering on the roof, rushing out of the gutters.

I closed my eyes. I saw the trail at Beachwood Canyon.

Had it really been less than a week?

I saw the dust, the craggy slopes, the scrubby vegetation.

The rain would wash away the soot caked onto the grasses, and in the morning everything would be new again. In the spring, the cottontail rabbits and mule deer would come out. And the flowers. I could see the lavender of the lantana. The white sumac. The red Erythrina.

I opened my eyes.

Anita would never see the flowers.

I slammed the window shut and walked toward the bathroom door.

I needed a shower.

Chapter 28

The bathroom was small, but spotless. The white tile glowed blue under the fluorescent light.

I tore up the piece of paper I'd used to work out my finances and flushed it down the toilet.

The water swirled in circles, then disappeared.

Indoor plumbing. Truly a marvel.

I slipped my robe off my shoulders and let it fall to the floor. Then I yanked open the plastic curtain, stepped inside, pulled the curtain closed, inhaled the lemon scent of antiseptic, unwrapped the soap, turned the handle marked *H* to the right, and screamed as the water hit me like a thousand knives.

For ice-cold water I was paying $59.99 plus tax?

Beggars can't be choosers, I supposed.

I wrapped myself in a towel and walked back to the TV, trailing fat drops of water on the dun-colored carpet.

Oh, yeah. No premium channels.

A person could always read.

I got out the phone book.

That was when the banging started.

It was rhythmic. Slow, then fast. Slow, then fast.

I flopped onto the bed and pressed a pillow over my ears.

I could still hear it.

Then the banging stopped, and a voice came from the room next door. "You okay in there? We heard you screaming a minute ago."

Jeez. "I'm fine."

"You sure?"

"Yup."

"You don't need anything?"

Solitude. Hot water. Cable. Vindication. "Nothing."

"Good night." Then they turned on the television. Sounded like a World War II movie. Lots of sirens and explosions.

I kicked my suitcase off the bed and stretched out.

Back to the yellow pages.

I was going to find Anita's sister, Gloria. There weren't many other options left.

First, I went to the section marked *Toys* and flipped to *H.*

No listing for Hello Kitty.

Then I tried *S* for Sanrio.

Nothing.

C for Children.

Nothing.

N for Novelties.

No luck.

Then the phone rang.

I leapt to my feet. Who could possibly be calling me here? I picked up the receiver.

"Anita? Roy from the office, here. Listen, if somebody's holding you hostage, just say, 'Sweet dreams, Henrietta,' and I'll have the cops there in half a second."

"Please don't call the cops, Roy," I said. "I'm perfectly fine."

"I heard there was screaming."

"There was no hot water."

"It takes five minutes to warm up. I should've warned you."

"Don't worry about it. Good night."

"You have anybody in there with you, Anita?"

"No. Why?"

"Because you're paying single occupancy. If there's someone there with you, it'll be extra."

"I'm alone. And I'm not expecting anybody."

"Okay, then. Sleep well."

Excellent work. Reassure the kook at the front desk that you're all alone for the duration of the night. Well, he was probably harmless. Just a lonely guy with nothing to do.

I got back into bed and flipped open the *Bakotopia*. Saturday night in Bakersfield. Sky's the limit. There was a wet T-shirt contest at Brunhilda's, with two-for-one beers on tap. There was also a speed-dating event back at the Marriott. And the Buckaroos were performing at the Crystal Palace, to be followed by karaoke.

I bolted upright.

What was that?

Get a grip, Cece.

It was the rain. Or a branch hitting the roof.

I knotted my towel around me and tiptoed to the window, then lifted the middle slat of the blinds ever so slightly so I could see out. The rain was shooting down on the asphalt so hard it looked like electric sparks. Nobody in sight.

For now.

But Roy had a key. He could let himself in if he felt like it. While I was sleeping, even.

Or maybe Jonathan Tucci was on his way. For all I knew, he'd staged that entire chase. I never did see the driver of the other car. It could've been one of his coworkers from the lot. He could've been trying to spook me so badly that I'd fall for his cock-and-bull story about not being able to check into a respectable hotel without credit card or ID. And then I'd have no choice but to wind up here, exactly where he wanted me to be. In the clutches of his coconspirator, Captain Weirdo.

I ran back to my purse and got the remains of the trail mix—peanuts, mostly—and scattered them on the carpet. I'd hear them crunch if somebody tried to sneak in.

No. I had a much better idea. I got the desk chair and dragged it into the bathroom, then climbed up and unscrewed the light bulb. I was going to place the bulb under the mat outside the door. You couldn't miss the sound of shattered glass. Giddy with anticipation, I opened the door and stepped out onto the stoop.

In retrospect, it was my fault entirely.

If I'd thought things through, I would've grabbed the key to the room. Or propped the door open with the yellow pages. But I was impulsive. Had been that way since I was a little girl.

Anyway, back to where I left off.

Just as I was bending down to place the bulb under the mat, a huge gust of wind came up and slammed the door shut.

It took a moment for the picture to crystallize in my mind.

Me.

A Hitchcock blonde.

In a skimpy towel.

In the pouring rain.

Locked out of Room 10.

I ran over to Room 11 and knocked on the door, but my neighbors couldn't hear me over World War II.

I had no choice.

Cursing the gods, I sprinted across the parking lot to the office. The sign was still turned to COME BACK ANOTHER TIME, but the lights were on. Thank goodness Roy hadn't left. I pounded on the door, but he didn't answer. I ran around to the side and saw him sitting in an easy chair with his eyes closed and a copy of the *Ladies' Home Journal* on his lap. I banged on the window for a solid minute. He finally opened his eyes and gestured for me to go around to the front door.

I hopped from foot to foot, shivering, while I waited for him.

Gentleman that he was, he let me in without mentioning my attire. Or lack thereof.

"If you needed a new light bulb," he finally said, "you could've called."

"I got locked out."

"Then what's that in your hand for?"

I held the light bulb over my head. "I have a great idea, Roy.

How about you let me back in my room so I can put on my clothes and explain it to you then?"

"No need for sarcasm." He took a key from behind the desk, then grabbed his big, black umbrella. "What're you waiting for, Anita?"

Back in Room 10, I was grateful for the woman with Raynaud's disease. Covered in a blanket, I huddled next to the radiator while I waited five minutes for the water to heat up and my body temperature to return to 99.6 degrees (I run a little hot). My chignon had wilted (obviously) and my hair felt alarmingly starchy. Carmen had said that might happen. I needed to use double the amount of conditioner for a while. Luckily, I'd brought two bottles.

Two minutes to go.

I went over to the phone and dialed zero.

"Yes?" Roy was chewing. A roast beef sandwich, I'll bet. With chips and a pickle. God, I was hungry. I'd never had dinner.

"Roy, it's Anita. I forgot to ask you something. Do you know of a Hello Kitty store around here?"

He started to choke.

"You okay?"

"Fine." He cleared his throat a few times.

"So do you know where it is?"

"Uh-huh."

"Great! Can you tell me?"

Long pause. "You planning on going there now?"

"Not now," I said, glancing over at the clock on the nightstand. "They're not going to be open this late. I'm going to wait until tomorrow."

"Oh, they're open. Trust me."

"Really?" The store was probably located in one of those big malls that stays open until the wee hours. I could get something to eat in the food court.

Roy gave me the address.

Then I took my shower.

And lived to tell the tale.

Chapter 29

Hello Kitty was indeed open. But there were no cute Japanese trinkets for sale.

Hello Kitty traded in flesh.

Overflowing DDD cups of it.

Bikini-waxed, tattooed, and pierced expanses of it.

In colors ranging from lily-white to darkest ebony.

"You here for the audition?" asked a man with a ZZ Top beard working the front door. "Step into my office." He put his hand over the security camera and cocked his head toward the alley.

"How do you do? I'm here to see Gloria Colby." I was trying to be businesslike, which was difficult given that I was wearing high-waisted Yves St. Laurent harem pants. "Is she working tonight?"

"Don't think so. She's not my type, anyway," ZZ said with a leer. "If I'd wanted the girl next door, I'd have gone next door, you know what I'm saying? But you're my type." I wondered if he'd put glue in his beard to make it stay.

"Give it a rest, Leo," said the other doorman. "And don't fool with the camera." He turned to me. "You looking for Gloria?"

I nodded.

He unhooked the red velvet rope. "Go inside and wait by the DJ booth. I'm gonna send Chastity over."

I'd never been to a strip club before, but this had to be the platonic version: low ceilings, smoky, poorly lit, with Whitesnake's "Here I Go Again" playing on endless rewind. In the center of the room, a girl wearing a black light–sensitive bikini was slithering up and down a pole while guys in trucker hats ogled her and slurped beers.

The DJ booth was in the back. Two women were leaning against it, smoking and drinking Red Bulls. Between lap dances, I guess. They were in their twenties, but looked like they'd seen it all and then some. One was wearing a nurse's outfit with five-inch platform orthopedic shoes. The other had on a sexy cop costume, complete with handcuffs and a badge reading OFFICER NAUGHTY.

"Hi," I said.

"You're under arrest," said the cop.

"Not yet I'm not," I muttered.

"You here for the audition?" The nurse smiled. "You oughta put your hair up in a ponytail first."

"Yes, master." The cop tried to wiggle her nose.

"You're mixing it up," said the nurse. "That's from *Bewitched*. She's Jeannie. Look at the pants."

I decided not to explain about my 1970s odalisque phase. "I'm not a stripper."

"Exotic dancer," the nurse corrected me.

"Sorry. I'm waiting for somebody named Chastity."

"Coming up right behind you at two o'clock," Officer Naughty replied. "Shit."

I turned around. The woman was about my age, maybe older, but she had the body of a sixteen-year-old. She was wearing a skin-tight pink tracksuit and a rhinestone-studded Hello Kitty tiara, and had a miniature Chihuahua in her arms.

"Somebody here looking for Gloria?" Her voice was like a sugar cookie, gravelly and sweet.

"Me," I said. "You must be Chastity."

Her eyes seared into me like a laser beam. "The one and only. And I know exactly who you are."

How that was possible, I didn't know. But it didn't seem like the right time to inquire.

"As for you two, you are on probation as of right this minute." The cop and nurse were about to protest when she put up her hand. "Not a word. Not even a sound. Neither of you has made your minimum, and you damn well know it. Get to work. This isn't an office Christmas party." She linked her arm through mine. "You come with me."

Now Def Leppard's "Hysteria" was playing. A woman took to the stage wearing a marabou-trimmed robe with a teddy underneath. The room was packed, but at Chastity's approach the crowd parted like the Red Sea. Men tried to kiss her hand. Working girls quaked in fear.

"Look at her," Chastity said as we walked past the stage. "I have to literally pry the Ding Dongs out of her hand." The woman had shed the marabou robe and teddy and was doing cartwheels in a G-string and heart-shaped nipple tassels. Her breasts defied gravity and several other natural laws. "But she's got a big following. She was head cheerleader at her high school. And I was the one who stole her away from the Teaser Pleaser, thank you very much."

She led me upstairs to the locker room, which smelled like sweat and Chanel N° 5. There were a bunch of girls gathered around two long benches. Some were leaving for the night. Others were getting ready for their shifts. They didn't look particularly happy, either way.

"Let me introduce you around," Chastity said. "This is Mystery."

Mystery, clad in a pair of jeans and a tank top, was removing layers of cover-up from a tattoo on her arm. "Hi." She flashed a gorgeous smile.

"And Destiny." Destiny had on a silver lamé romper with a cut-out revealing an appendectomy scar. She, too, had perfect teeth.

Sitting next to her was an errant farmer's daughter with penciled-on freckles, a straw hat, and cut-off jeans.

"Meet Strawberry," Chastity said. "She's a professional dog trainer who did wonders with my baby." She gave her Chihuahua a sloppy kiss on the lips. "Everyone, I'd like you to meet Gloria's big sister, Anita Colby."

My life was getting stranger by the minute.

"Hi, all," I said.

"You look exactly like your sister," said Strawberry, "except for the hair."

"Blondes will be extinct by 2202," said Destiny.

"Oh, no," said Strawberry. "Why?"

"Because blond hair is caused by a recessive gene, which means two recessives have to do it to make a blonde. And there simply aren't enough of us."

Chastity rolled her eyes. "That's it for the chitchat. We have work to do, right, girls? I'll just get your stuff."

I nodded. My stuff. "Okay. That would be great."

Chastity disappeared into a back office.

"That Prince Charles is a pig." Destiny slammed her locker closed.

"I know," said Strawberry. "I got him to stop peeing in her roses, but he still goes on the couch. And she doesn't seem to care."

"What was that?" Chastity had reappeared with a small brown cardboard box in her hands.

"Nothing," said Strawberry. She looked terrified. Destiny and Mystery were staring at a spot on the floor.

"That's what I thought." Chastity handed me the box. It was wrapped all the way around with packing tape. Looked like somebody had used a whole roll.

"Thanks," I said.

"We're going to miss Gloria." Chastity didn't look like she'd ever missed anyone or anything.

"She enjoyed working with you," I said.

"Obviously," she replied breezily. "Anyway, tell her she's welcome back anytime. She always made her minimum."

"Did Gloria happen to leave you a number where she could be reached?" I asked.

Mystery and Destiny exchanged glances. Chastity turned the laser on me again. "Shouldn't *you* have her number?"

"I should, you're absolutely right," I said with a nervous laugh. "But I was on my honeymoon, now I'm traveling for work. My sister and I haven't talked in a couple of weeks. "

Chastity reached over and snatched the box out of my hands, "I forgot to ask you for ID." Her voice was all gravel now.

I reached into my purse and pulled out Anita's driver's license. "Here you go." But I knew she wasn't going to be as easy a sell as Roy. There was no way a seasoned flesh-peddler like Chastity was going to mistake me for a thirty-year-old.

She set down the box. I thought about crying fire again, but even if I managed to get the box away from her, I'd never make it past the goons at the front door.

Chastity stared at the driver's license, then up at me. "Wait here for a second. Girls, keep an eye on her." She took the box and disappeared into the office again. She was probably calling the police. The real police, I mean, not Officer Naughty.

Destiny stuck her finger in a pot of Vaseline and smeared it on her teeth. "I'm not security, for God's sake. If you try to leave, I'm not stopping you. Besides, I'm on next. I don't want to get frazzled."

"Remember last time," warned Mystery.

Destiny frowned. "That was your fault."

"Easy, now," said Strawberry, in the soothing tones you'd use with a pit bull.

All of a sudden Chastity was back and handing me the box. "Sorry, but we've got to kick you out now. I have to collect from a couple of these girls and then take care of a few things downstairs."

That was it? She had to have realized I wasn't Anita. So why had she given me back the box?

Then I noticed the tape.

It was no longer smooth.

It had been pulled off and stuck back on.

Chastity had taken something out.

Or put something else inside.

Chapter 30

I walked back down the stairs. The woman on stage was peeling off a skin-tight red suit that looked a lot like mine. ZZ Top was roaming the floor like a desperado.

It was definitely time to go.

I was pushing my way through the crowd when somebody grabbed me by the waist and pulled me down onto his lap.

"Let go of me!" I protested. But nobody could hear me over the music.

"It's just you and me, gorgeous," the man whispered into my ear.

"I said get your hands off me!"

"Why? My money's as good as anybody's. You got a problem with it? Maybe you need somebody to set you straight." He wrapped his arm tighter around me, pressing down hard on my rib cage.

"That isn't what I meant," I gasped. "It has nothing to do with you. It's me. I don't belong here."

"What makes you so special?"

"I'm not—"

"That's enough," said a voice.

I looked up.

Chastity had taken off the crown, but she could still command armies. The man released me instantly.

"There's obviously been a bit of confusion," Chastity said. "This young lady is not an employee. But I'd like you to meet Strawberry."

Strawberry tipped her hat. Prince Charles gave a low growl.

"Quiet!" Chastity said. Prince Charles buried his head in the crook of her arm. Then she turned to the man. "Strawberry here can take you somewhere a little more private and buy you a drink, if you'd like. That'll be our way of apologizing." She turned to me, and there was no mistaking her message. "Goodnight, Anita."

"You Can Keep Your Hat On" was playing as I walked through the door.

My car was parked at the far end of the lot. The rain had stopped, but the ground was still wet. I walked as fast as I could without slipping, hugging the box to my chest. Then I heard steps behind me.

It was him.

I picked up the pace, clasping my car key between my two middle fingers so I'd be ready to plunge it between his eyes if I needed to.

"Wait!"

A woman's voice.

I turned around.

Mystery stood in front of me. "Sorry. I didn't mean to scare you."

I could see her tattoo now, a bunch of terrified little yellow chicks running from a bloody cleaver, with the words "Meat is Murder" inscribed on the blade.

She followed my gaze. "I used to be a vegan."

"What do you want?" I asked.

"I need to talk to you."

She opened her hand. A rubber band circling her fingers held a wad of bills. She counted out forty of them.

"Sorry they're all ones." She handed them to me. "That's how they tip you at Hello Kitty. You get fives at the Teaser Pleaser, but not everybody makes it to the big time."

"I don't understand."

"Gloria loaned it to me. I would've given it to you in the club, but Chastity has this thing about money. Thinks everybody's trying to rip her off. Didn't you notice the cameras? She watches the whole night's footage when she goes home. I don't think she ever sleeps. Anyway, would you give this to your sister when you see her next?"

I pushed the money back at her. "I don't know when that's going to be. Look, I just want to get out of here. Please."

Mystery nodded. "You don't trust me. Why should you? You've gone to hell and back. I know what you've been through."

"How would you have any idea what I've been through?" I could still feel the man's hands on me.

"Gloria talked about you a lot."

"She did?"

Mystery nodded. "Yeah. Her big sister and all."

I'd always wanted a sister. "What did she say?"

Mystery leaned against the hood of a parked car. "Oh, I don't know. How you were always there for her. How you'd had this piece of shit life and never believed anything good was going to come your way. And all of a sudden you were getting the wedding you'd always dreamed of, and a real honeymoon, and this great guy who thought you were the sun and moon and stars combined. She was afraid you might mess it up."

"I'm not going to mess it up," I snapped. "And if I do, it'll be because I want to." Then I bit my lip.

"Don't get angry," she said softly. "That's not what she meant. Gloria's just worried about you. She told me you haven't been alone since you were a kid. That you pick bad men. That you sell yourself cheap."

I leaned against the car alongside Mystery. "I've changed."

"Sounds like it. And I admire what you're doing. Sounds like a lot of people got hurt. But it must feel good not to be a victim anymore. To be in charge of your own life. Finally."

I didn't understand. I needed more information. "You and Gloria must've spent a lot of time together."

"Yeah, we did. We trusted each other. We told each other everything." Mystery looked both ways, then lowered her voice. "She even told me about your name." She hesitated a second. "How you had to change it. How it's not really Anita."

She and I locked eyes. "What is my real name?"

Mystery's voice fell to a whisper. "Cece."

I stood up so fast the box fell to the ground. Mystery bent down and picked it up for me.

"I have to go," I said. "Right now."

"Are you okay?"

"Fine." I took a deep breath. "I'm just tired." But I didn't need sleep. Just the opposite. This was a nightmare and I needed to wake up.

"Take the money," Mystery said one last time.

I shook my head. "Gloria told me to tell you to keep it. And to give you some advice."

She looked at me hungrily. "What?"

"To change your life while you can. To start over."

If only Anita had had a chance to do the same.

Chapter 31

The box was lighter than air. Was it empty? Or full of secrets?

I didn't want to be alone when I found out.

I sped down Buck Owens, looking for signs of life. Anything but Denny's. Here was something. Zingo's. Open twenty-four hours a day. Famous for their cinnamon rolls. I chose a booth in the back and sat facing the door, like a mob enforcer.

No more surprises.

The menu was not exactly heart-healthy: chicken fingers, chicken-fried steak, zucchini sticks, batter-dipped onion rings. On the back cover was a picture of the famous cinnamon rolls, which resembled the ziggurat Richard Dreyfus builds in *Close Encounters of the Third Kind*.

I tried to catch the waitress's eye, but she was behind the counter chatting with the cook. Fine. I guess I wasn't all that hungry. That trail mix eight hours ago really filled me up.

I turned back to the box. Heart pounding, I grabbed the knife and slit it open, then peered inside.

There was a single piece of paper there, crumpled into a ball. Maybe this was Chastity's idea of a joke. I pulled it out and flattened it with my hand, but the ends kept curling up, so I used the salt and pepper shakers as paperweights.

"Ahem."

I looked up, startled.

"You ready?" The waitress dropped a glass of water onto the table.

"Yup."

"You're not from around here, are you?"

"How could you tell, Betty?" Her name was sewn onto her pink uniform in purple thread.

She clicked open her pen. "Your bloomers."

"They're harem pants," I said.

"You work for the circus?"

"Is that a rhetorical question?"

"Listen, hon, why don't I take your order? We're real busy tonight."

There were five people total in Zingo's, and Betty and the cook were two of them. I ordered a Monte Cristo and a glass of milk. When in Rome.

Once she was gone, I studied the piece of paper.

It was a list of names and phone numbers. I counted. Nineteen. Men and women. There were small red checks next to all of them.

Blackmail.

It seemed like the obvious explanation.

But was Anita the perpetrator, or one of the victims?

None of the area codes were familiar except one. 661. That was somewhere around here.

Unfortunately, I'd lost my hot pink cell phone, somebody had stolen the other one, and a Hummer had run over my BlackBerry. I slid out of the booth, found a pay phone by the bathroom, and dropped in some change.

A man picked up on the second ring. He sounded old and tired. I glanced at my watch. It was almost ten. I'd probably woken him up.

"Sorry to disturb you," I said, "but I'm looking for"—I checked the list again—"Dorothy Johnson."

"She don't live here no more."

Damn it. "Do you know how I can reach her?"

"Sure, but I can't give her phone number out to a stranger, not after everything she's been through."

So she was another one.

Just like Anita.

"I understand. That puts me in a bit of a bind, though. I'm an attorney here in Bakersfield, and we've been trying to track Ms. Johnson down for some time. It's nothing bad, don't get me wrong. Ms. Johnson has come into some money, and we need to get it to her."

The moment the words came out of my mouth, I regretted them. Now I was going to be another thing Dorothy Johnson had to get through.

"Well, that is good news," the man said.

"Good news? It's great news! When Dorothy hears what I have to say, she's going to be jumping up and down!"

He was quiet. One more push would do it.

"No one would want to miss an opportunity like this," I said. "At least no one in their right mind."

The old man's chair scraped against the floor. "Dorothy could sure use a break."

I was going straight to hell.

A minute later, I dropped some more coins into the slot. This time a woman answered.

"Dorothy Johnson?"

"She's not here. This is her daughter. Can I help you?"

"I'd rather speak to her directly. Do you know when she'll be home?"

"Not until tomorrow. Give me your number and I'll have her call you then."

"I'm going to be hard to reach. When tomorrow?"

I heard ice clinking in a glass. "Who is this?"

"I'm an attorney. It's about some money she inherited."

"Nobody we know has any money." Dorothy's daughter wanted to be convinced otherwise.

"It's someone your mother worked with a while back. She may not even remember her. I can't say much more. When tomorrow will she be home exactly?"

"Late."

"Can I catch her someplace during the day?"

"Don't take no for an answer, do you?"

"Never lost a case."

"Fine. She'll be at work tomorrow. In Wasco, near the 155."

I jotted down the address and took my seat just as Betty arrived with my sandwich and glass of milk, which radiated a strange kind of blue-green light. But maybe that was the fluorescent light here at Zingo's.

Hitchcock concealed a light in the glass of poisoned milk Johnny (Cary Grant) brings to Lina (Joan Fontaine) in *Suspicion*. The eerie glow was meant to underscore the menace the handsome ne'er-do-well poses to his rich and very naive wife. Unfortunately, the effect was undermined when the head of RKO insisted on tacking on a happy ending. He was convinced nobody would believe Cary Grant a murderer. But Hitch knew he could make anybody believe anything.

There's nothing more seductive than the impossible projected in Technicolor.

"What's the matter?" asked Betty. "You wanted nonfat?"

I peered into the glass, then sucked down the milk.

It was ice-cold and delicious.

As for the Monte Cristo, it was like what the divine Cary Grant said about working with the egomaniacal Joan Fontaine.

Never again.

Chapter 32

Room 10 was like a cave, warm and dark. I'd been planning to sleep until spring, but was startled awake by the sound of a key turning in the lock.

I jumped up, gathered the sheets around my naked body, and was fleeing for the nearest closet when a small gray-haired woman appeared in the doorway pushing a cart piled high with sheets and towels.

The new day was filled with surprises of both the pleasant and unpleasant variety.

Maid service at the E-Z Nights, to begin with.

Followed by cinnamon rolls at Zingo's, which were moist and flaky at the same time.

The sun was shining brightly, another happy surprise. After breakfast I went back to the room and changed into my version of lawyerly attire, which consisted of a black silk shantung suit, matching faux fur stole, and large gold envelope clutch.

My blond hair, however, undermined the general effect, so I tucked it into a military-inspired beret.

Wasco was thirty-five miles away. I threw my bag into the car and took off.

It was Sunday. Everybody must've been in church because there was nobody around. Even better. I took off my dark glasses and sped with impunity.

Within twenty minutes, I was in the middle of nowhere. Golden fields of rural nothingness, stretching as far as the eye could see. The occasional tumbleweed, drifting in the wind. A blackbird. A corn maze. Some of these are incredible. If you see them from above, they make patterns, like a map of the United States or a butterfly in its larval stage. But this one was closed for the season.

I put down the window and took a breath of fresh air. That was when the chugging began.

One minute you're driving along, minding your own business, taking in the sights. The next minute, your Camry is making odd noises and refusing to accelerate before churning up a cloud of dust and rolling to a dead stop.

Running out of gas was the first surprise of the unpleasant variety.

I sat there for a minute in shock. Then for another minute, willing a tow truck to appear. When that didn't happen, I opened the glove compartment and flipped through the manual, looking for the chapter on what to do when your life is falling apart, but they'd left that chapter out.

I got out of the car and walked over to the shoulder. Then I saw somebody coming. A minivan. My kind of people.

"Hey!" I screamed, waving my arms frantically as it zoomed past me.

I waited another ten minutes, but not a single car drove by.

I was marooned.

With no cell phone.

I had to find a gas station.

But where?

I'd gone probably twenty miles already, so it was no more than fifteen until Wasco. Could I walk that far in the midday sun in high-heeled black mesh ankle boots without risking dehydration and possible death?

First things first: I had to move the car over to the shoulder.

I got back in the car and hit the hazard lights, then shifted into neutral. Then I got out, leaving the wrecked driver's side door ajar. With my left arm on the door frame, I summoned every ounce of strength I had in an attempt to push the car forward. But I couldn't get any traction because the soles of my boots kept slipping, so I took them off and tried again in bare feet, keeping my right hand on the steering wheel so I could guide the car as it rolled.

You know how they say a mother can lift a car off of her baby when it's a life-or-death situation?

It's a lie.

I put my boots back on and started down the road. At least I had money. I was going to bribe the gas station attendant into driving me back here. If I found a gas station, that is.

Another car whizzed past me without so much as slowing

down. A damsel in distress didn't mean what it used to. People are so suspicious these days. God, it was hot. I whipped off my fur stole. My feet were hurting already.

Only fourteen and a half miles to go.

I passed a roadside shrine, piled with dead bouquets and a teddy bear wearing a faded red ribbon.

Too bad I believed in omens.

I turned around. I couldn't see the car anymore. Had I remembered to leave the hazard lights on? That probably wasn't a good idea, anyway. What if a cop drove by? I had no idea whose plates Jonathan Tucci had given me. They could be another ex-con's. Maybe somebody who'd done a lot worse than fleeing a jurisdiction. But I couldn't dwell on that now. What I was going to dwell on instead was the fact that I'd had a full tank of gas last night.

Somebody had wanted this to happen.

Then I tripped on a pebble and just missed falling flat on my face.

"Oh, shit!" I cried out loud. "Why me?"

In the vain hopes of alleviating the sudden intense throbbing in my ankle, I sat down for a minute by the side of the road. At least silk shantung is washable. I had Advil but nothing to drink, and I'm not the kind of person who can swallow a pill without water. I stood up, put a little pressure on the ankle, then a little more. All right. I'd live.

Five minutes later, I'd reached some kind of intersection. And what was that sign? I half-sprinted, half-limped toward it.

A bus stop!

I was saved!

I slowed my pace, put my stole back on, straightened my skirt. Now all I had to do was wait for the bus to show up, then ride it to civilization, where I could find somebody to drive me back to my car and fill it with gas. Maybe give me an ice pack.

I was in front of the sign now. The schedule was posted. The bus to Ellerbee came through every fifteen minutes. No, that was Monday through Friday. On Saturdays, it came once every thirty minutes. But today was Sunday.

The day of rest.

No bus service on Sunday.

I sat down by the side of the road and explored my options.

That didn't go well.

Then my luck took a 180.

I'm talking about Jean-Claude.

The only Frenchman within hundreds of miles of here.

He'd stopped because of my beret.

Jean-Claude hailed from Lyon. He'd come nine years ago to visit the Mojave Desert and had fallen in love with the area. He'd settled in Joshua Tree and opened a *patisserie-boulange-rie*, which had proven surprisingly popular with the Marine Corps wives stationed in Twentynine Palms. He was on his way to Fresno, the aforementioned raisin capital of California. Business trip. He'd be delighted to drop me at the next service station.

Jean-Claude's Ford truck was spotless. He gave me a bottle of Fiji water to wash down my Advil and a *tarte au citron* to take the edge off until lunch. After promising to come visit him someday, I bid him a grateful adieu.

Phil's Fill 'er Up was a humble establishment. There was a kid working the pump. I explained my plight. He filled up a bright red five-gallon gas can and handed it to me. I almost sank under the weight. There was no way I could walk back with that. The kid offered to drive me, but he wouldn't be available until the end of his shift. At six o'clock. Which would be too late. Dorothy Johnson would've left work for the day.

I started with fifty, and went up to two hundred, but he was unwilling to desert his post. So I called a taxi.

Dmitri showed up twenty minutes later.

Dmitri was Russian and didn't speak a word of English, but when we pulled up to my car and I pointed to my gas tank, then to him while smiling encouragingly and waving a twenty, he seemed to understand.

But then Dmitri got a call on his cell phone and much screaming ensued, following which Dmitri threw his cell phone on the ground and stomped on it. Then he picked it up, shaking his head sorrowfully at me, and got back into the taxi and zoomed off.

Fine. I'd seen people do this a million times on TV.

But they'd had funnels.

I crawled into the back seat of the car and found an old piece of newspaper. Then I dug through my purse and found a piece of Bazooka bubble gum, which I unwrapped and popped in my mouth. When it was nice and chewed, I rolled the newspaper up, then secured the ends with the wad of gum.

Now I had a funnel, too.

I took off my jacket and stole to allow for sufficient freedom of movement.

There was a long tube attached to the cap of the gas can.

I removed it and inserted it into the gas tank. Then I stuck the funnel into the end of the tube, hefted the heavy can into place, and started to pour, as slowly as I could.

When the can was empty, I pulled out the funnel and the tube, put the cap back on, sat down in the driver's seat, and turned the key in the ignition.

Incroyable.

I turned the car around so I could return the tank to the kid at Phil's Fill 'er Up.

And that was when I heard it.

Inside the car.

In the back seat.

A phone was ringing.

I pulled over, killed the engine, and slowly turned around, afraid of what I might see.

A hot pink cell phone.

Oh, no.

How had it gotten here?

I didn't have to pick it up. Not this time.

It was still ringing.

Damn it.

I reached back and flipped it open.

"You shouldn't leave your car unlocked," said the person on the other end of the line. "It's dangerous, Cece."

Cold as ice.

Hard as a stone.

My hand flew up to my blond hair. So much for the security measures.

"Where are you?" I asked. "How'd you find me?"

"We've had this conversation before, haven't we?"

"What do you want from me?"

"It's too late for that. I'm just checking in, that's all."

"Leave me alone," I said.

"Is that an order?"

I squared my shoulders. "It's a threat."

He laughed. "You're threatening me?"

"Yes. I'm going to find out who you are, and you're going to pay for what you've done. Good-bye."

I hung up. I was shaking all over. But I also felt strangely liberated.

Then I looked at the phone.

It was my phone. The one I'd thought I'd lost. It must've been in the car all along. How had I missed it?

I hadn't missed it.

He'd put it here.

When I was getting gas?

When I was at the E-Z Nights?

When it was parked in the driveway of my house?

I had no way of knowing.

But I did know one thing.

He wanted to be able to reach me.

He knew I'd pick up.

I couldn't be sure I wouldn't.

I started up the engine and pulled back onto the road. Once I was going sixty, I opened the window and felt the cool rush of air against my skin. Then I hurled my cell phone as far and as hard as I could.

Then I closed the window and turned on the radio to drown out the voices in my head.

Chapter 33

It isn't every day you meet a bearded lady and the world's fattest man. No, that was a once-in-a-lifetime experience. Of which I'd experienced several lately.

Sugar Beet Amusement Park rose out of the dust like a cut-rate mirage, featuring twenty-five different games and shows, a farm-themed carousel, and an adults-only Tunnel of Love.

I pulled the car into an empty spot, then made my way to the entrance.

The bearded lady and the fat man were having a smoke under the neon sign.

I coughed to get their attention, then asked if they knew where I could find Dorothy Johnson.

After one last drag, the fat man crushed his cigarette under his floppy red shoe. "Nasty habit, sorry."

The bearded lady said, "You're a heart attack waiting to happen, young man."

"Shut up," he said companionably. "Your whiskers look like crap."

She whacked him on the shoulder, then licked her fingers and twirled the ends of her mustache. "We're disgusting. Like an old married couple. Take a right at popcorn and another right at Chicago-style dogs. Dorothy does spin art."

The place was packed. A boy in a cowboy hat bumped me as he passed.

"Where'd you get the cotton candy?" I asked. "It looks good."

"Dentist says it rots your teeth." He reached into his holster, pulled out a gun, and pointed it in my face. "You get me?"

Ah, the impertinence of youth.

I followed the sound of fresh corn popping, then the scent of Chicago-style dogs, which come on a poppy-seed bun and unless you say otherwise are topped with mustard, onion, sweet pickle relish, a dill pickle spear, tomato slices, peppers, and a dash of celery salt. I got mine fully loaded.

While I was eating, I watched the people trying their luck at the Hi-Striker. There was a father with a trio of adoring daughters. A skinny cowboy whose girlfriend was holding a huge stuffed bear, which the adoring daughters eyed enviously. An older man wearing his Sunday best. After draping his suit jacket over the fence, he picked up the mallet, raised it over his head, and slammed it down with all of his might, ringing the bell. He won a bag of freshly pulled taffy, which he gave to the little girls.

Spin art was just opposite.

"You can use blue, too, if you want." The woman behind the counter handed a squirt bottle to a kid with chocolate all over his face. "Three colors for two dollars."

The kid throttled the plastic like he was draining the life out of it.

The machine stopped spinning. The woman removed the piece of paper. "There you go," she said, smiling.

"Looks like guts," said the kid with satisfaction.

I took a step forward. "Excuse me?"

She studied me with clear blue eyes. "My daughter told me you called. I've been waiting."

The first thing I noticed about Dorothy Johnson was her hair. It was silvery gray and glittered like tinsel on a Christmas tree. She wore it pulled back off her face, like she had nothing to hide. But she was tired. You could see that in the set of her mouth. Tired of having to smile.

"Give me just a minute." Dorothy walked over to the ring-toss booth. "Emma," she called out. "Can you take over for a little while?"

A young woman with a Mohawk handed a large man three metal rings and tucked the five-dollar bill he gave her into the pocket of her apron. "No problem," she said, revealing a mouth full of gold teeth.

"This way." Dorothy took my arm. "Let's find someplace a little more private."

It was crowded. We pushed our way past teenagers traveling in packs, mothers pushing strollers, kids clutching giant cups of soda.

"I once rigged a spin art machine for my daughter out of a salad spinner and some paper plates," I said. "Man, did that make a mess."

"I'll bet."

"Have you been working here long?" I was trying to make conversation.

"Nope."

"Pop the balloon, Miss?" a man in yellow overalls called out. "Five dollars for three tries. Your choice of prizes!"

"It's rigged," Dorothy said with a sudden flash of anger. "The balloons are underinflated and the darts' tips are dull. And don't even bother with the milk throw. One of the bottles in the bottom row is always weighted. Come on."

We passed a display of the local produce, which included sugar beets, potatoes, corn, and barley. Then the carousel, which had pigs, sheep, and goats instead of the usual prancing ponies. Just beyond that was a small dock and a glistening man-made lake with an island in the middle, surrounded by lush palms.

Dorothy walked up to the kiosk and got two tickets.

We were going to the Isle of Enchantment.

The kid manning the dock helped us into a small rowboat. "Hands and feet inside at all times. Remember to be courteous to your fellow travelers, and no drinking and driving." He gave us a hard push.

The boat drifted away from the dock. We glided for a minute or so. I watched a stray balloon turn into a dot, then disappear.

"Nice day," I said.

Dorothy didn't respond.

I reached down to touch the water. The cold pricked my fingers. I shook off the drops and closed my eyes. I felt the sun on my face, the soft breeze against my cheek.

When the boat came to a stop, we picked up the splintering oars and started rowing. It didn't take long to get into the rhythm. Oars lifting, pausing, slicing into the water, then dragging against the current until they reached the sweet spot where they could be lifted out again. Before long we were bumping up against the shore.

Dorothy got out first, picking her way through the tall grasses clustered along the bank. "This way."

I could still hear the sounds coming from the other side of the lake: the carnival barker, the carousel music, bells ringing, whistles blowing. But they were faint now, just echoes. We followed a path of moss-covered stepping-stones through a shady grove of trees, past some empty picnic tables and an abandoned stand that had once offered fresh lemonade for twenty-five cents. Now all I could hear was birdsong and the wind whipping up the fallen leaves.

The Isle of Enchantment was deserted.

All of a sudden, Dorothy turned around. She had a strange look in her eyes.

And a gun in her hand.

"What are you doing?" I gasped.

"This is the last time anybody's going to take advantage of me." She leveled the gun at my head.

I did not have a good feeling about this. "Can we talk, Dorothy?"

"Nothing to talk about. It's over."

"Put the gun down, Dorothy. Please. Shooting me isn't going to solve anything."

There was no point in screaming. We were alone. As for making a break for it, I could try. But most people can't outrun a bullet.

"I lost my house, my job, everything," Dorothy said. "But you'd know that, wouldn't you? And I wasn't the only one. A lot of people got hurt."

I took a step back. If I could distract her for a second, I could duck into the trees. It was dark in there. She wouldn't be able to find me. "I'm sorry, but I don't understand. "

"You're a lawyer. You've been trying to find me. All you need is my social security number, right? Maybe the number of my bank account? Then you'll wire me my inheritance, isn't that how it goes?"

I took another step backward. "Look, I'm sorry I lied to you. I didn't want to, but I had no choice."

"Oh, you had to? You're just another innocent victim?"

"I swear I don't know what you're talking about."

"Liar." She pulled back the release.

A lot of people got hurt.

That was what Anita's sister had said to Mystery. But she'd also said Anita was finally taking her life back. That she was done being a victim.

"Wait," I pleaded. "Do you know somebody named Anita Colby?"

"Quit stalling."

"Anita Colby lost everything, too."

I thought about what the tiny yellow-haired girl at the Andalusia had told me. That Anita was finally getting out from under.

"Anita Colby is the reason I'm here," I said. "She was murdered, and she left behind some papers. Your name was on them. I think she knew what was going on. I think she was trying to stop it."

"I don't know anybody named Anita."

I reached into my purse.

"Stop!" Dorothy cried. "Don't even think about it!"

I put my hands up and let the purse fall to the ground. "I just wanted to show you something. I have a picture. Maybe you'll recognize her."

"I'll get it." She bent down to pick up my purse, never taking her eyes off me.

"It's in my wallet, a driver's license. Anita Colby. Blond hair, five foot ten."

Dorothy reached into my wallet, indiscriminately tossing credit cards and papers onto the ground. Then she stopped. "Is this what you're talking about?"

I took Anita's driver's license out of her hand. I'd picked it up on the trail less than a week ago. So much had happened since then. I looked deep into Anita's brown eyes. She was trying to tell me something. But what?

"Yes," I said, handing the license back. "This is what I'm talking about. This is Anita."

Dorothy shook her head. "This isn't Anita."

"I don't understand. Who is it, then?"

"This is Cece."

I felt my stomach lurch. "Cece Caruso?"

Dorothy nodded. "You know her?"

I sighed. "I am her."

Chapter 34

Cece Caruso turned up one day like the proverbial bad penny.

She was a tall, willowy blonde in some kind of crazy wraparound kimono dress. Big eyes. Looked like a movie star.

Yeah, Dorothy said, remembering. She was some kind of actress.

It had been close to nine o'clock in the morning. Dorothy was late to work. She was in a hurry. She'd been reprimanded twice the week before. Her job was on the line.

Not to worry, Cece said. I'm going to make it worth your while.

She worked for a Hollywood studio.

Flashed a fancy business card.

Said they were shooting a movie in the area, and her job was to scout locations.

Cece needed a house just like Dorothy's. A house with a white picket fence and an American flag and a couple of bikes in the driveway and a rose garden that could maybe use a little pruning.

The house was where the family lived. Dad worked for the city and Mom stayed home with the kids and baked cookies. On weekends, the neighbors came over for barbecues. Then Dad got laid off and Mom stopped baking. Dad started drinking. And late one night, after a delicious pot roast, he waited until everyone was fast asleep, knocked back a fifth of Scotch, stumbled out to the garage, and blew his brains out.

But that was getting ahead of ourselves, Cece said. She promised Dorothy a copy of the script. It had Oscar written all over it. Then she pulled out a contract. Her boss would be by the next day. He'd pick up the paperwork and go over any questions Dorothy might have.

They were going to pay Dorothy ten thousand dollars for the first week, and an extra five for every day after that. Cece anticipated it would be twelve to fifteen days' shooting time, meaning Dorothy was going to get close to fifty thousand dollars.

Fifty thousand dollars? Dorothy asked where to sign.

Cece laughed, then asked if she could peek inside for a minute. Dorothy invited Cece into her home. And that was when she did it. Found something. Some piece of mail or some old bill or some loose check or something with Dorothy's private information on it. Dorothy still didn't know what it was. But whatever it was, Cece found it and took it and tore Dorothy's life to pieces. Not that Dorothy knew that yet. That was back when she still thought she was lucky.

Cece's boss showed up the next day to pick up the signed

contract. He was a handsome fellow. Said that he liked what he saw. That Cece had picked the perfect place. He shook Dorothy's hand and promised the check would arrive by messenger within the week.

The check never arrived.

Dorothy called the number he left, but it was not in service. Dorothy looked up the production company, but couldn't find it. She figured they'd found another house with a white picket fence and roses that maybe needed pruning and promptly forgot about her Hollywood dream.

The trouble started six months later.

When the phone rings at three in the morning, it's never good news.

It was somebody from a collections agency. They said Dorothy's account with some bank she'd never heard of was four months in arrears. If she didn't immediately make a payment of $9700, they were proceeding with legal action. When Dorothy tried to protest, the man on the other end of the phone started yelling, then hung up.

When Dorothy arrived at work later that morning, she had a note on her desk saying her supervisor wanted to see her. Dorothy was nervous. The supervisor had a bad temper. Her name was Mary Alice. Mary Alice said that they were doing a routine check on their employees and had learned that Dorothy had several delinquent accounts, a judgment against her, and a warrant out for her arrest. Mary Alice fired Dorothy on the spot.

On the way home, Dorothy stopped for lunch. After she'd finished her burger, she put down a credit card. The waitress took it with a smile, then came back frowning. The card was declined. So were the rest of them.

Dorothy paid cash.

When she got home, she had four messages on her machine. The first was from the collections agency. The second was from the bank. The third was from the mortgage company. The fourth was from the police.

Dorothy put her head in her hands, and wound her fingers around her long silvery hair. She couldn't go on.

She didn't have to. I handed her a tissue and put my arm around her. I was starting to understand.

Which meant the nightmare was almost over.

Chapter 35

Dorothy lived in a trailer park not far from Sugar Beet Amusement Park. On the way there, we stopped at the grocery store and picked up steaks, baking potatoes, lettuce, and a bottle of Cabernet.

"Special occasion?" asked the checker, taking the hundred-dollar bill out of my hand.

"Could be," I said.

"Somebody's birthday? Don't see no candles."

"Better," said Dorothy. "The day of reckoning."

The checker handed me a bag and sixty-seven cents' change. It'd better be the day of reckoning. I was down to eighteen hundred dollars. If I'd been thinking, I would've taken that forty from Mystery.

Dorothy's trailer had flower boxes in the windows, wall-to-wall carpeting, and wireless Internet access.

"The resident manager set it up," Dorothy said, flipping

through her mail. "She's constantly on eBay. Collects owls. Owl salt and pepper shakers, owl cuckoo clocks, owl brooches. I have no idea where she keeps them. When I lost my house, I threw everything away. Didn't stop until I'd filled ninety-seven garbage bags. Jesus. Don't you hate junk mail?" After tearing the whole stack in half, she reconsidered and threw it up into the air. "Look. It's confetti."

Somebody was in a party mood.

"You can sit over here." Dorothy picked a folding chair off a hook on the wall and carried it over to a wooden desk wedged into the narrow space opposite the bathroom. A daisy had been carved into the desk with red ballpoint pen. "I'll be right back."

The tiny space was a miracle of organization. There were twin Murphy beds, a Lilliputian kitchen unit with a pop-up Formica table, and a leather loveseat with swiveling armrests that doubled as TV trays.

"Do you take anything in your tea?" Dorothy asked.

"Black is fine." I pulled Anita's list out of my purse and laid it down next to the computer monitor.

There were eighteen names and phone numbers besides Dorothy's. Ten of them had the same area code: 785.

Dorothy's screensaver was a mystical gazebo, complete with unicorns, fairies, and tinkling wind chimes. I killed the fantasy and opened Safari.

Area code 785 stretches from the Colorado state line on the west to the Missouri state line on the east, but does not include the Kansas City metropolitan area. The largest city covered by the area code is the state capital of Topeka.

Kansas.

That must've been where this had all started.

Kansas?

Something rang a bell.

My best friend, Lael, grew up outside Topeka, but that wasn't it.

Kim Novak's character in *Vertigo* is from Salina, but that wasn't it, either.

It would come to me.

Back to the list. I decided to start at the top.

Elaine Harris, from New Haven, Connecticut.

I typed the name into Google.

After reading through most of the thirty-plus hits, I pieced together Elaine's story from articles in the *New Haven Advocate*, the *New Haven Independent*, and the *Yale Daily News*.

Elaine had met him at the mall. Her mother had always warned her not to speak to strangers, but this man was different. Soft-spoken. Professional-looking. He gave her his card. It was on nice paper stock. Heavy. Expensive.

As one of the principals of A-1 Celebrity Management, he was always on the lookout for girls with that special something, and Elaine had it in spades.

He bought her lunch. They talked about everything under the sun. He told her she was not only beautiful, but also smart. The world, he said, was her oyster. Right there and then, he prepared a contract for her to sign. Exclusive representation for a year.

Elaine spent much of her savings having her hair straightened and her lips plumped. Then she had head shots taken and sent them to a post-office box, as instructed.

Two days later, he called. He'd gotten her an agent and a

paper towel commercial. She was going to be a young house-wife whose marriage is saved by double-ply double rolls. All he needed to process her advance was a social security number.

Schuyler Kramer of Sandy Point, Maryland, met him while she was walking her dog, Lucifer, an uncommonly attractive Afghan hound.

He told Schuyler he ran a company that represented animal actors, who were always greatly in demand. Had she ever thought of registering Lucifer? She could make a tremendous amount of money.

From Schuyler, he got a bank account number.

Joe Schwartz, from Tampa, Florida, was an aspiring science fiction author. His hero was Philip K. Dick.

There were two of them this time.

Joe met them at a reading he gave at the community center. A good-looking man and a nondescript woman. Dishwater blonde. Big, staring eyes. That's how he'd described her to the police.

During the Q&A, the woman had asked a lot of questions—how he'd gotten started, what inspired him, where and when he did his best writing. The man with her was quiet, but took copious notes.

Afterwards, they approached the podium. Asked Joe if they could take him out for a drink. Said they ran a publishing house based in the Midwest, and were interested in putting out a small run of his short stories.

The man and the woman accompanied Joe back to his apartment. They had another drink while Joe printed out his life's work. The woman asked if she could use the bathroom. Joe and the man stood at the door, chatting, while she freshened up.

After they left, Joe waited to hear from them. When he didn't, he assumed they hadn't liked the stories after all.

The call from the collections agency came eight months later.

I looked up from the monitor, aghast.

Who could do such things?

Taking people into their confidence.

Preying on their vanity.

Leaving them with nothing.

Never worrying about the trail they'd left behind because it would be cold by the time anybody could put two and two together.

"More tea, Cece?" Dorothy asked.

I rubbed my eyes. "I'm fine. The steaks smell great."

"They'll be ready in ten minutes." Dorothy had draped an oilskin cloth over the pop-up table and was setting it with plastic utensils. "I'm sorry about this. It's going to be hard to cut with plastic."

"It isn't easy to start over," I said. "I admire you."

"Drink your wine," she said, bringing it over.

"Here's to." I clinked my glass against hers.

Then I typed in the words, "identity theft."

Identity theft and fraud.

Identity theft prevention.

Surviving identity theft.

Fighting identity theft.

The last one was a news item.

In New Mexico, Wells Fargo Bank was inviting people to bring up to fifty pounds of paper documents to their local branch for free shredding.

I suddenly remembered the stack of preapproved credit-card solicitations on Anita's desk drawer. She'd gone through other people's trash to get them. No wonder she had all those pairs of rubber gloves under her sink.

And the change-of-address forms. When she got sick of going through other people's trash, she'd simply rerouted their mail.

Anita was guilty. That seemed fairly evident now. But she wasn't working alone. There were at least two of them.

She wanted out.

He wanted to keep things as they were.

Maybe she blackmailed him, thinking it was her only option. Maybe not. In either case, he decided to kill her. But he didn't want anybody asking questions. He had to make it look like an accident. For that, he needed a witness.

It was dark now. I looked out the window. I couldn't see anything except my reflection in the glass.

I was the witness.

But why me?

Why had Anita been using my name? Was she the only one? Were there other Ceces out there wreaking havoc on innocent people's lives?

"Anybody here?" somebody called out.

Dorothy's daughter was home. She resembled her mother, except for the hair. Hers was straight out of a bottle, a glossy blue-black, and hung down on either side of her pale face. She had a Bettie Page tattoo on her forearm. The girl took one look at me, then turned to Dorothy. "We rich now, Mom?"

"Erin," Dorothy began.

"Didn't think so." Erin tossed her purse on the couch.

"I'm afraid you don't understand," I said.

"Oh, I understand plenty." She pulled a Coke out of the refrigerator. "Nice steaks. She buy those for you?"

"It's not what—"

Erin grabbed her mother by the shoulders. "You said you were going to teach her a lesson. And now she's in our house, and on your fucking computer! It's happening all over again. Wake up, Dorothy! You're not in Kansas anymore!"

Kansas.

Kansas.

Jesus.

Now I remembered.

Chapter 36

I leapt to my feet.

Dorothy frowned. "Everything alright, Cece?"

"Can I use your phone for a minute?" I asked. "It's a California number."

She was tossing the salad. "But we're just about to eat."

"I don't want any croutons, Mom," Erin whined. "They make me sick, as you very well know."

"It'll only take a minute," I said impatiently. "It's extremely important."

"Give Cece the phone," Dorothy said to her daughter.

Erin grudgingly handed it to me, and I dialed Annie's number. When she picked up, I said, "It's me."

I could hear the relief in her voice. "Mom? Thank God. Somebody named Detective McQueen called me today. She wanted to know if I'd heard from you. Where are you? What is going on?"

I had to keep it short. "Is Vincent home?"

"Who's Vincent?" Erin hissed.

"Quiet!" her mother commanded.

"Are you in trouble, Mom?" Annie asked.

"Everything's going to be fine if I can just talk to Vincent. Please. Then I have to hang up."

I heard her call him into the room.

"Cece?"

"Vincent. I have a quick question. Remember the other day when you emailed me the images that were on my phone?"

"Yeah."

"You only sent me seven. I think there were more."

"There were. I downloaded them onto my computer. But you only wanted the nature shots. For your Christmas cards."

"I need all of them. Right now." I looked at Dorothy. She wiped her hands on her apron, then scribbled her email address on a piece of paper and handed it to me.

"No problem," Vincent said. "I'm sitting at my computer. Tell me where to send them."

That was one of the many things I loved about my son-in-law. He didn't ask a lot of questions. Not because he wasn't curious, but because he respected a person's privacy.

A minute later, the pictures turned up.

A dry hillside.

Scattered leaves.

An abandoned truck parked on the trail.

The Hollywood sign.

The Hollywood sign again.

More dead leaves.

Dirt.

Those I'd already seen.

I was looking for the two pictures I'd taken the previous night.

In the parking lot of the Orpheum, right after Bachelor Number One had rear-ended my Camry.

And here they were.

A blurred shot of the back of my car.

And a crystal-clear shot of the front of his.

There were California plates on his black Mercedes. Just what you'd expect from an agent who grew up on a cul-de-sac in Tarzana and swore he'd never been anywhere near a prairie.

But the frame surrounding the license plate told a different story.

I stared at it for a minute, just to be sure.

It wasn't from California, the Golden State.

It was from the Sunflower State, the place Dorothy is desperate to return to after her ill-fated trip to the Land of Oz.

Dorothy wanted to go home.

Home was Kansas.

Chapter 37

I got back to the motel at nine. Roy was in the front office playing solitaire.

"Boo!" I said.

He looked up from his cards and glared at me.

"Just getting into the holiday spirit," I said. "Halloween is tomorrow, after all."

Roy pointed to a sorry-looking candy dish filled with Necco wafers, Smarties, and those unspeakable circus peanuts. "Help yourself, but watch out for razor blades."

I gave him a look. "Key, please."

"Have you decided when you're checking out?" Roy put a five of hearts on top of a six of spades.

"Tomorrow. Can I get my key?"

"I heard you the first time." He turned around and plucked the key to Room 10 off its hook.

"Thank you," I said.

"Thank you, *Roy*."

"Sorry, *Roy*." I headed for the door.

"Anita."

I turned around.

"You sure you wouldn't like to stay a little longer? Just to talk?" He pulled a stick of gum out of his pocket, and folded it in half and then into quarters before popping it into his mouth.

"So now you want to be friends?" I supposed I could have one Necco wafer. Just to be sociable. And to postpone the inevitable.

"Nah." He moved a seven of clubs on top of an eight of hearts, then moved the whole pile over to the left. Then he waved me away.

Back in the room, I thought of a million things I'd rather do than make a call to Ben McAllister.

Eat crap candy with Roy.

Spear trash along the highway.

Walk through a graveyard at midnight.

Steeling myself, I picked up the Chinese menu he'd scrawled his number onto. It had been sitting in the glove compartment of my car for almost a week.

"Hello?"

I gave a start at the sound of his voice. "Ben. It's Cece. Don't hang up."

He took a deep breath, then exhaled. "It's late. What can I do for you?"

"I wanted to apologize for the other night."

"Apology accepted. Good night."

"Wait! Please. I can explain."

"There's no need."

"Yes, there is. There's no excuse for how I behaved."

He waited.

"I haven't been myself these days," I said. "But I guess that's an excuse."

"Sounds like one."

"It's just that I'm so confused. I broke off my engagement a couple of weeks ago, and I know I'm not ready to get involved with anyone right now, but I can't help myself." I felt my stomach turn. "Being with you—I don't know. I guess the way you make me feel scares me."

"Go on."

Greedy bastard. "I want to see you, Ben."

"When?"

The room was stifling. I cracked open the window. "As soon as possible."

"How about tomorrow?" He had to attend an auction at Bonhams & Butterfields in Hollywood. One of his clients had put something up for sale. It was an obligation he couldn't get out of. I was going to meet him there, and then we were going to have dinner somewhere quiet, where we could talk.

That was perfect.

Because *B is for Ben* is a good talker.

And I am a good listener.

Chapter 38

I was packed and showered before the housekeeper showed up the next morning. Including the tip I left her, the grand total for my two-night stay at the E-Z Nights came to just under two hundred dollars, which is about the same amount of money it would've cost me to buy the Maud Frizon black silk *peau de soie* pumps with the pleated indigo bows I'd been eyeing at Bridget's for two months. Not that I was keeping track.

On the way out of town, operating on the premise that it would be a long time before I returned to Kern County, I decided to check out the giant white shoe at the corner of Chester and Tenth, former home of Deschwander's Shoe Repair, which opened in 1947, the same year as the first UFO sightings over the U.S. I'd read an article in the *Bakotopia* listing the area's top ten sights. The giant white shoe was #1. And deservedly so. #2 was a ten-foot-tall man made out of air-conditioning ductwork standing in front of American Air, Heating and Air Conditioning, and #3 was a giant Native American with arrows poking out of his head who used to stand guard over the Big O tire shop. I couldn't find either of them. I did, however, manage to locate Yolanda's (#5), home of the three-foot churro, but they were closed for Halloween. I considered making a detour to Kingsburg, home of the Swedish Coffee Pot (#6), which is five hundred times larger than its real-life counterpart, however Kingsburg was almost to Fresno, and that seemed excessive. The last place James Dean stopped for gas (#8) was not far from Wasco, but I was hungry now.

I stopped at an In-N-Out Burger halfway down Highway 5. There was a long wait, so I had plenty of time to map out my strategy.

Tonight I was going to ensnare Ben. First I'd hang on him a little, giving him a false sense of security. He liked to play the tough guy. Then I'd ambush him. Once we were seated in our chairs at Bonhams & Butterfields, that is, and there were hundreds of people around. He wouldn't dare try anything with hundreds of people around.

I'd accused him once before, but I hadn't had the facts. Now I did (more or less). There was Anita's list. Dorothy's story. The hot pink cell phone. And then there was Kansas. As Gambino liked to say, it wasn't enough to hang him, but it was enough to get a warrant.

There were six hours until seven o'clock, however, and I couldn't exactly go home. Anybody could be watching. Detectives McQueen and Collins, for example. Officers Lavery and Bell. The SWAT team, perhaps. It wasn't like my neighbors Lois and Marlene could be counted upon for discretion. They had noses like bloodhounds. The minute they got a whiff of me, they'd be on the phone to the local news, primping for their close-ups.

I was pumping mustard in a little paper cup when they called my number.

Burger and fries in hand, I hopped back into the car.

I could always go to the movies. Or go shopping. I still had over a thousand dollars in my purse. Or how was this for a novel idea? I could work on my Hitchcock book. No actual writing, of course. That would require ideas, organization, a beginning, a middle, and an end. But I could go on a little research expedition. Do some field work.

I finished my burger, then eased onto the 405 South.

After exiting in Westwood, I headed straight for the Wilshire Palms.

The year was 1939. Producer David O. Selznick had wooed them relentlessly. And they'd finally given in.

The Hitchcocks were coming to America.

Hitch was, of course, already a success in his native England. He'd directed such hits as *The 39 Steps* and *The Lady Vanishes*. But he wanted more. The Brits saw him as a fat, unglamorous young man from Essex who'd learned how to work around the British film industry's technological limitations to churn out winning entertainments. But they didn't consider him an artist.

Hitch wanted to be taken seriously. And Selznick knew just what to say.

The studio rented the director, his wife, Alma, and their eleven-year-old daughter, Pat, a three-bedroom apartment in the Wilshire Palms, a new high-rise with views of the mountains and ocean located just ten minutes away from Selznick International in Culver City. It was a chic address: Franchot Tone, recently divorced from Joan Crawford, was shacking up there. Mickey Rooney and Ava Gardner moved in as newlyweds three years later.

The apartment was all white: white draperies, white carpet, white furniture, white walls. Pat said it reminded her of a snowstorm. Alma told her daughter it would be a long time before they saw bad weather again. But she hadn't foreseen the trouble with Selznick. *Rebecca* was their first collaboration, and Selznick wanted everybody to know who was boss.

Take the script, based upon the novel by Daphne du Maurier. After the final draft was submitted, Selznick responded with a memo that Hitch joked would make a very good film: "The Longest Story Ever Told."

Then there was the casting. Selznick had a crush on Joan Fontaine, so she got the female lead, as the tormented second Mrs. de Winter. For the part of Maxim de Winter, Selznick chose Laurence Olivier, mostly to placate Olivier's lover, Vivien Leigh, whom Selznick was holding hostage in Hollywood for postproduction work on *Gone With the Wind*.

Oh. Here we were.

I slowed down and squinted at the numbers. I was looking for 10331.

Number 10531 was the Mama Royale, or maybe the something-else Royale. I couldn't tell because of all the curlicues.

Next door to that was a deserted pumpkin patch. Guess everybody who wanted a jack-o'-lantern already had one.

Next door to that was a moody chateauesque number with

turrets and spires and gables. I couldn't see an address, but this had to be it.

I parked just up the street and walked back.

The place reminded me of Manderley, the mansion Hitch said was the true star of *Rebecca*. It was dripping with atmosphere. And foliage. There were probably a lot of spiders in there.

I approached with trepidation. You never knew who might be lurking in the shadows. Mrs. Danvers, the sadistic housekeeper obsessed with the first Mrs. de Winter, was a first-class lurker. She was also my favorite character in the movie. I loved the part when she forced the poor, pathetic second Mrs. de Winter into wearing Rebecca's ruffled white ball gown. Mrs. Danvers understood the mystical allure of the right dress. She had a lot in common with Bridget.

But no, I suddenly realized, this couldn't be 10331. The Wilshire Palms was a high-rise. Was it this hideous beige twenty-story condo next door? I hoped not. I couldn't commune with Hitch's spirit in a beige condo. It looked too new, anyway. They must've torn down the Wilshire Palms. These things are known to happen in Los Angeles.

I got back into the car and headed up Beverly Glen.

Bel Air was just on the other side of Sunset Boulevard.

That was where the Hitchcocks moved next, to a cozy, English-style cottage they'd visited when Carole Lombard was living there. The couple had befriended the blond comedienne soon after they'd arrived in Hollywood. She'd shared Hitch's taste for practical jokes. When they'd worked together on *Mr. & Mrs. Smith*, Lombard had installed a miniature cattle pen on the set complete with three young heifers wearing banners emblazoned with the names of the three stars of the film (herself, Robert Montgomery, and Gene Raymond), her comeback to the director's infamous quip that all actors were cattle. When Lombard decided to move into boyfriend Clark Gable's ranch house in Encino, Hitch and Alma jumped at the chance to take over her lease.

I was at Sunset now. All I had to do was remember Carole Lombard's address.

Was it Saint Pierre Road?

St. Bertrand?

St. Peter Claver? No, that was my parish church in Asbury Park.

I waited for the green light and turned right, then slammed on my brakes to avoid hitting a Bride of Frankenstein who'd plowed through the red light going seventy. An early reveler, I supposed. What was her hurry? Ah. She was buying a map to the stars' homes. There were hand-painted wooden signs advertising them propped all along Sunset between Westwood and Beverly Hills.

I wondered.

Would Carole Lombard's address be listed on one of those maps?

Carole Lombard died in a plane crash in 1942, but I doubted they updated those things regularly. I slowed down a little so I could peer down the next side street. Sure enough, there was a guy sitting in a lawn chair in front of somebody's massive Tudor mansion. He had a pile of maps by his side.

I put on my turn signal. And that was when I saw them in my rearview mirror.

The dreaded flashing red lights.

Known to make the innocent feel guilty, and the guilty play innocent.

I couldn't say exactly where I fell in the continuum.

But some might find it telling that as I pulled over, my first thought was that I only had fifteen hundred and forty three dollars left for bail.

Chapter 39

The policeman got out of his car and walked around to my window.

I rolled it down, terror washing over me. "How are you, today, Officer?" If he asked for my license, I was done for.

He didn't take off his sunglasses. They were that cop kind, dark and opaque. "Not good."

Might as well get it over with. "What's up?"

"What's up," he repeated. "Five years I'm on the job, never had anybody ask me what was up."

I laughed nervously.

Now he took off his glasses. "It's not funny."

I shook my head. "No."

"You were going twenty-five in a forty-five-mile-per-hour zone. That's illegal."

"Was I really?" I batted my eyelashes.

"Stop that."

"Yes, sir," I said, embarrassed. "I was just trying to turn onto this street here to buy a map to the stars' homes." I pointed to the guy sitting on the lawn chair, who gave me a little wave.

"Not too many stars in your neck of the woods," the cop said.

"Excuse me?"

"Arizona. There's Jenna Jameson, the porn actress, of course. Her father was a cop. She lives in Scottsdale."

"I'm from Phoenix."

"Those pornmeisters are into all sorts of illegal activities. Drugs. Guns. Gambling. She must've broken her dad's heart."

I nodded, thankful he wasn't reading me my rights.

"It's a slippery slope," he said. "You start small, but things can snowball—excuse me." He'd received a call on his radio. "314 on Rodeo Drive," he said. "Right away."

He leaned into the window again. "Duty calls. Indecent exposure at Gucci. I'm letting you off with a warning this time."

"Thank you, Officer."

He put his shades back on. "Drive safe, Miss. And welcome to Bel Air."

The guy with the maps wanted to hear the whole story, but I wasn't in the mood for conversation. He was. Before I could stop him, he recounted the entire history of the star map industry, which began in 1936 when a man named Wesley Lake parked himself at the corner of Baroda Drive and Sunset to sell his maps to sightseers eager to meet their matinee idols. His daughter Vivienne took over the family business in the mid-fifties. She was so beloved that Glen

Campbell, who lived up the street, used to have her over regularly for tea. Nonetheless, in 1973 she was charged with violating the law by conducting her business along the roadside. It went all the way to the California Supreme Court, which in a landmark decision affirmed Vivienne's right to free speech. "She was Beverly Hills's own Patrick Henry," the guy said, waving an arm in the air. "You know, give me liberty or give me death?"

It was a hell of a sales pitch. I handed him a twenty and took the map.

Sure enough, there was Carole Lombard. 609 Saint Cloud. Also on Saint Cloud were Louis B. Mayer, Ronald and Nancy Reagan, and the Fresh Prince. Small world.

With the map spread out on my lap, I followed the red arrows into the verdant, faux-gated paradise that is Bel Air. The "faux" means the gates don't actually close. They're there to remind you that you don't belong. The topography reiterates the message. Houses are hidden from view by looming hedges and high walls. Streets wind around one another like pretzels, meaning if you don't have a chauffeur you might as well forget it. Not to mention there are no sidewalks. In fact I didn't see anybody around except gardeners, pool men, and security guys in vaguely menacing white cars.

Considering the neighborhood, 609 was a dump.

I wasn't sure anybody was even living there anymore. The driveway was strewn with leaves and yellowed newspapers. The gate stretching across it was covered with brown canvas so you couldn't see in. However, somebody had cut a little hole at the bottom. Someone with an avid interest in the former residents, perhaps. Or maybe it was for the dog. Claustrophobia is common among animals. If I accidentally close Buster into the bedroom, I pay for it, believe me.

I got down on all fours and peered through the hole.

The Hitchcocks's former home was brick, modestly sized, and shrouded by overgrown trees and bushes—eucalyptus, yucca, eugenia. The bottlebrush was enormous, with fuchsia blossoms rather than the usual red. I closed my eyes for a minute and tried to imagine myself pulling into the driveway in my Studebaker (or whatever the 1940s equivalent to a Camry was), wearing my periwinkle silk doupioni cocktail dress with the pleated bodice that wraps around the front obistyle, for one of Hitch's famous blue dinners, where he served blue soup, blue venison, and blue ice cream.

I opened my eyes again. Then I rubbed them. Then I screamed.

There was an arm in the bushes at the far end of the driveway, by the trash can.

Mottled but still pinkish.

With a hand at the end.

I spun around.

On the other side of the street four gardeners in green coveralls were pruning some gorgeous climbing roses.

"Hello!" I yelled. "¡Hola!"

"Beverly Hillbillies and Barry Manilow?" one of them asked, putting down his clippers. "Go straight."

"No, no!" I dashed across the street. The place where they were working looked like the White House. "There's an emergency!"

They gathered around, murmuring to one another in Spanish.

"Elizabeth Taylor," said a younger one. He had a crew cut and spoke excellent English. "On Nimes. That is the same street as Mac Davis."

"You don't understand. I'm talking something awful. A disembodied arm!"

They looked puzzled

"Does anybody live in that house?" I pointed to 609.

They went into a huddle.

"No," said the crew cut.

The first guy said something to him in Spanish.

The crew cut turned back to me. "My dad says there were some people here yesterday, but just visiting."

"Where there's an arm," I cried, "there's bound to be other body parts!"

They had nothing to say to that. I ran my finger across my throat. "Dead. *Muerto?*"

The fourth gardener, who had a double chin and braces, reached into his pocket and pulled out a cell phone. The others followed me across the street.

I crouched down in front of the peephole. "Look."

I moved out of the way, and the crew cut kneeled down. Then he turned to me and said, "Dummy."

"That's not very nice," I said.

"It's a dummy, Miss. *Maniqui*," he said to the others.

"That's impossible," I said, pushing him out of the way. I peered in again, then felt my cheeks get hot.

That arm sure did look plastic. Kind of shiny and all.

Just then, I heard a car screeching to a halt and a door slamming.

Not the police, thank God. Bel Air Patrol. Piece of cake.

The patrolman had John Wayne fantasies. You could tell by the way he walked, like he had a saddle between his legs. "What seems to be the trouble?"

"No trouble," I said, standing up. "None at all."

"April Fool!" said the gardener with the double chin. He was trying to help me out, which was nice.

"Today's Halloween, my friend," said John Wayne.

"Trick or treat!" I said, brandishing a Necco wafer.

The patrolman shook his head. "Not while I'm on duty."

"We have green cards," said the crew cut.

"What about you?" he asked me. "What's your business here?"

"Just a tourist," I said, smiling. "Visiting from Tucson. Go Suns!"

"I think all of you had better be moseying along," he said.

"Would you look at the time?" I glanced at my watch. "Do you know the way back to the Bel-Air Hotel?"

"You a guest there?"

"Um-hmm."

"Don't leave before trying their tortilla soup," John Wayne said. "It's out of this world. The secret is the tomato base."

The first gardener started yelling in Spanish.

The crew cut nodded vociferously, then stepped forward. "Tomatoes are not the secret. Masa flour is the secret." He nodded. "My dad just wanted you to know."

The Hitchcocks didn't stay at 609 Saint Cloud for long. In the spring of 1942, they purchased an elegant colonial shaded by lush trees that backed directly onto the Bel-Air Country Club's golf course. Number 10957 Bellagio Road was in move-in condition, but it took twenty years to complete the redesign of the kitchen.

For Hitchcock, eating was serious business.

His father, a grocer in London's East End, insisted on potatoes at every meal. The habit stuck. Hitch wolfed them whole, halved, diced, sliced, boiled, baked, fried, sautéed, cottage-fried, double-baked, and, in his waning years, mashed. At age twenty-seven, he weighed two hundred pounds; at forty, he weighed close to four hundred. At forty-four, by his own admission, his ankles hung over his socks and his belt reached up to his necktie. Not that he particularly minded.

His weight was his armor, his insulation.

Which makes it doubly odd that in his work food is so unfailingly gruesome: the milk poisoned, the eggs scrambled to resemble brains, the ketchup explosive. Murder victims are baked into pies, then devoured. Corpses are concealed in sacks of potatoes. Chickens have necks meant to be strangled, and breasts—don't ask.

But 10957 Bellagio Road would have to wait for another day.

I had a date in less than an hour.

I drove directly to the Hotel Bel-Air, known for its blue lake filled with white swans, beloved of brides and Oprah Winfrey, who threw a slumber party here when she turned forty. And for its tortilla soup, I hear.

"Checking in?" asked the valet, handing me a ticket.

"Um-hmm." I grabbed the suitcase out of the trunk.

"Can I get that for you?" he asked.

"I can take care of it myself."

I sailed past the registration desk and a bouquet of creamy

white calla lilies, and walked downstairs to the bathroom, done up in pretty pinks and greens, where I proceeded to set up shop.

Out came the blue-black mascara, the black kohl liner, the baby pink blush, and the very berry gloss. The brush, the curling iron, and the mousse. The bronze ankle-wrap sandals and clutch. The plum, crimson, and fuchsia tiered dress with plunging neckline. The matching bolero. And a nearly empty bottle of Serge Lutens's Fleur d'Oranger, which smells like the first day of spring.

Nobody bothered me for twenty minutes. After that, a maid came in with a feather duster and the wherewithal not to say a word. She dusted around my makeup, then disappeared, returning moments later with a garment steamer for my dress.

When I was ready, I went over to the concierge and asked for directions to Bonhams & Butterfields.

"Ah. The sale of Very Important Celebrity Memorabilia." He checked his watch.

I nodded. It was almost seven.

The concierge said he'd be happy to provide me with a map. He wondered, though, if I knew about the complimentary limousine service, available for guests of the hotel for destinations within a five-mile radius. Before I could say a word, a man with a very black cap took my suitcase and led me out to a very black car with a very full bar in the back seat.

I poured myself a Diet Coke, put on some music, and sunk back against the plush leather seat.

Blondes may be nearing extinction, but they still know how to have more fun.

Chapter 40

The limo glided to a stop in front of Bonhams & Butterfields. The driver ran around to open my door. "When would you like me to come back for you, Miss?" he asked, extending a hand.

I had trouble pinpointing an answer. It depended on so many things. Whether or not I could muster up the nerve to confront Ben. Whether or not he'd admit what he'd done. Whether or not he'd try to get away. Whether or not he'd try to kill me.

I.e., could be thirty minutes, an hour, or don't bother, I'll be seeing you in the hereafter.

I stepped up onto the curb, opened my purse and pulled out two hundred-dollar bills. "Can you keep the motor running?" I was starting to believe I was rich. That couldn't be good.

He tipped his hat and nabbed the dough simultaneously. "My pleasure."

Inside, a pack of women wearing expertly tailored pantsuits

prowled the Berber carpet. When they saw me, they bared their whitened teeth. Three of them tried handing me catalogs. Another proffered cocktail wieners. A fifth popped open a bottle of champagne. A sixth, all business, asked if I'd like to register to bid.

After photocopying the driver's license I handed her (Anita's), she gave me a paddle.

"The sale started a couple of minutes ago." She gestured toward the open door. "But there are still some seats down in the front."

I stood in the doorway, surveying the room. It reminded me of church. There were maybe seventy-five people seated on hard wooden chairs. Most were dressed in sober tones of black and gray. There were numerous hats. Half a dozen small dogs. At least two people dragging portable oxygen tanks. All eyes faced front, where the auctioneer was taking bids for Lot 1009, an unused check from the account of Marilyn Monroe and Arthur Miller at First National City Bank of New York. A photograph of the wrinkled check was projected on a flat screen TV over the podium, along with a snapshot of the unhappy couple on the set of *The Misfits* in 1961.

I turned to the young woman. "I need to know where the exits are." Just in case.

"Are you a fire marshal?" All color drained from her face. "I didn't know you people worked on holidays."

"No, I'm an agoraphobe," I replied, fanning myself with the paddle. "This is the first time I've left my house in seven months."

"Good for you." She pointed to two exit signs at the rear of the room, then fled.

No sign of Ben yet. I found two seats on the far aisle and squeezed past six annoyed people. "Sorry," I said. "Almost there." I sat down on a pair of glasses that apparently belonged to the woman on the other side of me.

"They're Cartier," she hissed, grabbing for my bottom.

"Allow me." The frames were covered with tiny gold spikes. Good thing they hadn't damaged my dress.

Now there was spirited bidding underway for Lot 1010, a pair of false eyelashes worn by Barbra Streisand in *Hello, Dolly!* They were handmade in Spain and came with adhesive. One of the combatants was a short woman wearing a ruby ring the size of a turkey gizzard and a triple strand of pearls you could barely see because of her chins. The other was an older gentleman who waved his gold-tipped cane in the air each time he wanted to increase the bid.

At $2800, the woman nodded her head.

At $3000, the gentleman's cane shot skyward.

"Do I hear three thousand three hundred?" the auctioneer called out.

The bejeweled woman's husband, who was wearing an ascot, began wrestling his wife for the paddle. She protested audibly. Everyone in the room was now aware he'd never made a dime of his own and had married her only for her money.

"Fair warning and last call," the auctioneer cried.

The husband was still attempting to restrain his wife. He'd be sleeping on the couch tonight, that was for sure.

The hammer came crashing down.

"Yes!" came a voice from the front row. The old gentleman had gotten the eyelashes. With tax and the twenty-percent buyer's premium, he was in for almost $4000.

"Next up is Lana Turner's violet silk moiré makeup case from the fifties," said the auctioneer. "We'll start the bidding at one thousand two hundred."

I loved Lana Turner. She was discovered drinking a Coke. Most people know that, but don't know that her high school boyfriend was Judge Wapner from *The People's Court,* nor that she left the bulk of her estate to her maid, not her daughter, even though her daughter killed the mobster Johnny Stompanato to protect her. Also, Lana Turner wore a turban better than anybody except maybe a Sikh.

The bidding escalated rapidly to $4700.

I looked around the room. Who were these people? Oh, my God. Was that Jilly? My neighbor? How odd. I waited until she turned her head. Yes, that was definitely her. The sunburn still hadn't faded. What was she doing here? I turned the pages of the catalog. Maybe she needed another hideous item for her bedroom. Another pink patchwork quilt? Something lacy with gingham? Oh, yes. Here it was. No doubt in my mind. She was after the last item in the auction. A four-poster Gothic Revival oak bed from the late nineteenth century, carved with nine full-figure saints. The previous owner was Cher.

Still no Ben. I picked up the paddle and started fanning myself again.

"With the lady on the far aisle now, one thousand eight hundred for Sammy Davis Jr.'s tortoiseshell snuffbox!" the auctioneer called out.

I turned around to see who the sucker was.

The man sitting behind me gave me the thumbs-up. "It's a beaut," he whispered. "I saw one owned by Peter Lawford on eBay for double the price."

I turned around and cried, "No! I'm not bidding. I'm an agoraphobe!"

The auctioneer glared at me. "I apologize, ladies and gentlemen. It seems we are back at one thousand seven hundred, one thousand seven hundred with the gentleman in the fedora for this wonderful piece of Rat Pack memorabilia. Do I hear one thousand eight hundred?"

This was my first auction. I didn't like the atmosphere. No windows. No air. That was how they confused you. By cutting off blood supply to the brain. No wonder those people needed oxygen.

Was that Gambino in the third row? It looked like the back of his neck.

God, I was hallucinating now. This entrapment thing was clearly a terrible idea. I wasn't prepared. I'd never even been a Girl Scout. My mother always steered me away from anything that reeked of female empowerment. Oh, why had I been so rash? If I'd been thinking I would've called Detective McQueen this morning and convinced her to put a wire on me. Maybe there was still time.

"Hey," Ben murmured, sliding in next to me.

Too late.

"I almost didn't recognize you." He lifted a lock of my blond hair. "Va-va-voom."

My heart started pounding, but not in a positive way. He was wearing jeans, an untucked white shirt, and a black sweater vest, which made me immediately suspicious. And cologne. Something outdoorsy, like hay. Or maybe wheat. I looked down at his feet. That was where it all fell apart. He should've been wearing Timberland boots, not those god-awful Gucci loafers. Those were the shoes of an unregenerate criminal.

I had to focus. I was supposed to be giving him a false sense of confidence. I channeled Lana Turner. I tossed my hair like this was a shampoo commercial. "I'm glad you like my new look."

"Oh, I do."

"Yeah," I said, nodding. "I got it done at a fabulous salon in Bakersfield. You ever been to Bakersfield, Ben?" So much for reeling him in slowly.

"Bakersfield? No, I don't think so." He checked his phone. "I thought there might be a message from my client. He seems to be running late. Can I see that catalog for a second?"

He flipped through it. "Cece, did you see this? Lot 1038? Rhonda Fleming's costume for the dream sequence in *Spellbound*!"

Now that would be something to own. Salvador Dali himself spent two hours with a large scissors cutting up a four-hundred-dollar Dior negligee to create it, but when it was shown to the Hays Office, the censors insisted on additional shreds to cover Fleming's exposed midriff, thighs, and breasts. Hitchcock pretty much washed his hands of the whole scene once Selznick butchered it further. Still, the costume would look amazing in the window of Bridget's store. She'd been talking about wanting to do a Hitchcock-themed display for Christmas, with beautiful fifties suits and hundreds of tiny coffins. Hitchcock loved to give tiny coffins as holiday gifts. He gave one to a young Melanie Griffith, with a minieffigy of her mother, Tippi Hedren, inside. Sweet.

"Here we go," said Ben. "This one belongs to my client."

He tapped his finger on the page in question. "Brown leather football, signed and inscribed to Lynda Carter, TV's *Wonder Woman*, by Joe Namath, reading in full, 'Hi Lynda/Stay Happy!/Love/Joe Namath.' Lot 1224. One of the last items. I'm sure Tom will be here by then."

Like there was a Tom.

"I think you'll enjoy meeting him," Ben said. "He's great. His wife, Jeri, loves vintage clothing, too. Maybe they can join us for dinner?"

Tom and Jeri? He was going to have to do better than that.

Ben took my arm and pulled me to my feet. "Let's go outside and see if we can find them."

"No," I said, sitting back down. My heart started pounding again.

"Why not?"

"Why not?" I repeated.

"Yeah," said Ben. "Why not?"

"Because I want to bid on the next item."

Lot 1062 was a custom throw pillow with needlework on one side reading, "Q: Name Two Things That Will Survive a Nuclear War," and on the other, "A: Cockroaches and Celine Dion." Just my luck.

The auctioneer said, "Do I hear five hundred?"

Ben looked at me.

"Oops," I said. "I dropped my paddle. Now where is that thing?"

He bent down to get it. "Here you go, Cece."

I raised the paddle in the air as slowly as humanly possible.

"I have five hundred with the lady on the far aisle. Do I have that correct this time?"

I gave him a weak approximation of a smile.

"How about six hundred? Six hundred dollars for this wonderful novelty pillow, once owned by the late Tiny Tim?"

Not a single paddle went up.

"Lucky girl," said Ben. "You're going to get it."

I turned to the woman with the killer Cartier glasses and whispered, "Wanna go halfsies?"

"Sold!" said the auctioneer, bringing down the hammer. "For five hundred dollars."

Maybe my accountant, Mr. Keshigian, could call it a business expense.

"No more excuses," said Ben, taking my hand. "We're getting out of here."

Chapter 41

Walking down the aisle at Bonhams & Butterfields felt like walking the plank. I tried to catch as many eyes as possible, thinking it couldn't hurt to have witnesses.

I could always twist my ankle. I was good at that.

Or I could try the old make-a-grab-for-the-lady's-turkey-gizzard-ring trick. The husband with the ascot would apprehend me; he and the wife would kiss and make up; somebody would call the authorities; and I'd be safely in cuffs in no time.

Jail time sounded infinitely better than alone time with Ben.

"Here we are," he said.

The lobby was empty.

"No Tom and Jeri here," I said, turning on my heel. "Let's go back inside where all the people are."

"How about some champagne first?" He walked over to the buffet table, pulled a bottle out of an ice bucket, and poured us two glasses.

"Champagne's the best," I said inanely.

"Cheers." He raised his glass.

I waited until the glass was at his lips, then cried out, "Oh!"

The champagne sprayed all over his sweater vest. A few droplets landed on the Gucci loafers. He tried unsuccessfully to maintain his cool. "What is it, Cece?"

"Over there! In the corner!"

When he turned his head to look, I dumped my champagne into a potted palm. I'd watched him pour it, but a person couldn't be too careful.

Ben turned back to me. "I don't see anything."

I wiped my lips daintily. "Must've been my imagination."

He took my empty glass, drained his, and set them both down. "We should check outside." He pushed open the heavy door. A blast of night air slapped me in the face. "The parking lot is around back."

"The parking lot?" Parking lots tend to be dark and deserted. How many shootings, maimings, and kidnappings have taken place in dark and deserted parking lots? Too many to count.

"Why are you repeating everything I'm saying?" he asked.

"I'm not repeating everything you're saying," I said, shivering. Sudden changes in temperature can cause colds. Too bad I'd left my bolero inside.

"Hold on a second." Ben pulled a pack of cigarettes out of his pocket.

"The nicotine patch is very effective," I said. "You should try it."

"I did," he replied. "But I'm no good at breaking bad habits. Do you have a match?"

"Give me a second."

The limo was double-parked in front. I walked around to the driver's side door, watching for oncoming cars. Traffic was heavy tonight along Sunset. Everyone was headed to the Halloween parade in West Hollywood. I wished I were at the parade right now. I wished I'd bought a costume for Buster at Petco. I wished I were home. But I couldn't go home. Not yet.

The tinted window came down.

"Do you have a light?"

The limo driver reached over to the glove compartment, popped it open, and pulled out a Hotel Bel-Air matchbook.

"Thanks," I said. "Listen." I lowered my voice. "I'm almost ready to leave. I just have some quick business with this gentleman in the vicinity of the parking lot. If I'm not—"

Ben was suddenly at my side. I tossed him the book of matches, then looked back desperately at the driver. But he already had his head in a car magazine.

"So," said Ben, striking a match. "We're trying this again, are we?" He lit his cigarette and took a long drag.

"Looks that way." We'd come to the end of the block and were about to turn the corner. There were cars all around us, and people walking up and down the street. I was perfectly safe. As long as we didn't go to the parking lot.

"Is this really what you want?" He blew one, then two smoke rings.

"What I really want," I said, mustering every bit of courage I had, "is to ask you a couple of questions."

He tossed his cigarette to the ground and stubbed it out with his shoe. Then he pulled me close. "Forget that. You didn't ask what *I* really want."

We were so close now I could smell the tobacco on his lips. I could see the stubble on his chin and the fine threads of blood in the whites of his eyes, like fault lines.

"Can you guess, Cece?" he asked.

Yes. "No."

His pupils dilated. "What I really want is to—"

"Freeze, douche bag!"

Both of us spun around. It was the limo driver, and he was pointing a gun at the place where Ben's heart would be, if he had one.

"I came just in the nick of time, right?" The limo driver's eyes were wide. "Man, this whole thing is such a coincidence. I'm studying to be a private investigator. It's a correspondence course, but still. Man, I'm so frigging excited!" He was smiling so wide I thought his face was going to split open.

"Who the hell is this?" Ben asked. "Your bodyguard?"

"I think it's about time you stopped asking questions." I moved next to the limo driver. "The only person asking questions now is going to be me."

"Cece, I suggest you stop while you're ahead," Ben said evenly. "We are standing on the corner of Sunset Boulevard. Somebody's going to drive by and call the cops. They're going to be here any second."

I didn't think so. This was Hollywood. We were obviously rehearsing a scene for our extremely low-budget film.

"I just want to know one thing," I said. "Why did you pick me?"

"Hell if I know," said Ben. "It was obviously the biggest mistake of my life."

"That's for sure," I said defensively.

"You know that night I met you, at the Orpheum, I should've known better. All the signs were there. But I didn't pay attention. Now, it seems so obvious. You are some piece of work."

The limo driver took a step forward. "Show some respect for the lady, bad ass, or you're going to be sorry."

I leaned over to the limo driver and whispered, "Excuse me, what was your name?"

"Larry," he said.

"Larry, let's not get carried away, okay?"

"Sorry," he said.

I cleared my throat. "Why don't you tell me about Kansas, Ben?"

Just then a middle-aged woman wearing librarian glasses and a flowered Marimekko shift appeared out of nowhere and grabbed Larry the limo driver around the neck. Then she kneed him in the rear, flipped him around, and let loose with a flying kick to his hand, knocking the gun to the pavement.

"Jeri!" Ben cried.

"I've been taking Krav Maga," she said with pride. "The martial art of Israeli commandos."

Some instinct deep inside my reptilian brain told me to run for it while I had the chance, but I dove for the gun instead.

Unfortunately, a short guy wearing a leather baseball jacket and spotless white sneakers got there first.

Tom, I presumed.

"Pretty nifty," he said, pointing the gun straight at his wife. "What do you think, Jeri?"

She nodded. "Our eight-year-old has that one. It comes with secret agent glasses."

I turned to Larry, who was lying on the sidewalk, legs akimbo.

"I'm not licensed yet," he said sheepishly. "What did you expect?"

I stuck out my hand and pulled him to his feet.

"What's going on here, Ben?" Tom asked.

"He has no luck with women," said Jeri, shaking her head. "I want to fix him up with my sister, but he says no."

"We didn't miss my Joe Namath football, did we?" Tom pulled his cell phone out of his pocket. "I have to buy it back. My kid is threatening to kill me."

"No," said Ben. "But we should get inside." He turned to me. "Cece, I think it's fair to say that this date is officially over. Not to mention our relationship."

"Wait," I said. "I want to know about Kansas."

"Three more lots until my football," said Tom, hanging up the phone. "We gotta make tracks."

"What about Kansas?" Ben asked.

"You said you'd never been anywhere near a prairie. Why does it say Kansas on your license plate frame if you've never been there?"

Ben sighed in exasperation. "I have no idea why I'm telling you this. My ex-wife is from Kansas City. The car used to be hers."

"She is a very well-known actress," said Jeri in a conspiratorial whisper. "She pays *him* alimony."

"Jeri!" said Tom, pulling her away from me. "Now!"

And just like that, everything fell to bits. My plan. My theory. Everything.

Larry the limo driver waited until they'd gone inside. "I

hate to be a pill, but I have to be getting back to the hotel. My shift is almost over."

"Fine," I said, in a daze. "I'll just get my bolero."

I had no idea who had killed Anita Colby.

I had no idea who had ruined Dorothy's life.

I had no idea what to do or where to go once I got back into my car.

Or even if the Hotel Bel-Air was going to give me a validation.

I pulled open the door to Bonhams & Butterfields. There were a lot of people milling around the lobby now. I was going to get a glass of champagne for the road. Drown my sorrows. And smuggle a glass out for Larry while I was at it. He meant well. But I never got the chance. Because on my way to the buffet table, I saw someone I recognized.

A woman.

Young, twenty-five at the most.

Tiny.

I couldn't place her at first.

She was wearing a white halter dress wrapped as tight as a bandage, a silver slave bracelet high on each arm, and flat silver mesh sandals. Her black hair was pulled back into a sleek ponytail.

Was she a client of Bridget's?

A friend of Annie's?

Then I noticed the tattoos. One on each ankle.

A fairy and Betty Boop.

It was the woman from the Andalusia.

Anita's friend with the neon yellow bob.

Which had obviously been a wig.

I ducked behind a pillar.

She was standing by the reception desk sipping a glass of champagne like she didn't have a care in the world.

Then someone approached her from behind and gave her a hug.

A man with sexy muscles and messy blond hair.

She turned around, laughing, and planted a kiss on his lips.

That would be Connor's lips.

I clapped my hand to my mouth.

I'd had it all wrong.

Totally and utterly wrong.

It was them.

Jilly and Connor and the rest of them.

They'd killed Anita and made me their fall guy.

It had been so easy.

They'd watched my house. They'd seen the people who came and went. They'd figured out my life was in shambles. That I was at loose ends. Feeling guilty and vulnerable. They knew what I did for a living. That I couldn't resist a mystery.

I was such a fool.

They'd gone ahead and stolen my mail, and, with the information they'd gleaned, bought a hot pink cell phone in my name.

The rest followed like clockwork.

And now here was Jilly. After all that hard work, who could deny her a night off? She definitely deserved a splurge. Something big and oak and Gothic to add to her inexplicable Cher collection. Which meant I had just about an hour.

As I whipped open the door, one of the predatory females

working at Bonhams & Butterfields grabbed me by the shoulder and turned me around. "Excuse me? Anita? Anita Colby? You wouldn't want to forget your purchase. How exactly will you be paying for it?"

I gave her five hundred dollars in cash and grabbed my Celine Dion needlepoint pillow.

It was pink with lace trim.

It would make the perfect housewarming gift for the new neighbor.

Chapter 42

"You looking for parking?" shouted a six-foot-six, three-hundred-pound Velma, wearing the largest orange turtleneck sweater I'd ever seen. A smaller man dressed as Scooby-Doo was trailing his mistress on a leash.

I rolled down the window of my car. "That'd be great. I've been circling the block for twenty minutes." Leaving me forty-five minutes, tops.

"The Mystery Machine is just up here," said Scooby, pointing to a Lexus convertible. "We're packing it in for the evening."

"Too much tequila," explained Velma.

"I love your costumes, ladies!" cried a man wearing a yellow-flowered bathing cap and coordinating paisley sarong. He was walking down the sidewalk arm in arm with another man who was wearing the same outfit in pink. They were carrying a boom box and blasting the theme song from *Grease*.

"Ditto!" Velma unhooked Scooby's leash and they clambered into the car.

As they drove away from the curb, I pulled the Camry in.

After reapplying my lipstick, I put on my bolero, got out of the car, and started down Croft. It was a six-block walk to my house.

I could already hear the commotion up on Santa Monica Boulevard. It was closed from La Cienega to Doheny to accommodate the revelers. The grand marshal of this year's parade was Mariah Carey. I passed at least three men dressed up as the petite songstress, in Members Only jackets and black spandex minis.

In West Hollywood, we revere Halloween kind of like they revere Easter in Vatican City.

At the beginning of October, around the same time the jacaranda trees start filling with their beautiful ultraviolet blooms, the windows at Trashy Lingerie start filling with trashy Cinderella, trashy sailor, and trashy schoolteacher costumes. Two weeks later, there's a line around the block just to get in. A week after that, the more entrepreneurial homeowners on Orlando Avenue begin auctioning off their parking spaces. Lois and Marlene got $120 last year from a weirdly desperate couple from El Segundo. Then there's the citywide doggie costume contest in the park, followed by the drag race and pageant (to take the crown, you must wear minimum two-inch stilettos), all leading up to the main event, which locals get to celebrate with half a million of their best friends.

I turned onto Orlando. There was my house. It looked so sad. So dark. I missed the place.

The lights were off at Jilly's, too. They'd left out a bowl of candy with a sign that read TAKE ONE. After nabbing a Mounds bar, I rang the doorbell, just in case. Nobody answered. I slipped my hand between the pillar and gate and felt around until I found the latch. Then, glancing over my shoulder one last time, I let myself in, the gate swinging closed behind me.

The courtyard was covered in gravel. I walked on tiptoe for good measure. The front door was locked, which didn't surprise me, so I decided to try the sliding glass doors around the back, which led directly into Jilly's bedroom.

The side yard was covered by a wooden overhang crawling with morning glory vine, which Javier calls the vampire of flowers. He's good with metaphors. As I passed, I heard a squeaking sound, followed by the pitter-patter of tiny mouse feet. No wonder the neighborhood cats liked to hang out here.

There was a series of switches by the back fence. I hit each one, illuminating, in rapid succession, the back office, the dining table, the ornamental shrubbery, and a spectacular yucca tree. The last switch triggered the pool's waterfall. Perfect. If they came home unexpectedly, they'd hear it and head straight to the backyard, giving me just enough time to hightail it out the front door undetected.

Unfortunately, the sliding glass doors were locked.

I tried a couple of the windows, which were also locked.

I had half an hour now.

Maybe there was a spare key somewhere around here. With all the guys coming and going, you'd definitely need a spare key.

The first place I checked was underneath the mat in front of Jilly's French doors, but that was too obvious, of course.

Then I stuck my hand inside each of the terra-cotta urns flanking the table.

No dice.

Nothing in the fuse box, either.

I knelt down and stuck my hand underneath the super-expensive chaises longes. Talk about an ideal place to hide a magnetized key holder.

No luck there, either.

But while I was on all fours, I came upon something even better than a magnetized key holder: a can of Solarcaine Aloe Extra spray, for nonstinging sunburn relief.

Jilly and I had obviously shopped the same aisle at Home Depot.

I stood up, dusted off my dress, and unscrewed the bottom of the can. And there it was, wrapped in tissue paper: a brand-new, gold-toned spare key.

I hustled over to the sliding glass doors and let myself into the house.

There wasn't much time. I figured the war room was my best shot.

I turned on the lights and closed the door behind me. The desk took up most of the space. There were three monitors on it, arranged in a semicircle. It looked a little bit like a cockpit. I took a seat on the fancy office chair and hit the three on switches.

While waiting for the system to boot up, I went through the drawers.

I was looking for change-of-address slips, stolen utility bills, preapproved credit-card offers, bank statements. Best of all would be a credit report. If you want to commit identity theft, a credit report is the golden ticket. All you have to do to get your hands on one is pretend to be someone's potential employer or landlord.

The top drawer was a bust. Paper. Envelopes. Clips. Staplers. Tape. Stamps. Nothing incriminating there.

The second drawer was full of receipts. Home Depot was a favored destination. Also, the local hardware store. Truck rentals. Electronics. Software. Adapters and cables. Mounts and brackets. I couldn't make heads or tails of it.

The third drawer I could barely open. It contained half a dozen overstuffed yellow folders, held together by industrial-strength rubber bands. I pulled out the folder on top, slipped off the rubber band, and laid it on the desk so I could look through it more easily. It was full of large black-and-white photographs. Maybe of potential victims. Jilly and her commandos probably stalked them for a while first. The picture on top was of a middle-aged man with a Fu Manchu mustache. His name and number were printed on the back, but I didn't recognize them from Anita's list.

The screens were up and running now.

And would you look at that.

The first screen showed the front of Jilly's house: the bowl of candy, which was empty now; the leaves blowing; a SpongeBob and Ali Baba strolling by.

The second screen showed the back of Jilly's house: a couple of cats sprawled on the superexpensive chaises, but otherwise, nothing much going on. Not any more, at least.

Jilly had the place under surveillance.

I couldn't believe I hadn't noticed the cameras.

If I'd been more observant, I could've smashed the lenses with the barrel of my shotgun. At least that's how gangbangers holding up bodegas do it on *Law & Order*. But I'm no professional. And more's the pity.

The doorbell rang.

I jumped up and turned off the lights. Then I cowered in a corner because it seemed the thing to do.

"Anybody home?" someone yelled at the top of his lungs.

I glanced over at the first screen. Two teenaged zombies carrying bulging sacks of candy were at the front door.

The bell rang again. "Trick or treat!" they bellowed in unison.

The first zombie yanked open his sack and pulled out a forty-ounce bottle of beer. He took a slug, then passed it to his buddy, who finished it off.

I walked over to the intercom pad by the door and pressed the button so I could hear what they were saying.

"We got another, man?"

"That's it."

The first zombie rang the bell again. "There's no more candy out here! And we're in need of sustenance."

There's a 7-Eleven a block away. Go get yourself a Slurpee.

The first zombie started pounding on the gate.

"Shut up, man."

"You shut up." The first zombie peeled off his jacket, shoved it at his friend, and started climbing over the wall.

Jesus.

I hit the intercom button again. "Sorry, guys. We didn't hear you."

The first one slapped his thigh. The second one shook his head. "It's Halloween, man. You're supposed to be listening for visitors."

"Yeah, well, we were in the back," I said. "Inspecting our underground bunker. The end is near, I'm afraid."

The zombies looked at each other, then tossed the empty beer bottle on the sidewalk and started running.

I sat down at the desk again, scooted the chair over to the third screen, which was in fact a computer monitor, and opened Word.

The first couple of files I checked out appeared to be financial stuff. Accounting spreadsheets, tax filings, workman's comp—did Jilly actually pay workman's comp? I guess her guys were more likely to get injured on the job than your average Joes.

Next I went to Safari. I wanted to check the history.

Odd.

The last ten hits all had to do with *The Twilight Zone*. Fan sites, episode guides, DVD sales. I never thought *The Twilight Zone* was as good as *Alfred Hitchcock Presents*, except I did like the one where a mean-spirited Telly Savalas makes an enemy of his stepdaughter's new doll, Talky Tina. But that was hardly as chilling as the Alfred Hitchcock one where the husband is driving his wife home from the hospital after she's been attacked and she says, "Stop! That's him!" and the husband beats the man to death, and then they drive off and see another man, and the wife says, "Stop! That's him!"

I went a little deeper into the history.

Sunday, October 30.

Here's what Jilly and the guys were looking at yesterday:

Alfred Hitchcock Scholars Meet Here! The MacGuffin Web Page!

BBC Audio Interview—Hitchcock

Strangers on a Train Plot Synopsis

North by Northwest: Trailer
Horror Asylum/ Psychoanalysis, Norman Bates/Horror
    Movie News
Lavender Blond: Kim Novak
A Tribute to Kim Novak
Suspicion: Hitchcock's Original Ending
Hitchcock: Truffaut
Vertigo Movie Tour of San Francisco

I was starting to get a bad feeling. In the stomach area. Like when you've been kicked.

I closed Safari, then Word. Then I stared, open-mouthed, at the desktop.

There was one little picture of a file folder up there. All alone in the corner.

Underneath the little picture were the words VERTIGO A GO GO.

I clicked on it. A two-page document opened. I read it once. Then I read it again. Then I laughed out loud.

And then I got really, really angry.

Chapter 43

Imagine waking up one morning and finding your tidy existence shaken to the core, your ordinary life stranger than fiction, your humdrum existence suddenly as thrilling and terrifying and glittering as one of Alfred Hitchcock's classic suspense films!

Meet Cece Caruso, an accidentally sexy, forty-something everywoman. Cece spends her days holed up in her funky bohemian bungalow in West Hollywood with no one to talk to except her dog and cat, living vicariously through her work researching the greats of mystery and suspense.

Suddenly, her overactive imagination starts to run wild—or does it?

Caught in a classic wrong-man scenario, Cece is the innocent plunged into a maelstrom of misunderstanding, forced to race against the clock to prove her innocence, with no one on her side and nowhere to hide.

Welcome to Cece's world!

We call it "Vertigo A Go Go!"

Cece thinks she's going crazy, but that's because she hasn't read the script!

Suspense, glamour, intrigue, black humor: it's all there, just like in your favorite Hitchcock movies: North by Northwest, The Man Who Knew Too Much, *and of course,* Vertigo!

You'll laugh, you'll cry, you'll be astonished as our unwitting heroine attempts to solve a murder and save her own skin at the same time.

What will Cece do next?

"Vertigo A Go Go" is the must-see debut episode of Deja-Vu!, *brought to you by the people behind last season's runaway hit, the Emmy Award-nominated* Rich and Strange!

Deja-Vu! *is a ground-breaking new reality television series which places an unsuspecting person into a fictional universe that he or she may or may not recognize. Think* Candid Camera *but more outrageous;* Punk'd *but smarter.* Deja-Vu! *is tailor-made for nostalgia buffs while speaking to today's millennial generation, which refuses to recognize the old lines of demarcation between entertainment and so-called real life.*

"It's all real, baby," laughs creator and executive producer Jilly Rosendahl.

Upcoming episodes of Deja-Vu! *include, "Twilight-Zoned;" "The Godmother;" and "Octowussy." The season finale,*

"Fear and Bloating in Las Vegas," will be shot on location at the Four Diamond Award-Winning Mandalay Bay Resort and Casino.

I finally understood the famous "vertigo effect," invented by a second-unit cameraman for Alfred Hitchcock.

The camera pulls back and zooms in at the same moment. The truth is on a collision course with a lie. The past crashes into the present. And everything is up for grabs.

It happened to Scottie when he realized that Madeleine and Judy were the same person. Now it was happening to me. I thought I was in one story, but I was in another one entirely.

My nightmare was Jilly's cosmic joke.

I sat there for a moment, my mind reeling.

They were so unspeakably clever.

The hot pink cell phone. What a perfect MacGuffin. They knew me well enough to know I wouldn't be able to resist. I'd show up at the hiking trail, and they'd be ready.

One blonde on the top of the mountain. Another blonde at the bottom. And a driver's license that just happened to blow my way.

There was no danger.

No bad guys.

No dead body.

Not even an Anita Colby. That was just a name they invented.

And the police. Those two young bumblers. The pretty detectives with their perfect smiles. They were never really after me. They were fakes, all of them.

I shook my head in disbelief as the past few days unspooled before my eyes.

The kid in the park and his obnoxious mother.

The cop that showed up afterwards, with the friendly advice.

Roy, the freak at the E-Z Nights.

Actors.

I grabbed the yellow folder stuffed with black-and-white photographs.

They were commercial headshots.

I studied the picture of the man on the top, with the Fu Manchu mustache. Of course. It was ridiculous, blustering Sy. He deserved some kind of award. They all did. They'd been amazing.

I yanked open the drawer and pulled out the other folders and spilled them all over the floor.

They were all here.

Dorothy with the silvery hair. Living in a trailer, her life a shambles. She looked good in a sexy halter dress and full makeup. I flipped over the picture. She could do foreign accents and tap dance.

And Jonathan Tucci. His real name was Kyle Black. He didn't look like an unsuccessful used car salesman. He didn't even look Italian. He looked like every handsome waiter in West Hollywood, serving chicken breasts and Caesar salads, hold the anchovies, while waiting for his big break.

Chastity took a great picture. She wasn't a tough-as-nails madam; she'd gone to frigging Julliard. The *New York Times* had singled out her performance as Lady Macbeth in an off-Broadway revival ten years back. But acting gigs were obviously few and far between for women of a certain age. She must've jumped at the chance to make a fool of me.

They'd led me on a wild goose chase, all of them.

And I hadn't caught on.

I hadn't seen any of it.

Those beautifully orchestrated Hitchcockian locations.

The amusement park, straight out of *Strangers on a Train*.

The deserted highway, courtesy of *North by Northwest*.

The chase in the Thai temple, as close as they were going to get to the Marrakech street scene in *The Man Who Knew Too Much*.

It was beyond embarrassing.

I'd made a complete spectacle of myself with those gardeners in Bel Air.

And with Connor. What an idiot I was about the break-in at my house, which obviously had never happened. There had been no cops that night. No cruiser. No lights. Connor must've seen where I kept the spare key, and let himself right in.

And the Andalusia. I groaned inwardly. That was not my finest hour. Did they have me on film in those hideous rubber gloves? Rifling through the desk? Hiding in the closet? No wonder the place looked like a film set. The art director had even remembered to stick a cigarette in a plate of eggs, just like Jessie Royce Landis does in *To Catch a Thief*. How could I have missed that? I hoped they'd shot those eggs from above for maximum visual impact.

The cameras.

They were everywhere.

At the strip club.

In the waiting room at Thai Orchid Massage.

In Sy's office.

Oh, God.

It couldn't be.

I dashed over to the door, threw it open, and ran down the hallway, out the sliding glass doors and over to the wooden fence between Jilly's house and mine.

It was too high.

I needed a chair.

I shooed away the cats, grabbed one of the superexpensive chaises, dragged it over to the fence, climbed up on top of it, and reached out for the big, brown, furry creature with the horrible, rat-like snout.

He wasn't playing dead.

He was stuffed.

They'd suckered me with an opossumcam.

All of a sudden there was a light shining in my eyes. Shit. They'd come home early. What was I supposed to do?

Confront them. Make them pay.

But it wasn't Jilly and her guys.

Not even close.

It was my ex-fiancé, Detective Peter Gambino of the L.A.P.D.

"Long time no see," he said, turning off his flashlight.

Chapter 43

ambino gave me his hand and helped me down. We stood facing each other for what felt like a very long time. Seeing him made me feel calm. Centered. All right, less hysterical.

And then, out of nowhere, Jilly's backyard was suddenly filled with the jazzy strains of "Spanish Flea" by Herb Alpert and the Tijuana Brass. Somebody in the neighborhood must've been watching a rerun of *The Dating Game*.

Or maybe the sound was coming from inside my own head.

"Hi," I said, smiling.

Even when I was a kid, I'd known *The Dating Game* was rigged. The third bachelor was always the charm.

"Nice opossum," he said.

"Nature's own Dustbuster. Would you mind?" I handed the wireless varmint to Gambino, who dusted him off a little and put him back on the fence. "It's a long story."

He nodded, lips pursed. "It always is."

"How are you?" I asked.

"Fine. You?"

"A lot better, now that you're here."

It was dark, but I saw something flicker in his eyes.

"So," he said.

"So. Are you going to arrest me?"

"Depends on the story," he said. "I'm still waiting."

"Let's go to my place." I took his arm. "The new neighbor is kind of unfriendly."

"BYEBYE," he said. "Definitely hostile."

"You know her?"

"I'm a cop," he said. "I keep track of these things."

I glanced over at the house. At least I'd remembered to turn off the lights. "She's going to be back any second."

He bent down and picked up the can of Solarcaine Aloe Extra spray. "Then you'd better put the key back."

"How did you—?"

"*Cherchez la blonde.*"

My hand flew up to my hair. "Do you mean me?"

He reached out to stroke my cheek. "Who else, Cece?"

My story was a bit rambling. Maybe it was the bottle and a half of Merlot we drank. Also, Gambino kept interrupting me.

Like when I told him about the message they'd left on the hot pink cell phone, where I'd threatened to kill Anita.

I couldn't understand how they'd done it until he told me about the outgoing message on his partner, Tico's, answering machine. It was Marilyn Monroe, breathily informing all callers that Tico was giving her a backrub and couldn't be disturbed.

Voice changer software.

It allows users to mimic other people's voices. All you needed was a recording of the person you wanted to imitate. Looked like *B is for Ben* was not the only person who'd listened to my KPCC interview.

Then there was the name of the erstwhile murder victim, Anita Colby. Gambino pulled me off of the couch and out to my office, where we Googled it, and a whole lot of other things.

Turned out Anita Colby was a real person—a tall, blond ex-model, known as the Face, who was hired by Selznick in the forties to teach his contract players about beauty, poise, and fashion. She became a great friend of Hitch's, and the inspiration for Grace Kelly's character in *Rear Window*. That was another clue I'd missed.

Along with the Andalusia Apartments. I hadn't known that Theresa Wright, the star of *Shadow of a Doubt*, had once lived there.

Nor had I known that the desolate road I'd walked down looking for a gas station was the precise location where the crop duster sequence in *North by Northwest* was filmed.

Nor that the used car lot Janet Leigh goes to in *Psycho* was in Bakersfield, on the exact strip where I'd found All-America Auto.

They'd done their homework.

Now it was my turn.

"Revenge is dangerous," Gambino warned.

"No, it's a dish best served cold," I said, my brain whirring.

"Did Hitchcock say that?"

I wasn't sure so I Googled it.

"It comes from an eighteenth-century French novel, *Les Liasons Dangereuses*." I pointed to the screen.

"See, I told you. Dangerous."

I wheeled around in my chair to face him. "Will you help me?"

"I already have." He grinned. "You know Jilly's surveillance cameras?"

"Oh, shit, I forgot all about them! I was supposed to smash them with my shotgun. Now they're going to know I'm onto them."

He put his hands on the arms of my chair and leaned down so his face was close to mine. "Your neighbor's whole system went on the blink for some reason between nine and ten this evening. Nothing salvageable. Nada. It's a real shame."

"Thank you," I said, meaning it.

"For what?"

"For even talking to me. For not hating me."

I saw that flicker in his eyes again.

This was it.

Nobody could take care of this for me.

It was now or never.

"I'm sorry." I stood up and threw my arms around his neck and whispered into his shoulder, loud enough so that I couldn't take it back, "It's you I want. It was always you."

He pulled back, holding me at arm's distance. "Say that again."

"It was always you," I said. "I never stopped loving you."

"I knew that," he said. "I meant the first part."

"I'm sorry?"

"Are you asking or telling?"

"Telling," I said. "That I am so sorry for everything."

"Then why'd you leave like that?"

I looked down at the floor. I was afraid to look into his eyes. But I had to. "I don't want to be married. I'm not cut out for it. I realize that now. But I know it's what you want. And what you deserve. So I left."

"How was the Caribbean?"

"Overrated. The sunsets looked like cheap postcards."

He smiled despite himself. "So where does that leave us?"

"I don't know," I said. "I guess it's up to you now."

"Come with me."

He led me back into the house to the living room, where he'd dropped his jacket. He reached into the pocket and pulled out something pink and filmy. Then he handed it to me.

It was the cut-up Dior negligee that Rhonda Fleming wore in *Spellbound*.

A wisp of silk, as delicate as anything I'd ever touched, yet it had survived Hitchcock's perverse imagination, Dali's scissors, Selznick's backseat driving.

And time. It had stood up to the hardest test of all.

"Happy birthday, Cece," Gambino said.

In all the tumult of the day, I'd forgotten it was my birthday. But Gambino hadn't.

Of course he hadn't.

Just outside my door, half a million people spent the rest of the night celebrating in the most outrageous costumes they could think of.

Inside, two people spent the rest of the night celebrating in next to nothing at all.

Chapter 45

At eight o'clock the next morning, I kissed Gambino good-bye, then paid a visit to my friends next door.

Connor didn't look especially happy to see me.

"Good morning," I said cheerily. "How are you?" I inhaled deeply. "Beautiful day, don't you think?"

"Yeah," he said, yawning. "Beautiful."

Poor thing was tired. He and the guys must've had a late night, what with getting the video equipment up and running again and devising even more audacious ways to humiliate me. Not to mention hauling home Cher's bed and making it up for their shameless, sunburned, madwoman of a boss.

I hoped Jilly had enjoyed a deep sleep. It would be the last one she had for a while if I had anything to say about it.

Connor yanked up the waistband of his sweats. "It's like the crack of dawn. What are you doing here?"

I handed him a stack of mail. "The mailman delivered it to me by accident."

"Weird," he said. "But thanks."

I didn't budge.

"I'd invite you in," he said, turning to look over his shoulder, "but I kind of need to shower."

"Oh, I understand. No problem at all." I held my ground.

"Okay, well, I'll be seeing you later, I guess. I mean, I *hope*." He looked uncomfortable now. "I stopped by a couple times the last few days and you haven't been around. I've missed you, Cece."

"You're such a sweetheart," I said, staring into his lying eyes. "You haven't said anything about my hair."

He turned red. "You look hot."

At least as hot as an accidentally sexy forty-something everywoman can look. "Aren't you going to ask me why I did something so drastic?"

He scratched his head. "You needed a change?"

Funny. "I needed to disguise myself. Make sure I wasn't recognized."

"What are you talking about?"

"C'mon, Connor. You know."

"No, I don't." He turned to look back over his shoulder again. "Listen, do you want to come in and talk about this or something?"

Hmm. The backyard might be a nice setting for our penultimate conversation, with the waterfall going and everything. But I was anxious to move on. I had a lot to do today.

"You don't need to pretend," I said briskly. "You're a smart guy. It's the police. They think I've done something. Something really bad. That's why they keep showing up here. Don't tell me you hadn't figured that out."

"I don't like to judge people."

I dropped my voice to a lower register. "Then you believe I'm innocent?"

"Of course I do."

"Oh, God." I pulled him to my accidentally sexy, forty-something bosom and gave him a hug. "You're amazing. Thank you so much for saying that. It means the world to me."

"No prob," he said with his usual eloquence.

"You know, I'm really looking forward to spending more time with you."

He nodded uncomprehendingly.

"Yes, after today, my life is going to take a whole new turn. I'm going to be able to breathe again. Turn a new page. Build rewarding relationships with deserving people. Get the monkey off my back. I'm really excited."

He took a step back. "What exactly is happening today?"

I shook my head. "I don't want to talk about it."

"Why not?"

"Because." I paused. "Let's just say *que sera, sera*."

Connor took my hand, which reminded me I needed a manicure before this afternoon. I wouldn't want to get caught on camera with chipped polish. "We're friends," he said. "Good friends. Maybe even more, right?"

"Right."

"Which means you can trust me."

"Well . . . It's hard for me." I looked off into the distance.

"I understand. You've been burned."

"My skin is raw," I choked out. Yeah, too bad about the

backyard. They could've done some fancy cutting between the waterfall and the tears welling up in my eyes. Would've been great.

"You gotta have some faith," he said. And then, the clincher: "In us."

"You're right. Faith can move mountains." Please. He wasn't that dumb. Well, maybe.

"So this afternoon?" he prompted.

I wiped my eye. "We're having a little family celebration. Around four. Everybody's going to be there." I blew my nose. "Which makes it the perfect time to straighten things out. Lay my cards on the table. Confront the enemy. Clean house. Get rid of dead wood."

"Is everybody coming over to your house?" Connor asked, wide-eyed. "Because if that's the case, I can make sure the guys park their cars down a couple of blocks so there's plenty of room. Or are you getting together someplace else? A restaurant, maybe? Somewhere in the area? Somewhere I might've been?"

Nice try. I glanced at my watch. "Oh, would you look at the time! I have to run." I leaned forward and kissed him on the cheek, then dashed down the sidewalk. "See you!" I called out, waving. "Sooner rather than later!"

Connor stood there in his saggy sweatpants looking kind of sick and dizzy.

Perhaps he didn't know that vertigo was contagious.

When I got back home, I went into the bedroom, yanked open the curtains, and smiled beatifically for the opossumcam.

After that I put on my prettiest apron, which also happens to be my only apron, and skipped through the rest of the house, throwing open the windows and letting in the fresh air. Then I did a load of laundry, collected the wine glasses from last night, cleaned up the remains of this morning's coffee and English muffins, and dusted. I decided to pay my bills another day.

At 11:00 a.m., I took off the apron and went to pick up my dog and cat from Lois and Marlene, whose front lawn was littered with beer bottles and candy wrappers, which is par for the course on the morning of November 1.

The ladies were beside themselves. It'd been some night. Just after midnight, a pair of chubby teenaged zombies carrying bulging sacks of candy had made the error of relieving themselves in their prizewinning rosebushes. A quick-thinking Lois, concealed behind the living room curtain, managed to snap an incriminating photo with her ancient Polaroid. She called the police, and the zombies were picked up for vandalism. From one to three this morning, the ladies had been at the station house, identifying them in a lineup. At nine, the ladies' masseur Rodney had arrived to help them manage the stress. They were feeling much better. Rodney had also examined the pets and felt confident that Buster and Mimi had suffered no trauma from being in such close proximity to a crime scene.

At 11:30, I pulled out of my driveway and headed south on Orlando. At Melrose I turned left and drove to Crescent Heights, where I took another left. At Santa Monica Boulevard I took another left, and when I got to Orlando, another left again.

It made a nice square.

I did that three more times, just to make sure nobody was following me, then drove straight to Bridget's store.

We were meeting there at noon: me; Annie, Vincent, and baby Radha (Alexander was at preschool); Gambino, who'd taken the afternoon off; my long-lost best friend, Lael, who gasped when she saw me (because of the bleached hair), and cried when she saw Gambino (for obvious reasons); Larry the limo driver; Esperanza, not an actress but an actual Cosmoluxe rep who knew Terence, Jilly's supposed nephew, from Pilates class and for the tidy sum of four hundred dollars had agreed to let her office double as Gersh Investigations whenever I eventually showed up, which I didn't hold against her as she had a seven-year-old she was putting through parochial school with no help whatsoever from his deadbeat dad; and, of course, Bridget, to whom I returned the five hundred dollars, with my sincerest gratitude.

Annie brought individual Tupperware bowls, each containing a breaded seitan cutlet and a side of chickpea "tuna" (secret ingredient: kelp powder).

Bridget's assistant, Bernadette, made iced tea.

"I just love mine with mint sprigs," said Bridget.

Bernadette said she'd be back from the market in fifteen minutes.

I cleared my throat. "Can I have everyone's attention, please?"

I went over the plan and doled out the props.

Bridget was in charge of the costumes. "You've gotten so fat," she said, holding a pair of tangerine-and-purple-striped raw silk cigarette-leg pants up against my body. They came with a matching bustier and trapeze coat.

"This outfit is a size four." I showed her the label.

"Excuses, excuses," she tut-tutted.

"The colors are garish with my hair, anyway," I muttered.

Bridget pulled a pair of owly blue-tinted sunglasses out of her pocket and slipped them on. "Look! I'm Edith Head! I won eight Oscars! Don't tell me what looks garish!"

Edith Head wore blue glasses to help her envision what colors would look like on black-and-white film. We were in the age of digital video, not that relevance was something Bridget gave much thought to when making conversation.

"The outfit will look better on Esperanza, anyway," Bridget said under her breath. "Her skin glows."

"Esperanza is wearing black, remember?"

"Enough about Esperanza," Lael said. "What about me? What do you think, Bridget, about a nice housedress? Maybe something floral with big pockets?" Lael had been around the block more than once, but she liked to play it down.

Bridget made a face. "We've spoken about your unhealthy obsession with housedresses before. You're going to wear this." She walked over to the rack and grabbed a silver crochet metallic jumpsuit from the late sixties, with a low scoop neck and narrow sleeves that flared at the wrist. "It's from the collection of Joey Heatherton, very Scandinavian ice queen, plus we'll be able to wash the ketchup out of it. Oh, look, Bernadette is back with the mint leaves!"

When Bernadette pushed open the celadon and gold door, the bell jingled, which woke up the baby, who started screaming.

Bridget threw her hands up to her ears.

"Why don't they give her a binky?" whispered Lael.

"They don't believe in pacifiers," I said as the screams intensified.

"Give them time."

Gambino lifted Radha out of her stroller and started bouncing her up and down. "Hey, hot rod. You're going to look good in a sixty-three Buick Riviera one day."

Larry the limo driver spoke up. "I like muscle cars."

"Who are you?" Bridget asked, looking at him for the first time.

"I work for Cece," Larry said, blushing.

Bridget put her hands on her hips. "Don't we all?"

Annie came over and put her arm around my shoulder. "I hate to bring this up, Mom, after all the effort you've put into this thing, but how do we know they're even showing up?"

Oh, they were showing up. I'd slipped an invitation to Alexander's fourth birthday party (which had in fact taken place six months ago) into the pile of junk mail I'd given Connor this morning. Jilly and her guys were resourceful. They'd find the invitation. And they'd show up at Bob Baker Marionettes at four o'clock this afternoon. Who can resist a puppet show?

I was rather pleased with myself for that one. The theatrical setting was classic Hitchcock (see *Stage Fright*, *Murder!*, *The 39 Steps*, and *The Man Who Knew Too Much*). Ditto the botched children's birthday party. In *The Birds*, Cathy Brenner's eleventh birthday celebration is ruined when a swarm of gulls swoops down on her right in the middle of a game of blindman's bluff. Mitch and Melanie (Rod Taylor and Tippi Hedren) are so busy prying the pecking beasts off the hysterical children that nobody gets so much as a bite to eat. But that wasn't going to happen to us.

Bob Baker Marionettes was providing ice cream.

Lael was making her famous butterscotch toffee angel food cake.

And I was bringing corn chips—bags and bags of them. I hoped Jilly would have a chance to kick back and have some. But you never know. She might be superbusy.

Tearing her hair out.

Ruing the day.

Stuff like that.

Yeah, payback's a—well, let's just say it rhymes with Hitch.

Chapter 46

The Bob Baker Marionette Theater is located in a white concrete box of a building just under the First Street Bridge, in a nondescript neighborhood somewhere between Silverlake and Bunker Hill. Founded in 1963, Bob Baker's is one of those venerated L.A. institutions, like the Venice boardwalk or Pink's hot dogs. I'd taken Annie for the first time when she was twelve, which turned out to be too late. She'd already seen the first two Chucky movies, and puppets gave her the creeps.

We drove over in a caravan.

Annie, Vincent, and the children led in their Prius. Lael was at the wheel of her brand-new, fully loaded Honda Odyssey. Bridget came next in her two-seater convertible, which seated one plus her caramel-colored Hermès Birkin bag. I brought up the rear, with Larry the limo guy and Esperanza in tow. Seemed like there might be some chemistry there.

After convening in the parking lot to go over last-minute

details, we filed into the theater and found seats on the folding chairs circling the horseshoe-shaped rug. Lael's son August
and baby Radha slept in their car seats.

"Fancy," said Alexander, wide-eyed.

Indeed. There were crystal chandeliers dangling from the
corrugated tin ceiling. Also disco balls, silver garlands, and a
red velvet curtain, with two four-foot tin soldier marionettes
standing sentry.

The room quickly filled to capacity. When the lights went
down, a chubby-cheeked young woman dressed in black came
bounding out. She looked like a cross between a kindergarten
teacher and a cat burglar.

"Welcome!" she said. "I am your master of ceremonies,
Jolene, like the bleach. I have a couple of announcements before
we begin. Parents, please turn off your cell phones and pagers,
and children, please stay on the red portion of the carpet. The
blue at the center is our stage and must be kept clear for the
marionettes at all times."

"Did you hear that, Auden?" the woman sitting behind us
whispered to her son. "The blue carpet is hot lava. You'll burn up
if you touch it." She made a sound like bacon sizzling on a pan.

"Looks like we have a couple of birthdays today." Jolene
clapped her hands. "Let's see—where is Millie?"

A tiny girl wearing a beautiful polka-dotted dress started
to cry.

"Millie," Jolene coaxed, "I have this wonderful gold birthday crown and you get to wear it for the whole entire show!"

"Nooo!" Millie wailed, making a break for the door.

"Okay, then, how about Alexander, the birthday boy?
Where are you?"

Alexander turned to Annie, confused. "But—"

I reached across Lael and wrapped him in a bear hug. "It's your half-birthday. Go with it."

He nodded solemnly to Jolene, who placed the crown on his head.

Now the lights came all the way up and the bouncy rhythms of "The Teddy Bears' Picnic" filled the room. Teddy bears on roller skates and in mini-Model Ts emerged from behind the curtain, maneuvered by unsmiling, black-clad puppeteers. They were all boy bears. Then a girl bear with pretty long eyelashes came out and started making sandwiches.

"That's called sexism, dear," said Auden's mother. "In our family, Daddy cooks and Mommy earns all the money."

Auden nodded before turning his attention back to the show, where a trail of ant marionettes was making off with the food.

I kept my eye on the side exits. After the teddy bears took their leave and the glow-in-the-dark skeletons began their manic Day of the Dead dance, Jilly's guys showed up.

Terence the smart-ass and Ellroy the dropout. Dressed in camouflage, for God's sake. They slunk against the wall and took seats in the way back.

I whispered to Vincent, who was sitting on the red carpet in front of me with Alexander on his lap, "The eagle has landed."

He coughed once, which was the signal for Larry the limo guy to confirm that he'd spotted Jilly's cameras. Part of his P.I. training involved learning to locate concealed surveillance devices. Larry, however, was flirting with Esperanza and didn't hear him. Vincent coughed again, louder this time.

"What's wrong with that man?" Auden whispered to his mother.

"Probably a smoker," she said with distaste. "Like Daddy."

When Vincent doubled over choking, Larry finally got the message, at which point he pulled a hankie out of his pocket and sneezed into it.

"Gesundheit!" said Esperanza.

Larry blew his nose enthusiastically, then shot a quick glance up to the crown molding on the far wall, where the multicolored spotlights were lined up. Sure enough, right in the middle was the tiny blinking red light.

It was showtime.

"Look, Grandma!" said Alexander. "The lady has hair like yours!" He was referring to a three-foot-tall, bleached-blond Phyllis Diller marionette singing, "Send In the Clowns."

I held up my finger to my lips. When Phyllis got to the line "You in midair," I elbowed Lael off her chair.

"Ow!" she cried, falling to the floor in a heap. "What do you think you're *doing*, Cece?" She tucked an errant bosom into her low-cut jumpsuit and climbed back onto the chair.

"Nothing," I said, leaning forward so the camera could catch my expression, which was one of pure, unadulterated hatred. "Not a damn thing."

"Oh, yes, you are. You've got it in for me, don't you?" She glanced over at Vincent, who mouthed, "Louder." The smart-ass and the dropout had earpieces on, obviously, but we wanted to be sure they caught every nuance of our carefully crafted dialogue.

"What goes around, comes around," Lael said, raising her voice. "Karma'll get you in the end."

"Shut up, you hussy," said Bridget at the top of her lungs.

Pure improvisation, but I liked it.

"Keep it down," hissed the flame-haired woman behind us, who had come without a child, not that I'd hold that against a person.

"Yes," echoed Bridget. "You're always making such a scene. You're not the star of the show, Missy. We're here for the puppets."

And who could blame her? "Send In the Clowns" was over. Now it was "Turn the Beat Around," the original version as opposed to the pallid Gloria Estefan remake, with boogieing marionettes straight out of a blaxploitation film, done up in cornrows, white leather suits with fringe, and gold platforms. Bridget was galvanized by the footwear, I could tell. But I was amazed by the puppeteers. Their movements were so economical. A series of tiny lifts of the elbow, and the puppets were doing the moonwalk. A twist of the wrist, and they were rolling their hips suggestively.

Had it been this effortless for Jilly to manipulate me?

Now the tables were turned.

The puppet would have her revenge.

Vincent started tapping his watch. Right. We had a schedule.

"I'm stepping outside for a minute," I said to Annie, opening my eyes as wide as I could. I wasn't going to blink for at least two minutes. It's the best way to make tears come, especially when you are wearing contacts.

I stumbled out of the room, pausing in the foyer long enough to adjust my sleeveless dove gray shirtwaist with the full skirt and thick white leather belt, inspired by the one Doris Day wears in *The Man Who Knew Too Much,* in the scene in which husband Jimmy Stewart drugs her so she won't flip out when she finds out that their son has been kidnapped. Doris goes to hell and back in that movie, but she triumphs by using her wits. She was a fine role model.

On cue, I lurched into the cheerful Bob Baker party room. The walls were painted in rainbow colors and festooned with sparkly ribbons and bows. There were three white picnic tables decorated with bunches of balloons. In the center of one of them, pyramids of juice boxes and individually sized paper cups of ice cream (chocolate, vanilla, or strawberry, each imprinted with the slogan SAY NO TO DRUGS on the lid) had been assembled for after the show. After putting down my white rattan bucket purse, I swept the snacks to the floor in a single blow, then hurled myself across the table, weeping.

When I'd sobbed for the designated amount of time, I turned my head in the direction of the oversized cellophane-wrapped Styrofoam lollipops in the corner of the room, where Larry the limo guy had spotted the second hidden camera, and said, out loud, "One final thing I have to do and I'll be free of the past."

Which is precisely what Jimmy Stewart says to Kim Novak in *Vertigo* once he realizes how she's deceived him.

"Cece," said Lael, who'd appeared in the doorway. She'd been afraid she might dissolve into laughter when she saw me sprawled across the picnic table, but I'd instructed her to think of something very sad if that happened. Like the time she didn't stir her flan sufficiently and it turned into scrambled eggs. "What are you doing in here? You're going to miss the finale."

"Look, Lael," I said, rising to my feet. "You're terribly sick.

I don't know whether it's possible for you to realize it or not. I don't know much about these things, but why don't you go someplace where you can get some treatment? Not only for your own sake, Lael, but so you don't go on causing more and more destruction to anyone you happen to meet."

That little speech came verbatim from the screenplay for *Strangers on a Train*, written by Raymond Chandler after the book by Patricia Highsmith.

"I'm not sure what you're talking about," Lael said, her eyes darting nervously. "I'm going back into the theater."

"You're my best friend, Lael. I thought I understood you. That we understood each other. But in this last week, I've come to the sad conclusion that people are ultimately unknowable."

"Cece, I—"

"It's like this book I've been not writing on Hitchcock. No wonder I can't get anywhere. Everybody sees him as this sadist, this sociopath, a lunatic sexual aggressor. So how do you explain the fact that he was also a devoted family man who was home for dinner every night for sixty years? Tell me that if you can, Lael."

"Cece, you need to calm down."

"But I am calm," I said, pulling a slightly dented French star tip for decorating cakes out of my white rattan bucket purse.

Lael clapped her hand to her mouth. It might've been to stop from laughing. I hoped she was thinking about the flan again.

"I see you recognize this," I said.

Lael looked down into her ample cleavage and shook her head violently.

I nodded. "That's right. Buster found it on the hiking trail the day Anita was killed. It still had traces of frosting on it, which is why I couldn't get him to spit it out. He's addicted to sugar."

Lael's knees started to buckle. She grabbed onto the door frame for support.

"Don't you have anything to say?" I demanded.

"The French star tip is used for borders, wagging rosettes, piping, and drop stars," she recited in a daze. "The finely cut teeth make nice, tight ridges as the frosting is pushed through the top."

"Stop it, Lael. You were there, weren't you? You killed Anita Colby and set me up for it. It's the oldest story in the book. You needed money. I told you not to buy that Odyssey, much less spring for the rear entertainment and navigation systems. But you didn't listen. And why should you? You were already mixed up with the wrong people. Yes." I laughed bitterly. "You always had been. All the way back to Kansas."

"No!" Lael cried.

"Yes! Kansas! You think I'd forgotten that you grew up outside Topeka! So much for Midwestern values!"

"We all go a little crazy sometimes," Lael whispered, cribbing from Norman Bates.

And then I took something else out of my purse.

Larry the limo guy's gun.

"Goodbye, Lael." I pulled the trigger at the very same moment that the cymbals crashed in the puppet show's final number, an elevator music version of Duran Duran's "Hungry Like the Wolf." As Lael staggered backward, clutching spasmodically at her chest while squeezing the plastic capsule of

Heinz ketchup all over her Joey Heatherton jumpsuit, I caught a glimpse through the open door of the Little Red Riding Hood marionette successfully squirming away from her lupine adversary as the audience burst into applause.

"What the fuck—" cried Connor, who came sprinting in from the hallway, earphones still on.

Terrence followed, screaming, "Shit! Shit! Shit! Somebody give her mouth-to-mouth! I have a cold sore!"

Lael's lips curled almost imperceptibly. I gave her a little kick.

"Show some respect for the dead!" screamed Ellroy, who'd run into the room, ripped out his earpiece, skidded to a stop, and was now hopping from one foot to another. "You killed her, man! We're witnesses! You're going to prison for like the rest of your life. And you've fucked Jilly in the process. They're gonna sue her ass for sure. Count your lucky stars, Terence, that none of us has any equity in this miserable fucking waste of a show!"

Jilly was last, her clipboard in hand.

She was white as a ghost.

No more sunburn.

"What have you done?" she asked me in a tiny voice.

"Jilly," I said. "Hi! And Connor! What are you guys doing here?"

"Give me the gun, Cece," said Connor, stepping forward. "It's going to be okay." He dropped his earphones to the floor and put out his hand.

"Tackle her, you idiot," said Jilly, reverting to form.

But before he could make a move, the lovely, black-clad Esperanza marched into the party room dangling a satin-lined coffin marionette with my *Rear Window* homage doll lying in it, propped up on the Celine Dion throw pillow. Vincent, who was so good with his hands, had constructed it earlier this morning. Larry the limo guy followed, carrying a boom box blasting the familiar theme music from *Alfred Hitchcock Presents*.

"The music was written by Charles Gounod in 1878. Do you know the title, Jilly?" I asked. "It's 'Funeral March of a Marionette.'"

Just then, the audience came pouring in, hungry for ice cream. Little Auden stepped over the supine Lael and picked up a cup from the floor. "Vanilla is my favorite," he said.

Alexander skipped right up to Lael and kneeled down. "Did you get ketchup on your clothes, La-La?" That was his pet name for her. "Don't worry. I do that all the time."

Lael popped up and ruffled his hair. "Yup. But Bridget said it'll wash right out."

"Jesus H. Christ," said Connor, whipping around to look at me.

Jilly's eyes bugged at least an inch out of her head.

Ellroy, I kid you not, passed out. It was a warm day, admittedly.

Terence grabbed a juice box from the floor, pierced it with the tiny straw, and squeezed so that a stream of organic apple juice came squirting out all over Ellroy's face. Ellroy sputtered a little, then sat up.

Bridget walked right up to Lael with a bottle of Pellegrino in her hand. "If you wait too long, it'll set." She poured some on a napkin, then started dabbing at the ketchup on Lael's chest.

"Stop that," said Lael, wriggling away. "I can do it myself."

Bridget trapped her at the door. "That jumpsuit is listed on eBay for eighteen hundred dollars. I'll do it, if you don't mind!"

At that point, Jilly started to laugh. Her laughter accelerated and was quickly accompanied by thigh-slapping, head-rolling, and other unseemly behaviors.

Connor stared at her, openmouthed. When he caught her eye, he chuckled once, purely experimentally.

"That's right," said Jilly. "Laugh away! This is utterly fantastic!!"

Connor chuckled again.

"Utterly fantastic!" echoed Terence, giving a little snort of glee.

Even Ellroy joined in, a company man to the bitter end.

"We're going to make history!" Jilly crowed. "This is the absolute best! We're all going to be famous! Reality TV will never be the same after Cece Caruso!" Jilly handed me her clipboard. "This is the release. Just go ahead and sign it, and then we can celebrate for real."

"Nah," I said.

Jilly's eyes narrowed. "What do you mean, nah?"

I took the release form out of her hands and tore it up.

Annie and Vincent gave each other a high five.

"The thing is," I explained, "reality can be extremely dull."

Jilly's skin had reverted to its characteristic mottled pink. "Excuse me?"

I smiled as I saw Gambino come into the room. "Hitch said that. I guess you must've missed it in all your research. That's why we turn to art."

"What are you saying, Cece?" Jilly asked.

"That I don't sell myself cheap."

"Oh, we weren't going to pay you," said Connor. "I mean, we could probably work something out in terms of reimbursing you for your expenses."

"Don't be ridiculous," interrupted Jilly. "Of course we'll pay you. Industry standard, still to be determined." She smiled a lipless lizard smile.

Bridget poked me in the ribs. "Don't be hasty, Cece. Once you're famous, you could get a hosting gig, or endorsements. Or even do a clothing line."

"I know people at Mervyn's," said Jilly.

"Tempting. But the fact of the matter is, I'm a writer." I looked directly into the camera hidden in the oversized, cellophane-wrapped lollipops, so nobody would miss it. "And if anybody's going to tell my story, it's going to be me."

Who said another scrupulously researched biography would really get at the truth of Hitchcock?

Reality isn't all it's cracked up to be.

That's why we escape into fantasy, as Hitch understood so well.

And what could be more fantastic than a story of an accidentally sexy forty-something everywoman caught in the throes of an obsession with the greatest maestro of obsession who ever lived?

I already had my first line.

They write books about women like me, who cancel weddings and then go on the honeymoons by themselves.

I glanced over at Gambino, tossing baby Radha in the air.

The last line, it appeared, was still up for grabs.

BOOKS BY SUSAN KANDEL

I DREAMED I MARRIED PERRY MASON

ISBN 978-0-06-058106-0 (mass market)

Sex and the City collides with *Murder She Wrote*! All that writer Cece Caruso really wants to do is complete her biography of mystery legend Erle Stanley Gardner, find a vintage 1970s Ossie Clark gown, and fix the doorknob on her picturesque West Hollywood bungalow. Then, a chance visit with a prison inmate who knew Gardner lands her right in the middle of a 40-year-old murder...and another case where the blood is still warm.

NOT A GIRL DETECTIVE

ISBN 978-0-06-0581084 (mass market)

In her work on a book on the pseudonymous author Carolyn Keene, Cece meets a fascinating collector of "Blue Nancys"—early editions of the Nancy Drew books—who even offers her the use of his vacation house while Cece attends a Nancy Drew fan convention. But when Cece discovers her patron stone-cold dead outside the house he loaned her, she has to unmask a very sly killer...using wits that would make the original Nancy proud.

SHAMUS IN THE GREEN ROOM

ISBN 978-0-06-128487-8 (mass market)

Los Angeles writer Cece Caruso is thrilled that her biography of the legendary Dashiell Hammett is headed for the big screen. But when the dead body of one of the lead actor's old flames is discovered—and neither the "facts" nor the hunky star's alibi add up—Cece can't help but ask questions.

CHRISTIETOWN
A Novel About Vintage Clothing, Romance, Mystery, and Agatha Christie

ISBN 978-0-06-145217-8 (paperback)

A new suspense-themed housing tract on the edge of the Mojave Desert is about to open. For the grand opening weekend, Cece Caruso is staging a play featuring the beloved sleuth Miss Marple. But everything goes wrong...including a leading lady who ends up dead.

Visit www.AuthorTracker.com
for exclusive information on your favorite HarperCollins authors.

Available wherever books are sold, or call 1-800-331-3761 to order.